THE MEMORY TRAP

The *Memory Trap* is Anthony Price's nineteenth novel, about a Russian defection which takes a wrong turn for British Iintelligence and sends Dr. David Audley on a dangerous search for an old colleague. First published in England by Gollancz in 1990, this is the first American edition and features a new introduction by the author.

THE
MEMORY
TRAP

ANTHONY
PRICE

THE
ARMCHAIR
DETECTIVE
LIBRARY

Originally published in 1989 by Gollancz.
Published simultaneously in trade, collector and limited editions
by The Armchair Detective Library in June 1991.
1 3 5 4 2

ISBN 0-922890-87-0 Trade $18.95
0-922890-88-9 Collector $25
0-922890-89-7 Limited $75

The Armchair Detective Library
129 West 56th Street
New York, New York 10019–3881

Library of Congress Cataloging–in–Publication Data
Price, Anthony.
The memory trap / Anthony Price.
p. cm.
I. Title.
PR6066.R5M4   1991
823'.914—dc20   91–7305

Printed in the United States of America

INTRODUCTION

David Audley was brought up on Kipling, and is still a Kipling man first and last, not a Tolkien one. Indeed, in his later years he has identified more and more with his favourite Kipling character, Gilbert de Aquila, the Lord of Pevensey in *Puck of Pook's Hill*. For not only did old de Aquila prefer brains to brawn in a violent age, and loyalty in a time of confused loyalties, but he was frequently at odds with those whom he served and little appreciated by them. "'Tis all here," Audley says, tapping his head as de Aquila did. "But it hath no play in this black age."

In fact, he didn't even come to read Tolkien until 1970, via a gift from his old friend Theodore Freisler intended for his future wife. And even then his enthusiasm was somewhat muted: Tolkien's "dismal poetry" certainly did not compare with Kiplings "on a bad day". It wasn't until quite recently, in the aftermath of "The Memory Trap"—and after the Department of Intelligence Research and Development had finally been closed down and he had been given his wooden sword at last—that he began to quote chunks of "The Lord of the Rings" from his incomparable (but far from infallible) memory. Sometimes he will identify himself (and certain of his closer colleagues, like Jack Butler) with Aragorn's "Rangers",

i

the *Dunedain*, who had guarded the "simple folk" of Middle Earth ceaselessly and secretly through the Dark Years, customarily rewarded with scowls and scornful names from those who lived "within a day's march of foes who would freeze their hearts". On occasion, though, (and perhaps reassuringly for his former employers) he now promotes himself rather beyond his actual station: "The Third Age was my age. I was the enemy of Sauron; and now my work is finished . . . My time is over; it is no longer my task to set things to rights, nor to help other folk to do so."

In a sense, of course, that "Third Age"—the old-style "Cold War", which started for Audley in *The '44 Vintage* and *A New Kind of War* 1944-45—had begun to end with Gorbachev and *For the Good of the State* in the late 1980's. This—including *The Memory Trap*—was for Audley the Clearing–up Time , when the chickens determined to come home to roost and the skeletons which rattled too loudly in the cupboards had to be dealt with. It is possible that his time is as yet unfinished: it will be years before some of the relevant documents and papers of this period either come into the open or disintegrate safely; in Audley's case (since he was notoriously concerned to leave as little evidence as behind him as possible, at least of what *really* happened) the truth may never emerge. His former employers would probably prefer it that way; they are still uneasy about him—still afraid either that Someone will come to pick his brains about Something better forgotten, or even that he may not (as reported) be busy writing a life of King Harold II of England (the 1066 Harold) but is actually laying down a full record of his own life and times, 1944–89, for the instruction and amusement (and possibly enrichment) of his posterity.

Well, Time will tell, won't it?

Anthony Price

*For Sarah Ballard, Jim
Becket, Lawrence Cartright
& George Siemieniuch*

PROLOGUE:

Lunchtime in Berlin

Two things, the boss had told everyone to do: to act normal, but to report anything suspicious to the plainclothes cop just inside the doors to the kitchen. But for Genghis, the new Turkish waiter, those were contradictory orders. Because, if there was one thing he had learnt never to do, both back home in the old country and in Berlin, it was to help the cops. The less a man had to do with those bastards, the better. And maybe in this case the safer too, if the kitchen-rumour about two cops-with-rifles on the roof was right. Small guns were bad enough, but long guns meant marksmen. And marksmen meant big trouble for someone. So bugger them! 'Dumb Turk', they were always saying. So he'd be dumb, then!

All the same (and strictly for safety's sake, anyway), he kept his eyes open. And that eventually paid off in a double satisfaction: it was drugs-bust for sure, and he had two of the ring spotted; and neither of them was at one of his tables.

In the corner of the terrace was, for a guess, the supplier, who was from out of town (he looked more like a Czech or a goddamn Pole than a German), and who was scared stiff with the stuff on him, as he wouldn't yet have been if he'd been the buyer, because carrying money wasn't yet a crime.

But he wasn't the scary one, anyway: the one to keep well clear of was the hatchet-faced Arab two tables away, by the steps down to the lake, who was pretending to be a Turk, reading a good Turkish newspaper, but who for bloody-sure wasn't. You could always tell an Arab.

But he was the minder . . . though whether he was minding the sweating-pig Pole, or watching for the money-man, Genghis couldn't decide. All that was certain was that he had scrutinized every new arrival on the terrace, while he hadn't given the Pole a second glance since his arrival, and that (unlike the Pole) he wasn't scared, but sat very still — *too* still — only lifting his eyes from this unread paper.

9

The head-waiter snapped his fingers. "Table Four — Table Five — they are still waiting. Get a move on!"

"Yes, sir!" Genghis bobbed his head obsequiously. "At once, sir!"

Table Five was the fat Berliner, and his fatter wife and fattening daughter, who had their main course to come. (One day it would be he who would snap his fingers!) And Table Four was the big handsome Englishman with the very plain Englishwoman (not his mistress . . . but her clothes were good and her perfume was expensive; so maybe his Mistress, rather!): they had ordered only a snack and rot-gut wine. But none of them had business with the Pole, anyway —

He pushed through the kitchen-doors, meeting the cop's eyes blankly.

Dumb Turk!

"Five — three pike." The heat hit him. "Four — sandwiches, wine."

"Not ready — the pike." One of the cooks slid a tray towards him, rocking the bottle dangerously. "Anything happening?"

The temptation to be smart, and tell them that nothing would happen until the money-man arrived, reached the tip of Genghis's tongue. But then he remembered the cop behind him, and shrugged stupidly.

Somebody shouted something that he missed, but everyone laughed.

Dumb Turk!

He pushed out into the sunlight again, away from the heat into the gentle warmth of the sun: it was one of those good Berlin autumn days, when the bitter winter still seemed far off. Then he saw the head-waiter bending and nodding to the fat German.

And someone else was coming in — a tall, distinguished-looking man —

The head-waiter intercepted him, bowed him to a table, and then snapped his fingers at Genghis once more.

Genghis set down the sandwiches, and took his time over opening the bottle. Then he gave the big Englishman all his attention until the rot-gut had been tasted, allowing himself additional time then to smile at the plain Englishwoman as he filled her glass, if only to annoy the head-waiter. And, anyway, apart from smelling good, she had a fine pair of boobs under that string of pearls. "Thank you madam — sir . . ."

"The gentleman at Table Five, you idiot!" The head-waiter hissed in his ear. "What are you playing at?"

"It wasn't ready — his order." He saw the distinguished-looking man look round over his menu. He would be the one —

"Don't bandy words with me. *Get moving!*"

Again the doors.

Again the policeman. (If he only knew!)

This time a heavily-loaded tray, with the additional beers the fat German had ordered earlier, about which he had clean forgotten: he balanced it expertly, but then waited until Otto and Dieter, who had not been far behind him, came in for their orders. Otto, he remembered, had been providing the Arab with his third cup of coffee. But, not being a dumb Turk, he wouldn't have noticed anything, of course.

Into the sunlight again, with everything as busily normal as before, with the pigs all at their troughs, feeding their faces as though their lives depended on it (all except the Pole, who was still sweating, and the Arab, who was still not really reading his newspaper), and the sail-boats on the lake behind. And, inevitably, the head-waiter gesticulating at him.

He began to weave through the tables —

The money-man buyer was still there, studying his menu. So *he* hadn't seen anything (but Genghis had to hand it to the cops there, the clever swine: there wasn't a uniform inside or a suspicious car outside to be seen, they knew their business all too well, the drugs squad, evidently!) —

Then he swore under his breath as the big Englishman got up, pushing back his chair and blocking his chosen route, so that he had to swing to his left . . . only to find that avenue blocked by the head-waiter himself. And, of course, he wouldn't give ground to make things easier, any more than the damned Englishman: no one ever cared for waiters.

He re-routed himself automatically, pirouetting on paper-thin leather through which he could feel the unevenness of the terrace flagstones. But now the woman was also moving, damn her — not getting up, but pushing her chair back in order to keep her eye on her partner: with a face like that perhaps she was used to him straying.

He coughed politely, and began to squeeze past. But as he did so the Englishman came into sight again —

What! He was heading for the Pole — ? And —

He saw the Arab get up. And, simultaneously, the Englishwoman began to move, pushing him — almost unbalancing him — *what?*

Suddenly the Englishwoman went mad — and his ankle caught on something, so that the tray began to escape from his control: he had only a fraction of a second to catch up with it, or else — *what?*

Nothing mattered but the tray — *the Englishwoman was either mad or drunk, what she was doing, and glass and crockery was crashing, and the Englishman tripping up, and someone was shouting —*

But it was the tray that mattered!

No one saw Genghis's amazing recovery: his gravity-defying swoop, down and up, and the triumph of speed over impetus which caught up with and corrected the unbalance of his burden so triumphantly against all the odds, above Table Five. Or, if anyone did, the next moment obliterated the image, as the *Verfassungsschutz* marksman opened fire. Because then Genghis did finally drop the tray.

PART ONE

A Walk in the Sun

I

THEY WERE WAITING for him at Heathrow: they took him off the plane ahead of everyone else, like a king or a criminal.

"Dr Audley? Would you come this way please, sir."

"Mmm." He hated being stared at like this. But there was no help for it. All he could do was to come quietly. The uniformed man even took his hand luggage from him. And then the civilian took it from the uniformed man.

It had been obvious, of course, ever since the *Return Immediately* message had been delivered so apologetically by his CIA guard-dog/guide dog, that the shit was in the fan back home; that they had held the flight for ten minutes just so that he could be on it merely confirmed the obvious. But after that the old drug had worked on him as it always did, as it always had done over so many years, so that now he was neither flattered nor apprehensive, but only impatient.

"Oops!" The man in the suit had stopped suddenly, so that he had almost cannoned into him. "What —?"

"Hold on a moment, sir." The man didn't need to explain further, since the reason for their halt was blocking the passage ahead. "Could I have your identification, please?"

"Mmm." Audley watched as the young soldier, green-beretted, camouflage-jacketed and armed-to-the-teeth, scrutinized his passport.

The civilian handed the passport back to him, unsmiling. "Nothing to worry about, Dr Audley. There's an airport security exercise in progress, that's all. And we're in a restricted zone here."

"Yes?" He hadn't the faintest idea where he was, actually. But within all major airports there were gimcrack labyrinths like this. In fact, the Devil himself had probably re-designed Hell in the light of the information he had gained from observing airport layouts.

"We're almost there." Misreading Audley's expression of distaste as transatlantic weariness, the man nodded reassuringly. "Not far now."

He winced within himself. Those were almost the exact words he had been accustomed to feed Cathy on long car-journeys. Which reminded him that, however stimulating, this wasn't the home-coming he'd planned for next week, just in time for her birthday. And he hadn't even got her a present now.

Damn!

"Your bag, sir."

The civilian was offering him his hand luggage while standing outside an anonymous door on which the uniformed man was about to knock.

"Thank you." On the other hand, depending on the nature of this emergency, it might get him home earlier. And, however important his Washington job was supposed to have been, it had also been ineffably boring most of the time. So all this might yet be a time-bonus. "And my other luggage?"

"That's being transferred directly to your onwards flight, sir."

The words took a second to register. "My onwards flight —" He just managed to clip the humiliating question mark off the end.

"Don't worry, sir. I shall attend to it myself." The man was wearily accustomed to querulous questions from VIPs. "And I shall be returning here to collect you —" He looked at his wrist-watch. "— in exactly thirty minutes from now, sir."

If this was Hell, then he wasn't even properly in it, thought Audley irritably: he was in the limbo of transit to somewhere else. And wherever it was, he already didn't want to go there.

Then he realized that the uniformed man was opening the door for him — he hadn't heard either a knock or any reply to it, but the thunderous VIP scowl he had fixed on the poor fellow had rendered the man expressionless.

"Yes — thirty minutes. Thank you." He heard himself reply to them both as he strode into the room like the wrath of God. "What the devil —"

"Hullo, David," said Sir Jack Butler.

Audley felt the wrath of God deflate, collapsing him to his true size in an instant. "Hullo, Jack."

"Close the door, there's a good chap."

"Yes, Jack." He had expected an underling, he realized. Or an equal, anyway. But, equal or underling — or civil servant of any variety and seniority, bearing whatever instructions and orders, and whatever material to be quickly studied, and then signed for or returned — or even the Archbishop of Canterbury himself, with the Thirty-Nine Articles — it would have been all the same. But it was Jack Butler. So he closed the door.

"David, I'm sorry to pull you off a job like this — in this way."

"That's all right, Jack." What he hated about Jack Butler apologies was their sincerity. Anyone else's apologies he could treat with the disdain they deserved. But when Jack said he was sorry, then that was what he was.

"I wouldn't have done it if it wasn't necessary." Butler regarded him steadily.

"No? I mean — *no* —" From having been suddenly embarrassed, Audley became even more suddenly apprehensive: that Jack himself should come to brief him was not in itself too worrying, because knighthood and promotion hadn't changed him one bit; but this elaboration of his apology *was* out of character "— no, of course not, I mean."

"Sit down, David."

Audley sat down — only to discover that the chairs in this particular VIP safe-room were somewhat lower and very much softer than he expected, so that for a moment he felt that he was never going to stop sitting down until he reached the floor. "Ah —— yes, Jack?"

Butler had seated himself without difficulty. "You are here because I made a grave error of judgement," he said simply. "As a result of which we have lost someone."

Audley's brain went into over-drive. Taking responsibility for mistakes had never been one of Jack Butler's problems: he had been taking it for upwards of forty years, ever since he had first sewn his lance-corporal's single stripe on to his battle-dress blouse. But losing someone was always unsettling, and all the more so in these somewhat less violent days.

"Who's dead?" It came out brutally before he could stop it, as the possible names of those at risk presented themselves — names, faces and next-of-kin.

"No one you know." Butler drew a single breath. "But it should have been you, David."

"Me?" Taken together with that 'error of judgement' that had all the makings of a sick little joke. But Butler had never been a man for jokes, sick or otherwise. And he certainly wasn't joking now. "What d'you mean — me?"

"Jaggard asked us to make a contact with someone from the other side." Coming straight to the point was more Butler's style. "From the Arbatskaya Ploshchad."

"From — ?" That was even more precisely from 'the other side': it was from the other side of the Kremlin — not the KGB side (from which, in the Dark Ages, orders to kill had so often emanated), but the GRU . . . which, in the present climate, was even more surprising. "From military intelligence, Jack?" But then, coming from anywhere over there at this moment, it was not so much surprising as — what? Astonishing — ? Outrageous? The synonyms shunted each other almost violently enough to de-rail his train of thought, leaving him finally with *incomprehensible* for choice. "But — for Christ's sake, Jack! — what — ?" Only then he realized that 'What am I supposed to have done?' was redundant: Jack Butler knew as well as he did that neither his Washington activities nor any others in which he had recently been involved could remotely be tagged even as annoying to the Russians, let alone dangerous. "What sort of contact?"

"A defection." Butler was ready for him.

Well . . . *yes*, thought Audley, relaxing slightly. Defections were

18

certainly on the cards these days: ever since the winds of change had started to blow through the Soviet Union and its satellites the possibility of picking up a useful defector or two had been widely canvassed. He had even written a paper on that very subject for the use of station commanders. But that had been all of eighteen months ago, in the early days of *glasnost* and *perestroika*. And, in any case — but the hell with that! "Why us, though? Jaggard knows we're not usually into field-work. And, come to that, he doesn't even like us to be, anyway."

"Yes." In the matter of the duties and scope of the Department of Intelligence Research and Development, Jack Butler was at one with Henry Jaggard, however much they disagreed on other matters. "But, in this case, the defector asked for us." He sighed. "Or, to be exact, he asked for *you*, David. By name."

It *had* been that damned defection paper, thought Audley wrathfully: it had carried a routine follow-up request, for those who wanted more information or who had information to give, so that he could up-date it subsequently; and anyone with an ounce of knowledge could have traced it back to him from its style and content; so some imperial idiot down the line had been careless with it, and it had fetched up on someone's desk at GRU headquarters.

"His name was Kulik." Butler returned to his point. "Oleg Filipovitch Kulik."

Kulik —

Then the past tense registered. "Oleg Filipovitch Kulik . . . *deceased*, I take it?"

Butler nodded.

"Kulik?" That wasn't so very surprising, because defecting was a high-risk enterprise, as Oleg Filipovitch must have known. However, what Butler was expecting was that he would now pick that name out of the memory-bank. But the only *Kulik* he could recall from the paying-in slips of thirty years was a third-rate Red Army general who had never been close to military intelligence (but rather, from his long and disastrous career, the opposite); and who, in any case, must be long-since dead.

"Yes?" Butler looked at him expectantly.

"Never heard of him. What was he offering?"

"He didn't say. He merely said that it was of the highest importance." Butler stopped there, compressing his lips.

"And?" Audley recognized the sign. Beneath that worrying apology and the customary politeness, Sir Jack Butler was incandescent with that special red-headed rage which always smouldered within him, but which he never failed to control no matter what the provocation. *Hot heart, cool head*, as old Fred had been so fond of saying: Butler was the sort of man he had liked best of all.

"They're not sure that he was GRU." Butler released his lips. "But they think there was a man named Kulik in their computer records department, liaising with KGB Central Records. Only, since they aren't sure about the value of what he was offering they're not prepared to be certain."

'They' were Jaggard's Moscow contacts, presumably. And in this instance they were quite right. Because if Kulik's lost goodies were peanuts it wasn't worth risking their necks for him. But if the goodies really had been dynamite, then Kulik's bosses would be just waiting to pounce on whoever started to ask questions about him now.

But now, also, he was beginning to see the shape of the game, even though the ball was hidden under the usual ruck of disorderly, bloody-minded, dirty-playing players who knew that the referee was hovering near, whistle-in-mouth. "So we know sod-all about him really — right?"

"That's about the size of it, yes." Butler looked as though he was about to pull rank. With reluctance, of course (and especially with Audley, who had once been his superior officer; but with Kulik dead and thirty-minus-minutes at his back and a plane somewhere on the tarmac out there, if it had to be pulled, then he would pull it). "They're working on him now."

"I'll bet they are." Audley knew he would loyally do whatever Jack Butler wanted him to do. Because that was the way he felt about Butler, in spite of all appearances to the contrary: in an uncertain world, Butler had somehow become his sheet-anchor over the years, much to his own surprise. Only, in the meantime, he was going to have his pound of flesh, with or without blood. "But all they know as of now is that Kulik wanted me. And now he's dead — ?" Flesh with blood, he decided. "And, of course, you didn't offer me up for the slaughter . . . Was that the 'error of judgement', Jack? Because, if it was, then I forgive you for it — " He refused to quail before Butler's displeasure "— was that the way it was, Jack?"

Butler looked at his watch. "The way it was . . . was that I didn't think I could get you back quickly enough from Washington." He looked up again. "Besides which, Jaggard said it was just a routine pick-up."

There was no such thing as a routine pick-up. "So you smelt a rat, did you?"

"No. That was what Jaggard said. And I had no reason to disbelieve him."

"No?" No excuses, of course. Where others would be looking to avoid blame, if not actually seeking credit for prescience when things went wrong, Jack Butler was accustomed to tell it how it was. "But Kulik did actually ask for me, you say. So what form did this request take? What did he want us to do?"

"The message was passed at an embassy reception for one of our trade delegations. Low-grade technology — factory robotics for car production. And he didn't really ask us to do anything. He just wanted to be met — by you, David." Butler pursed his lips. "It was your name that sparked Jaggard's Moscow colleagues. They'd never heard of Kulik. But they had heard of you."

"Where did he want to be met?" Audley brushed aside such doubtful fame.

"In West Berlin."

"*In* West Berlin — "

"That's right. He was getting himself across. He said that he had something of the highest importance. He gave his name. And he named the place and date and time of the meeting. Just that — nothing else. Except he wanted you to meet him."

Too bloody simple by half! "Where was the place?"

"A restaurant beside one of the lakes. Well inside the city — nowhere near any crossing. And Jaggard said he'd have the place properly covered, so he didn't reckon on any complications."

Audley felt the minutes ticking away. Maybe that 'too-bloody-simple' had been hindsight. Because it did look reasonably simple, if not routine: Kulik himself had been doing all the risky work, and had in effect offered himself on a plate in the restaurant, free of charge and without advance bargaining. So, really, anyone could have picked the man up, since he had nowhere to go except further westwards after having come so far already.

Then a cold hand touched him between the shoulder-blades as he found himself thinking that, although anyone could have gone, he would actually have fancied a nice easy trip to Berlin, to meet someone who wanted to meet him. He'd always liked Berlin, even in the bad old days.

"And . . . Jaggard didn't mind, when you refused to supply me?" It occurred to him as he spoke that Henry Jaggard *might* have smelt a rat. In which case, if things went wrong, Jack Butler's intransigence could be blamed.

"I promised to produce you in due course, when they'd got Kulik back here."

"Uh-huh." He sensed that something was inhibiting Butler now. And it could be that, even if he hadn't smelt that rat, Butler might well have smelt Henry Jaggard's calculations, even though he would have despised them.

"Yes . . . Well, I thought it might be as well for us to have a representative there, David." Butler scowled honestly. "Just in case Kulik really wanted to deal with Research and Development, not with anyone else."

The cold hand touched Audley again. But then he remembered gratefully that Butler had already reassured him about the casualty list. "A very proper precaution, Jack!"

All the same, the coldness was still there, even while he grinned proper curiosity at Butler by way of encouragement. Because, with Kulik deceased (and no matter how frustrating that certainly was), there was nothing much anyone could do now. And yet here was Sir Jack Butler at Heathrow, like the mountain come to Mahomet. "So who did you send, then?"

"I sent Miss Loftus."

"Oh yes?" In matters of intelligence research, Elizabeth was razor-sharp. But her field experience was necessarily limited by her length of service. "A good choice." And, on the face of it, that was what it must have seemed to be — for Henry Jaggard's 'routine pick-up'. Only, from the granite-faced look of Mount Butler now, it evidently hadn't been. "She's okay, is she, Jack?"

"Yes —" The VIP cordless phone on the low table beside Butler began to buzz, cutting him off but not startling him. "Hullo?"

Audley took refuge in the echo of that reassuring 'yes' for a moment as Butler stared through him while receiving his phone-message. Then the departure/arrival flight monitors on the wall behind caught his attention. They gave him a choice of Stockholm, Athens, Naples or Madrid, but not Berlin, or even Frankfurt — there were no immediate German destinations at all, in fact.

"Thank you." Butler replaced the receiver.

It was just possible that they'd chartered a plane just for him, decided Audley, permutating the scheduled alternatives in order of possibility and then rejecting them all as unlikely. But then, since old Jack was quite notoriously tight-fisted with his Queen's revenue, a chartered plane was either out-of-character or another disturbing indication of extreme urgency.

Butler nodded at him. "Your flight's on schedule, David. They're boarding now."

Audley's eye was drawn back to the monitor. If it was one of those, then it would be Stockholm, with a Berlin connection, the boarding warnings suggested. All the rest were too far away to make sense, so far as that was possible. "You said Kulik was heading for West Berlin. How far did he actually get?"

"He got to the restaurant. He was killed there."

"Christ!" Audley began to make connections. There was a Catch-22 about old-fashioned field experience, rather like fighter-pilot's

23

combat-time: the more you had, the safer you were. But that meant surviving to become safer. "So Elizabeth was on the spot, you mean — was she?"

"Very much on the spot." Butler bit on his own bullet. "Kulik wasn't the only one killed in the restaurant. Jaggard kept his word — he arranged for an escort from Berlin station, to look after her. And the West Germans had the place properly staked out — the *Verfassungsschutz* special squad was covering every exit. All the liaison procedures were observed: Jaggard played it by the book."

Audley nearly repeated his previous blasphemy. "Who else was killed?"

"Our Berlin station man." Butler shook his head. "You don't know him, David. But . . . he was killed alongside her, anyway."

Some 'routine pick-up'! "And what the hell was the *Verfassungsschutz* doing —?" What made it worse was that the special squad was good — not to mention well-armed. "Enjoying their lunch?"

"They killed the assassin. He only got off two shots: one for Kulik and one for our man." Butler shook his head again. "It's no good blaming the Germans, David. But I'm not going into any of the detail now. Miss Loftus will put you into the picture soon enough."

"Oh yes?" What made it worst of all was that it didn't fit properly — in fact, it didn't damn-well fit at all at this moment. But that had to wait, with the way Butler was looking at him. "So now I go to Berlin to clear up the mess, do I?" He frowned at the departures monitor. The Stockholm boarding warning had gone off, and the remaining destinations were incomprehensible. "Or — what?"

"You go to Naples."

"*Naples?*" If it had been Timbuktoo, it would have made no better sense.

"Paul Mitchell will meet you — he's already there. And Miss Loftus will also be there by the time you arrive. They will each brief you. But you are in charge, they know that."

"I should damn-well think so —" A disorderly crowd of questions jostled Audley's brain, pushing in through the hole *Naples* had made in his concentration "— What's Mitchell doing in Naples?"

"His brief is to watch your back. But at the moment he's looking for someone I want you to talk to. Someone you know, David." Butler stared at him. "Do you remember Peter Richardson?"

The disorderly crowd stopped jostling as Naples suddenly became at least partially explicable. "Yes. I remember him." He decided to leave it at that with his Neapolitan boarding light winking at him behind Butler.

"I have his service record here."

Audley accepted the buff envelope automatically. But then he found he could no longer leave it at that after all. "What has Peter Richardson got to do with Kulik? He retired years ago. And he wasn't with us long, anyway."

"Kulik gave us Richardson's name before he died. His name and your name again, David." Butler continued to stare at him. "Is there anything you know about Richardson that we ought to know —" He glanced down at the envelope "— that may not be on record?"

So that was why he was here: to ask the old 64,000 dollar question!

"Without looking at the record . . ." Then he shrugged. Obviously there wasn't anything of significance in it, otherwise he wouldn't have been given it. And the only thing he did know about Peter Richardson which wouldn't be in there had nothing to do with security matters, but was well covered by his own word of honour. "But . . . I can't think of anything. Only, I haven't set eyes on him for years. Not since he up and quit on us. And that would be . . . '74, was it? Years ago, anyway. And I didn't know him all that well, even then." He lifted the envelope. "Isn't that clear from the record?"

"He once pulled you out of trouble, in Italy."

"He did — yes." No use denying what was on record. "And he was there up north, on that job of yours at Castleshields. But I still hardly knew him — he was Fred Clinton's man, not mine." It was Kulik's word against his, it seemed. "Fred's man — Fred's mistake, wasn't he?" That would also be in the damn record, even if Sir Frederick Clinton himself was honourably dead-and-buried, so he didn't need to labour the point. But Kulik's word was final, of course: there was no arguing with a dead man. "So you want me to talk to Peter

25

Richardson. So I'll talk to him." All the same he was still more than puzzled. "You didn't sweat all the way from the Embankment just to ask me if I knew more than was in this rubbish —" he held up the envelope again "— did you?"

"I want you to bring him in, David. We can't force him to come. But I think he may be safer under wraps for the time being. And he may listen to you, of all people."

There was a sharp knock on the door. And, on cue, the Neapolitan boarding light had become desperate.

"*Wait!*" Butler gave the man outside his old Army voice. "When I said that it could have been you in Berlin I meant it. That's why I'm giving you Mitchell to watch your back. And your front, too." The parade-ground volume had gone, but it was still Colonel Butler speaking, not Sir Jack. "Until I'm satisfied that that second bullet didn't have your name on it I can't be sure that there isn't a third bullet still unfired, with Richardson's name on it. So you must exercise due caution in Naples, David. Is that understood?"

"Yes, Jack." Or, as everyone was so fond saying, *See Naples, and die!* But, in the meantime, he had a plane to catch.

II

THEY WERE WAITING for him at Naples too, of course: they took him off the plane ahead of everyone else. Only this time, even though the stewardess treated him like a VIP, the rest of them were in two minds about him — even those who heard him addressed as *Professore* —

"Professore Audley? This way, if you please, Professore."

Everyone had looked at him when he'd arrived last and late. Now, regardless of the Italian custom of upping even the most cobwebby doctorate to professorial status, the suspicious expressions on the faces of those passengers nearest to him suggested that they were mentally bracketing him with *Professore* Moriarty, as another master-criminal caught at last.

But after that it was simpler, with no Heathrow labyrinth to negotiate, only a car waiting for him, with Paul Mitchell standing beside it.

Or, rather, three cars —

Or, rather . . . half the Italian army?

"Hi there, David." In dark glasses and open-necked shirt Mitchell looked like any late-season English tourist, in striking contrast to Audley's Italian escort, whose shiny crumpled suit had shouted 'Policeman' in confirmation of those recent passenger-suspicions. "Good flight?"

"What are all those soldiers doing?" Audley pointed past Mitchell.

"Don't worry. They're not your reception committee." Mitchell waved an acknowledgement to shiny suit, who was hovering beside the rearmost car. "There's some sort of anti-terrorist scare in progress . . . although they're calling it 'an exercise', like the SURE one you must have seen at Heathrow." He re-directed the wave to the

27

front car. "So everyone's being screened and searched." Now he opened the passenger door. "Everyone except us, that is . . . Get in, David, there's a good fellow . . . No, we're cleared to go out by the back entrance, with these special branch types for protection."

Audley regarded the small battered Fiat with distaste.

"Yes . . . well, I'm sorry about the transport." Mitchell grinned ruefully at him. "Only, I wanted to drive you, so we could talk. And this was all they could find at short notice. But . . . it is unobtrusive. And I have put the seat back as far as it'll go, anyway."

"What about my bags?" Mitchell's rather strained cheerfulness was almost as irritating as the Fiat. "And where's Elizabeth?"

"Elizabeth is chatting up the local cops and the *Guardia di Finanza*." Mitchell circled the car. "She'll be meeting us along the coast. And your bags are being held at the airport. Don't worry."

So that was the last of his luggage, thought Audley. But, although he couldn't see what the Italian customs service had to do with Peter Richardson, it was perhaps as well that Elizabeth was elsewhere, because there certainly wasn't room for her in the back of this car. "I'm not worrying. Just tell me about Peter Richardson."

The car started with a jerk which banged his knees against the dashboard.

"Damn! Sorry!" Mitchell struggled with the gear-box. "This isn't exactly what I've been used to — it drives in Italian . . . or maybe Neapolitan — ah!"

Mitchell's pride and joy at home was a second-hand Porsche, which he had got cheaply for cash after the stock market crash, Audley remembered. "Tell me about Peter Richardson, Mitchell."

"Major Richardson — ?" Mitchell flogged the car to catch up with the unmarked police vehicle ahead. "I thought you were the expert on the elusive Major, David?"

Audley's heart sank. So far from being an expert, he still thought of Peter Richardson as *Captain*, not *Major*. But, of course, that last promotion had been Fred Clinton's work at the time of the fellow's departure, as a sop to their mutual feelings of still more-or-less friendly regret. But that wasn't what mattered so much as the adjective Mitchell had added. "What d'you mean 'elusive'? Haven't you found him?"

The Fiat juddered to a halt, within inches of the leading car which had stopped at what was now a heavily defended exit, complete with a brace of light tanks.

"Yes . . . well . . . 'yes-and-no' is the answer to that, David." Mitchell peered through the dirty windscreen, watching the Italian special branch arguing with the Italian army. "Or, rather, 'no-and-yes', more accurately."

Audley felt his temper begin to slip, but then checked it. Of all his colleagues, apart from Jack Butler himself, he knew Paul Mitchell best. So now he could recognize the tell-tale signs under that accustomed casualness, for all that the man's eyes were concealed behind sunglasses. And the 30-millimetre cannon which was more or less pointing at them at this minute no more accounted for those whitened knuckles on the hands on the steering-wheel than did the little car's gearbox account for that bruising start.

"Uh-huh?" If Paul Mitchell was frightened, then perhaps Jack Butler was right — and perhaps he ought to be *properly* frightened too. But fear was in itself a debilitating influence, so whatever was scaring Mitchell, a display of Audley-temperament would serve no useful purpose.

"Uh-huh?" As Mitchell turned to him he just had time to compose his own expression into what he hoped was one of innocent inquiry. "Is he safe and sound, Paul?"

Mitchell frowned at him, as though such unexpected mildness was just another burden, and a rather unfair one. "I think . . . so far as I know he is — yes."

It was going to be very hard to keep up this Butler-like equanimity. And, in any case, overdoing it would only worry Mitchell more. "You *think* —?"

Activity ahead mercifully distracted Mitchell. The police seemed to have convinced the army that they were not terrorists making their getaway, and barriers were being variously raised and moved.

Audley braced himself, but this time Mitchell recovered his

Porsciie-driver's skill, launching them after the lead car as though they were at the end of a tow-rope, yet still leaving himself half-a-second in which to grimace at his passenger. "You know that all this has been happening rather quickly, David — hoicking you back from the States and me from . . . where I was — ?"

Where Mitchell had been was probably Dublin, thought Audley. And that wasn't a place for rest and recreation. So, until he'd met Elizabeth, he might actually have been cheering up. But after that he might suspect that he'd exchanged the frying pan for the fire. Only that wasn't what he was about to enlarge upon. "Something's already gone wrong, you mean." He tried to sound resigned to such an accustomed turn of events rather than angry.

Mitchell made a face at the thickening traffic ahead. "There was a misunderstanding, let's say."

"Oh yes?" Resignation was actually more appropriate: since no one yet understood what was happening, what else could be expected? "Go on."

"London sent an SG to Rome, warning them that I was coming — and that you were also en route, and that you wanted to talk to Major Richardson." Mitchell massaged the steering-wheel. "To be fair to them in Rome, David . . . the SG wasn't all that explicit. It didn't specify any sort of emergency in asking them to locate Richardson."

"It didn't mention Berlin, you mean?" That was hardly surprising. "So what did they do?"

Mitchell half-shrugged. "They had his address in Amalfi of course. And a bit more than that, seeing he'd been in the business himself in the old days. So they didn't think twice about picking up the phone and calling him up with the good news that you were about to drop in at his *palazzo* — " He glanced at Audley " — is it really a *palazzo* — ?"

"They mentioned my name?" Audley brushed the question aside.

"They didn't at first — " The slipstream of an enormous lorry made the little car shudder " — they didn't actually get through to him, only to some servant at the *palazzo* . . . what do *palazzos* have? Butlers — ? Major-domos?" The vision of a sun-bathed palace on the

Amalfi coast, complete with a uniformed staff, animated a curiosity tinged with envy in Mitchell. "And it's the old family place too, isn't it? His mum was a *marchesa* or a *principessa*, or something, wasn't she?"

"They mentioned my name?" There was no particular reason why Mitchell should know anything about Richardson. Except that Mitchell always knew more than was good for him.

"Only when he played hard to get. I think they rather thought he must be an old buddy of yours, David. And when the . . . major-domo, or whatever . . . when he kept telling 'em the Master was busy, or otherwise-engaged, and could he take a message *per favore* . . . then I'm afraid they did name-drop."

"And what happened then?" Audley still couldn't put that 'yes-and-no', 'no-and-yes', together.

"Then I arrived — in Rome. And I had a little talk with Jack. And, of course, he told me to play it by the book, and tell the Italians we were on their patch, looking to have a chat with an old comrade."

Audley's heart sank again as he imagined what the Italians would have on file under *Audley, David Longsdon*. It would have been all right if old General Montuori was still alive, albeit in well-earned retirement. But with no one to explain the truth between the lines recording his one-time Italian activities Montuori's successor would inevitably expect trouble once that name re-appeared on his blotter — just as Peter Richardson might also have done.

Damn! "Are you about to tell me that Richardson is now missing, Peter?"

"Yes — yes-and-no, David —"

"And just what the hell is that meant to mean?" As he turned on Mitchell the car plunged into a tunnel, startling him as it bathed everything in garish orange light.

"It's not quite as bad as it seems, maybe." The orange light flickered eerily on Mitchell's face. "The Italians got a bit up-tight at first."

Surprise, surprise! "They did?"

31

"Yes . . . They insisted on helping us — on finding Richardson themselves, and delivering him to us. I rather got the impression that he isn't exactly *numero uno* in their popularity stakes."

"What —?" They were in the midst of a deafening maelstrom of tunnel noise-and-traffic on a multi-lane autostrada which hadn't existed in his old Neapolitan days — the days of General Montuori and *Captain* Richardson. "Richardson —?"

"Uh-huh." Mitchell annexed Audley's own useful multi-purpose non-committal grunt for himself. "The elusive major himself — " He nodded " — only, as they apparently haven't found him themselves they're being nicer to us now — *God!*"

Audley's knees hit the dashboard painfully as the little car decelerated fiercely. "What — ?" He could hardly think for the noise.

"Some mad bastard — that mad bastard —" Mitchell stabbed a finger ahead " — has just cut in ahead of me." He looked up at his mirror. "They're all mad — stark, staring mad, David —" He frowned " — or . . . I hope they are, anyway — "

Audley massaged his bruises. He couldn't keep shouting 'What?', he had to find a more sensible question. "If no one knows where Richardson is . . . what makes you think he's safe?"

The car burst into sunlight. "Safe —?" For a moment he didn't seem to have heard the rest of the question. "That's why I think he's safe: because no one knows where he is." He peered into the mirror again. "I just hope the same applies to us, now that I've lost our escort somehow — "

Audley looked around. What was certain was that he didn't know where he was. But this was one bit of Italy where, on a clear day like this, that ought to be easily rectified once a sufficient gap in the buildings on his left opened up.

"Ah! There he is — phew!" Mitchell grinned relief at him. "Sorry, David. Really, I quite enjoy driving in Italy. It's the nearest thing to stock-car racing I know. But keeping in with our escort rather spoils it, that's all . . . But, as I was saying — what was I saying?"

Audley gave up trying to spot Vesuvius. "Richardson is safe. But you don't know where he is."

"That's right." Mitchell sounded almost cheerful. "So he knows where he is."

Audley could see another nightmare tunnel ahead. "What d'you mean?"

"I mean that he got in touch with us. The major-domo did his stuff, evidently. So now the Major's calling the shots, David. And we're going to meet him."

After Berlin that was an unfortunate choice of words. But the tunnel closed in on them before Audley could react. And this time, with an enormous sixteen-wheeler thundering beside them, no further words were possible, and even thought wasn't easy.

Light returned at last, yet Vesuvius was still hidden behind buildings. Except, by now they must be beyond it, with Amalfi still an hour or more ahead. But now he had thought of what he had been going to say. "You know about Kulik, Mitchell."

"Not a lot." Mitchell sniffed. "Does anyone know more than that?" He glanced at Audley quickly. "Have you pulled the rabbit out of the hat again, Dr Audley — *Professore* — ?"

"No."

Mitchell flicked another glance at him. "You're about to remind me that Kulik also called the shots — day, time and place — are you?"

Audley winced at the repetition of 'shots'. But, having talked to both Jack Butler and Elizabeth, Mitchell had it all pat, evidently. And meanwhile the car was beginning to slow down again.

"And it didn't do him a lot of good — is that it?" This time Mitchell didn't bother to look at him. "Don't worry, David. I haven't forgotten that. It's at the very top of my list that I'm your minder."

Audley was about to look away in exasperation. But then he caught a glimpse of the sea beyond Mitchell's profile.

The sea at last! 'The sea! The sea!' — the cry of Xenophon's ten thousand fellow-Greeks had been dinned into him so thoroughly at school by old Wimpy long ago that the words always came back to him at every first sight of it, at first almost triumphantly, and then almost sadly as he

33

became conscious of the length of years which now separated him from that first-learning!

"What is it, David?" Mitchell sat bolt-upright. "What have you seen?"

"Just the sea." The man was a bag of nerves. "That's all."

But it wasn't all. And it wasn't just the sea — it was the Bay of Naples . . . Old Wimpy's Bay of Naples — no, not Naples, but *Neapolis*, with Pompeii and Herculaneum close at hand, and Paestum just down the road: the happy hunting-ground of every Classics-master who had ever had to hammer irregular verbs into —

The sea —? This time he also sat bolt-upright. "What the hell — ?"

"What — ?" Mitchell's nerves had been jarred again.

Audley looked around as best he could within the maddening constraint of his safety belt and the ridiculous little car itself. "The sea's on the wrong side. This isn't the way to Amalfi."

"*What?*" Mitchell's voice cracked with exasperation.

"Where the hell are we?" He fumbled with the window-winder: if the sea was on *that* side — where were they going?

"We're in a traffic jam, is where we are — what d'you mean, 'the wrong side' —? *For Christ's sake, David! Don't do that — get your head in —*" The rest of the command was drowned by a cacophony of horns behind them.

Audley could see the jam of cars. But it was about all he could see: with one pantechnicon behind them and another trying to push them off the road, wherever Vesuvius might be, it could be anywhere. But they were undoubtedly in a traffic jam: they were on the approach to some sort of Italian clover-leaf junction, and that seemed to be a *sauve qui peut* invitation to every driver to assert himself, according to his courage if not the size of his vehicle.

"Get your head back in please, David." Mitchell ignored the noise behind him and recovered some of his cool. "*Please*, David —"

The very coolness turned Audley back towards Mitchell, because of its underlying panic: it caught exactly the final desperation of that Royal Sussex corporal on the grenade-throwing primary training exercise long ago, when Trooper Arkwright in front had held on to

34

his live grenade between them, instead of throwing it out of the drill-trench —

"Throw it." (Matter-of-fact, the corporal. Almost conversational.) *"Throw it —"* (No longer matter-of-fact: frozen-faced, rather — was that the face? But he couldn't remember the face: faces sometimes eluded him.) "THROW IT — !" (Memory blanked out at that point, as the Royal Sussex corporal and Trooper Audley had hit the dirt in the bottom of the trench, in an attempt to reach Australia before the grenade exploded) —

He found himself smiling as he turned. Time had quite washed away the sick horror of that moment, leaving in memory only the comedy of their undignified survival after Arkwright's belated throw, and then the wondrous flow of the corporal's invective, unleashed after a matching moment of speechlessness. But then he stopped smiling as he saw the half-drawn pistol in Mitchell's hand.

"Put the window up, David." Mitchell wasn't looking at him.

Just ahead of them, weaving between the gaps in the cars in the other lane, were a couple of Neapolitan urchins carrying trays of cigarettes and assorted junk.

"For God's sake, Paul! They're only — "

"Put the window up." Mitchell didn't take his eyes off the urchins.

"Throw it!"

Audley wound the window up.

"Only kids." Mitchell slid the pistol back under his armpit before completing his sentence.

The car moved again, leaving the children behind.

"Only kids." Mitchell nodded. "But that's the way it's done. Beirut . . . the West Bank . . . Belfast one day, I shouldn't wonder. All you need is a traffic jam in the usual place. Or, if not, they can easily cause one . . . And then a bit of carelessness, like an open window. And then, just pop a grenade in, and run."

35

"A ——" The coincidence with his own recent thought chilled Audley into silence. As of now, that would never be a jolly anecdote again. But meanwhile he had to reassure himself. "Aren't you being a bit over-cautious?"

"Probably." Mitchell breathed out heavily as they shook themselves free of the traffic jam, turning under the autostrada on to what looked like a minor road. "Maybe I'm a bit twitchy."

Too long in the trenches, thought Audley critically. Mitchell's problem was the reverse of Elizabeth's. And it was one thing (and a good one) to give Research and Development types like Elizabeth a bit of field-experience, but another (and a very bad one) to overstretch them just because they showed an aptitude for that too. In fact, seconding Mitchell to Henry Jaggard's Dublin operation was like chartering Concorde to fly relief food to Ethiopia: when he finally over-shot some inadequate runway — when his already-threadbare academic cover finally split under the pressure — all bloody-Jaggard's sincere regrets wouldn't put the clock back.

Mixed metaphors, he thought, also critically. But, trenches and Concordes and threadbare clocks aside, he must be gently encouraging now —

"I didn't mean that, Paul." He could see the sea again. "I know you're just obeying Jack Butler's orders." But not the sea: this was Wimpy's Bay of Naples, still — it had to be. And . . . and there was even a road sign ahead —

Baia — Bacoli — Miseno —

Not just Wimpy's bay: Wimpy's ancient *Misenum*, from which Admiral Pliny had heroically taken his fleet to succour the Vesuvius disaster-survivors of Pompeii and Stabia —

Damn!

"What I meant . . . I don't see how anyone can know that I'm here —" He almost added 'wherever I am'. But now he knew where he was, even if he didn't know why he was so far from Amalfi — "except Peter Richardson —?"

"And the Italians." Mitchell accelerated after the police car in front. "And the entire staff of the *Palazzo* Richardson —? And

Uncle Tom Cobleigh and All, thereafter?" He nodded at Audley without taking his eyes off the police car. "But chiefly Major — *Peter* — Richardson . . . yes."

Suddenly everything was turned on its head, upside-down, in a way which he'd never even considered. But which, of course, Mitchell had quite naturally taken as a possibility from the moment he'd been saddled with his orders. "Peter Richardson isn't a traitor, Paul."

"No?" Slight shrug. "Well . . . if you say not, David . . ." This time he managed a quick glance. "After fifteen years — or more, would it be — ?" Now he was on the *Miseno* road. "Are you willing to bet your life on that — never mind mine . . . which I still rather value — ?" Another shrug.

Audley waited.

"You're the boss." Mitchell finally remembered the rest of his orders, but with an unconcealed air of resignation. "And the expert."

There was more. And Audley wanted to hear it.

Shrug. "Just so you remember that Kulik must also have reckoned no one knew where he was, David."

That was the opening. "I haven't forgotten that. But you told me that Peter Richardson is arranging this meeting. And you also told me not to worry, Paul."

The police car ahead showed its brake-lights, and then turned off the road.

"So I did." Mitchell followed suit. "And so *he* has . . . more or less — yes."

'More-or less' was like 'yes-and-no': as unsatisfactory as it was imprecise. Only now they were running out of road — quite literally running out of it, as the final narrow stretch of tarmac ended and they bumped on to a pot-holed sand-swept track. And he could see the sea again, between a scatter of beach-cafés and kiosks, with a few parked cars and a jetty ahead: they had not only run out of road, they were running out of land, too.

Mitchell parked beside the police car, right on the foreshore.

"This is where we change horses, David. But you stay here for a moment."

"Why?" The next horse had to be a boat. But there was no craft in view belonging to the police or the customs, let alone the Italian navy. Indeed, what he could see from here suggested that this wasn't one of the Baia–Miseno peninsula's more fashionable anchorages.

"Because I say so." Mitchell started to open his door, but then stopped. "How much did Jack Butler tell you about Berlin, David? Apart from Kulik."

Audley could guess what was coming. "He said we lost a man."

"That's right. Name of Sinclair — Edward Sinclair. I met him once." Mitchell nodded. "Big chap. Not specially bright. But big. And a fluent German-speaker. That was why Ted was in Berlin, probably."

Audley couldn't place Edward Sinclair. But that merely confirmed what Butler had said. "So what?"

"Big like you, David." Mitchell paused, and looked around. "Elizabeth will tell you in more detail. But when she got to the rendezvous, Kulik was already there, sitting at a table all by himself. *And so was the man who shot him.*" He stared at Audley. "Do you get the picture? He was waiting for *you*, David."

Audley stared back at him as the picture formed in his mind.

"Okay." Mitchell nodded again. "So I'm just going to have a quick look round. And then we'll take a boat trip. And we'll just hope Major Peter Richardson has got his act together properly, and that he hasn't forgotten all he was taught. Okay?"

If there was one thing they could rely on, it was Peter Richardson's memory, thought Audley. But at that moment it also looked as if it was the only thing. "Where are we going?"

Mitchell grinned suddenly. "We're going to be end-of-season tourists, David." He swung his door open. "How would you like to visit old Tiberius's villa on Capri, eh?"

III

FOR A MOMENT, as he examined the 18-hour stubble on his chin in the mirror of the motor-cruiser's Lilliputian lavatory, Audley forgot about the dead. But then they crowded back into his thoughts, uninvited but insistent.

'It's bad luck, thinking of the dead': who had said that —?

The question, no sooner treacherously asked, was instantly answered by memory: it had been 'Daddy' Higgs — Troop Sar'-Major Higgs himself, no less, of course — of course! Old Daddy Higgs!

'It's bad luck, thinkin' of the dead when there's work to be done, Mr Audley, sir': memory expanded the superstition automatically, with the words perfectly recalled even though that grizzled face itself had become hazy. (Had it really been grizzled, even?) It had been 'Daddy' because the men complained that he was always fussing — but Old because he proudly wore the 1937 Coronation Medal . . . so that when he'd been burnt to a crisp on Fleury Ridge he'd been — what? All of 30-years-of-age, plus maybe a year or two, forever after? God!

He shook his head at his reflection and dried his hands on the dirty scrap of towel. Daddy Higgs was long-dead. And General Raffaele Montuori was five years' dead, alas! But Oleg Filipovitch Kulik and Edward Sinclair and one as-yet-unidentified assassin were very newly-deceased. And —

Damn! Daddy Higgs's theory, behind his admonishment to his youngest and greenest (and most stupid?) subaltern, had been that the dead always had a majority vote; so, by thinking of them, you invited them to vote you into their club —

Damn!

But he had to think of the newly-dead, all the same, while he could, with both Elizabeth and Mitchell somewhere out there, waiting for him under the tattered canvas awning at the stern, and the politely-suspicious senior Italian intelligence officer whom he'd so briefly just met also expecting an invitation — damn!

He scowled at himself. There could be very little doubt that his own invitation had been given, in Berlin. Kulik, all alone but no doubt sweating with relief now that he'd crossed the Wall safely, had in fact been comprehensively betrayed: date, time and place-betrayed, from the inside. But, with such exact information, all that bloodbath in the restaurant could have so easily been avoided that it must have been intended.

He shook his head at himself. Because all that, while it was enough to give Butler and Mitchell the frights, equally didn't make sense, either. So he was back to old Wimpy's despairing anger, when any of his pupils (but, it had always seemed, most of all one David Audley!) had bogged up the logic of the crystal-clear Latin language: 'This is nonsense, boy! And nonsense *must* be wrong!'

There they were, waiting for him.

"Elizabeth." He had already nodded to her, embarrassed that his most urgent need wasn't information, but a lavatory. But now he could come to the point. "Tell me about Berlin."

"There isn't much to tell, David." Her chin came up. "I'm afraid I made a hash of it."

"She didn't make a hash of it, actually," said Mitchell. "Henry Jaggard and our Jack mixed the hash. Lizzie never had a chance."

Elizabeth gave Mitchell a wooden glance, and then dismissed him without bothering to react. "It was supposed to be routine. But the Germans weren't happy with Kulik coming across under his own steam: they wanted to pick him up straightaway."

"But you didn't know how he was coming across." Mitchell again came to her defence. "No one even knew what he looked like, for God's sake!"

He should have foreseen that Mitchell would be a problem, thought Audley: there had been the beginnings of something between the two of them, Mitchell and Elizabeth, once. But now it was very much a one-sided thing. "Go on, Elizabeth, please."

"Yes." The jaw came up again, more determined than before: the Loftus jaw which, on her famous naval ancestors, must have struck terror into friend and foe alike. "As Dr Mitchell says, we weren't able to supply them with any information, except as regards the RV. So . . . maybe I should have expected trouble. But I didn't."

"It was . . . 'just routine', they told her," supplemented Mitchell.

Audley coughed diplomatically. "I take it you weren't armed?"

"The *Verfassungsschutz* was covering the place, David," said Mitchell. "They're always armed to the teeth. And they get uptight if anyone else is. They're always rowing with the Americans about it."

"Uh-huh —" As the cruiser rocked in the gentle Mediterranean swell Audley pretended to reach for one of the supports of the awning, but missed it and caught Mitchell's arm instead.

"Not like the Italians, fortunately — ouch!" Pain cut Mitchell off.

"Sorry." Audley kept his grip. "So neither of you was armed . . . How did you identify Kulik?"

"We didn't. Not for certain. He was there alone. And there was also an Arab, sitting alone, but we discounted him. So . . . Ted — I sent Ted over, David."

Babes and innocents! And now she was blaming herself — and quite rightly. Except that Henry Jaggard and Jack Butler had even more to answer for between them. "Uh-huh?" That was all he could say.

"It happened very quickly."

When it happened, it always happened very quickly.

"Ted reached his table. It was three tables away from where we were sitting. Kulik looked up at him." She stared through him. It

41

wasn't happening quickly now: it was happening frame-by-frame on slow advance, and she couldn't stop looking at it. "I think Ted said something."

"And the Arab?"

"He was by the steps." She continued to stare. "He'd got up. At least . . . he must have got up . . . when Ted Sinclair got up."

She hadn't been watching the Arab: it had been a routine pick-up, and Arabs hadn't featured in it. But now he was in the frame at last. And by then it had been too late.

"I saw the gun then." She focused on him suddenly. "He'd had it behind his newspaper as he walked — he was holding the paper across his chest when I first saw him by the steps." She frowned at him. "Then . . . he simply pointed it."

"What sort of gun?"

"What sort of gun?" She blinked at him.

"7.65 Browning — North Korean copy. Short silencer." Mitchell murmured the information. "A pro's gun, David."

"Yes?" Mitchell knew about guns. But to know so much about this one he must have been in contact with the Berlin security police on his own account. Or perhaps, in giving him his minder's job, Butler had obliged him helpfully. "Go on, Miss Loftus . . . You saw the gun —?"

"Yes." She drew another deep breath. "As I saw it . . . he dropped the paper and held the gun two-handed. And he shot Ted Sinclair with it first, David."

So that was why they were all so worried for him. "And then he shot Kulik?"

"Yes ——"

"No!" Mitchell had moved out of reach. "You're not telling it how it was now, Lizzie, damn it!"

"Mitchell —" Audley began angrily "— for God's sake!"

"No! He's right, David." Elizabeth shook her head, blinking again. "I saw the gun . . . and I don't know . . . I knew it was already too late, then . . . But there was this bottle on the table, the waiter had just brought —" After the hesitations the words suddenly tumbled out "— so I picked it up and threw it at him, David. At the Arab, I mean."

"That's more like it." Mitchell nodded. "And she bloody-hit him too, by God, what's more: that's the way it was! She's not an ex-games mistress for nothing, by golly — cricket as well as hockey was it, Lizzie?"

Audley held up his hand quickly before Elizabeth exploded. "All right! You threw the bottle, Elizabeth —"

Elizabeth breathed out. "Yes."

"And it hit him." He kept his hand in Mitchell's view.

"Not really." Her anger didn't subside, but she controlled it. "I don't know — I'm not really sure. Because . . . everything was happening at once. And there were tables in between, with people, David. They started to scatter and scream when I threw the bottle, before they knew what was happening."

"And Kulik —?"

"He was trying to duck under the table, I think." Her lips tightened. "The Arab shot him in the back — I saw him recover, and then aim again, slightly downwards . . . He — it was as though he shrugged the bottle off, and steadied himself again before he fired." She gave Audley a single decisive nod. "But I couldn't see Kulik by then, not properly. And that was when the German police marksman on the roof also fired — I heard the thump of the Arab's first shot, but not the second one: I only heard the rifle-shot. And it knocked the Arab down the steps — I wasn't even sure that he had fired, that second time — not right then."

"No, of course." It wasn't simply the bitter cocktail of professional misjudgement and personal guilt that was bugging her now: it was the imprecision of her own eye-witness recollections, which her training and her honesty were both requiring her to admit as he forced her to drain the cup — and in front of Paul Mitchell, too, of all people.

And Mitchell was just about to open his big mouth again, too —

"So what happened then?" The very last thing she wanted would be sympathy and understanding from Mitchell.

43

"I went to Kulik."

Good girl! If there had been two compressed seconds of consternation after she had hurled a full bottle of wine across a peaceful Berlin restaurant, it would have been nothing compared with the chaos after that rifle-shot. There would have been just one milli-second of silence, in which the meaning of the sound registered. And then it would have been pure panic. But she had kept her head, nevertheless. Good Girl!

Only she wouldn't thank him for saying as much. "You went to Kulik —?"

"He was in a bad way. I thought he was dead, actually. Or as good as."

"Which he was." Mitchell nodded. "As good as." He nodded again. "7.65 soft-nosed dum-dum: pro-gun, pro-bullet — went diagonally through him, upwards and then in all directions, David." Final nod. "He damn-well should have been dead — like Ted Sinclair already was."

Elizabeth was looking at Mitchell now. But she didn't seem to see him. "Yes."

Then she returned to Audley. "He opened his eyes. And he looked at me."

In surprise, it would have been. Whatever natural death might be like, unnatural and violent death always came as a surprise, even in war, where it had been neither surprising nor unnatural, Audley remembered: even those who had claimed to be resigned to the inevitable the night before, regardless of Daddy Higgs's superstitious outrage, hadn't believed that it was actually happening to them.

"He said something in Russian."

Yes. And, for choice, that would be 'Mother'. Even William Shakespeare, who was usually right about everything, had been wrong about that, in imagining that the dying thought about their wives and children, let alone their unpaid debts. Although, to be strictly accurate about what he could recall, it was the younger ones who had remembered their mothers, while the older — or the relatively older, anyway — had used words which Elizabeth might not have known in English, never mind Russian.

"Yes?" He realized that as he remembered Normandy he had been looking through her. And that had disconcerted her. "Yes, Elizabeth?"

She still looked at him strangely, frowning.

"Yes, Miss Loftus?" He felt the wind on his face, and the boat rolling under him in the swell: they were far out into the bay now, and he felt time at his back with Capri looming ahead somewhere. But together they sharpened his voice, from a gentle question to an order.

Still she frowned at him. "I said . . . 'You're going to be all right', David."

Good girl, again! (But perhaps it hadn't been him she'd really been looking at, by God!) "Yes —?" (But she was looking at him now.)

"He didn't seem to hear me." But looking at him seemed to steel her. "So I thought . . . first, I thought he was dead. But then he opened his eyes again — he'd closed them . . . But then he opened them again."

Audley waited. This, after all, was the important bit. "Yes —?"

"I thought . . . no, I knew he was dying, then . . ." She trailed off, almost as though ashamed.

If he'd been there he would have been dead by then. But then, again, he might not have been. Because he would never have just sat there in the open, waiting for Kulik to make contact, just because Henry Jaggard had pronounced the occasion to be mere 'routine', with Kulik making all the running, when he knew nothing about either the man or what he was bringing out. Only, Elizabeth hadn't known any better — and Henry Jaggard and Jack Butler had made their respective errors of judgement. So now he was here — in the bloody-middle of the Bay of Naples, and without the faintest idea what he was doing, as a result. (Except that he did know slightly more about Peter Richardson than about Oleg Filipovitch Kulik . . . which was almost nothing. So now he was

45

damn-well boxed in by that, and would have to let Richardson make the running this time, whatever the risk, damn it. Damn it!)

So now he was angry, because he was having to wait again. "Go on —" He caught his anger in that instant as it jolted him with a sudden insight: this was Elizabeth Loftus, and she was one tough lady — a real 'shield-maiden', if ever there was one. So by then, in the midst of that Berlin chaos, she would have been angry too . . . with all the shame-of-failure and guilt-for-Ted-Sinclair still in the future. "That was when he dropped my name . . . and Peter Richardson's, did he?"

The Loftus-jaw again. "I shouted at him." (Those Loftus-ancestors had hanged men on the yard-arm at the Nore, back in '98 — 1798!) "And he said, 'Tell Audley', David." (And the ones they hadn't hanged, they'd flogged.) "Then he said, 'Tell him Piotr Richardson knows.' And he tried to say more, but then he haemorrhaged — he coughed up blood all over me . . . And then he died."

Audley nodded. That was near enough what Butler had indicated: that Elizabeth Loftus would spell out what had actually happened.

"Famous last words," murmured Mitchell. "'Tell Audley'! So what is it that you know, David? What's the little shared secret you have with our elusive Major?"

Audley shook his head irritably. "What happened then, Elizabeth?"

"But that's the problem of course, Lizzie." Mitchell nodded to himself. "His problem — our problem . . . everyone's problem, eh? For once you don't know, do you David? Or you don't know what it is you're supposed to know, rather . . . all those years ago — uh-huh? Otherwise he wouldn't be here."

"Shut up, Paul." Elizabeth transferred her anger for an instant. "What do you want to know, David?"

What did he want to know? "What did the Germans do? Are they holding anyone? What sort of statement have they put out?"

"They haven't got any leads." She paused for a moment,

marshalling her answers. "Only the Arab's passport. Which doesn't actually prove anything for sure . . . except that it looks like one of a PFLP batch, according to the Israelis." She didn't quite look at Mitchell for confirmation. "But . . . they grilled everyone who was there. Only that didn't produce anything. Because most of them were regulars. And the rest were cleared easily, Colonel Schneider said."

"And the restaurant staff?"

"They were clear too. Except a new waiter, who was a Turk." She closed her eyes for an instant. "They held him for questioning. Because . . . they thought maybe he'd caused a diversion, before the shooting started."

"A diversion?"

"He didn't. He dropped his tray." Her mouth twisted. "But that was after the shooting, not before, I was able to tell them. But . . . they're still holding him."

"Why?"

"That was to do with their official statement. Because . . . what they're putting out — at least for the time being, David — is that it was a gangster shoot-out, involving Turks and drugs." She gave him a clear-eyed look. "The Germans were extremely helpful, David. But Colonel Schneider said he didn't think the statement would stick for long."

"Extremely embarrassed, more like." Mitchell sniffed derisively.

"Do be quiet, Mitchell." Audley silenced Mitchell, and then nodded encouragingly at Elizabeth. (They were both right, of course: Schneider was a damn good man. So he would have been hugely embarrassed by such a monumental fuck-up on his patch.) "How . . . 'helpful', Elizabeth?"

She studied him for a second. "I talked to Colonel Schneider. And then he contacted Jack in London. And they concocted a holding story between them, to which I agreed . . . after I'd talked to Jack — Sir Jack." The look was now clear-eyed. "Sir Jack told Colonel Schneider that I had been standing in for you, David. And . . . the Colonel knows you, doesn't he?"

That was an understatement. But it was none of anyone's business right now. "What story?"

"It's chiefly to do with Ted Sinclair." The mention of Sinclair hurt her. "Officially, they haven't put out any names, as yet — just that it was a criminal police matter, with no politics involved." Elizabeth blinked. "But Colonel Schneider has arranged for one of the Berlin papers to pick up a leak that an innocent foreigner was unfortunately killed in the cross-fire. And they've put out that he was a British Council officer who'd just arrived in Berlin from Frankfurt, who was lunching a . . . a visitor, David."

"A visitor?" Mitchell snapped the question. "With three people dead, Lizzie —? And the Berlin papers chasing everyone who was there?"

"The visitor was me." Elizabeth threw Mitchell off. "And I was representing the British Ladies' Hockey Federation, to arrange an exhibition match in the spring. And, if they check up on that, the BLHF will confirm they sent a committee member to Berlin, to examine the condition of the playing-fields." She tossed her head. "But that isn't important . . . even if they could trace me . . . I *am* a BLHF committee member because I'm a Ladybird —"

"A *what?*" exclaimed Mitchell.

"For God's sake, Mitchell ——" Audley joined her. "Yes, Elizabeth —?"

"Yes." Elizabeth dismissed Mitchell. "The name Colonel Schneider did leak was for you, David: Ted Sinclair has become 'David Ordway'. And the British Council in Frankfurt has been told that their head office and the BLHF were sending two people to Berlin. Do you see?"

"That won't hold for long." Mitchell shook his head at Elizabeth. "If we're lucky . . . maybe another day. But no more."

But Audley saw. And, although Jack Butler hadn't quite told him everything, he saw even more clearly. Because Butler and Schneider between them had conspired to buy him *time*, as Mitchell had emphasized. But, as neither of them was certain that they'd done that in spite of all their best efforts, they were letting him decide how

48

much those efforts might be worth: that, either if he failed to elicit this information . . . or, even if he did, and he judged the risk too great, and played it accordingly . . . then he would act accordingly anyway . . . with Elizabeth and Mitchell beside him, and the Italians breathing down his neck.

"Yes." He was here now, in the Bay of Naples. So the bottom line was that Jack Butler was relying on him to make the right decision without any footling restriction, as from company commander to second-lieutenant. And the years which separated him from Peter Richardson, also separated Jack from that: even though he was now back in the field, and far from home, Butler expected him to weigh politics and diplomacy, as well as survival, and coming-safe-home to Mrs Faith Audley and Miss Catherine Audley, into the bargain.

"So, in theory, you're not supposed to be here." Mitchell, with his responsibility for that survival, went one better. "Because, whoever put that *kamikaze*-Ay-rab into Berlin is supposed to be presuming that he took you out with his first shot, as per contract — eh?" But he sneered at his own hypothesis as he offered it. "Is that what we're supposed to assume?" He rocked with the boat's motion: coming back to England — or, actually, to Wales — from Dun Laoghaire (which was worse than this: which was frequently sideways as well as up and down . . . so he had his sea-legs now, from all those Anglo-Irish crossings!). "But you're not relying on that, are you?"

Audley held on to the stanchion which Mitchell had abandoned in moving out of his reach. What neither Butler nor Mitchell could imagine was that coming back to the sharp end was more interesting: that, however uncomfortable, it also reassured him that he was still alive, and not yet too geriatric for those duties to which he nowadays helped sentence others, for whom no scheduled flights were held, and who were not delivered to (or taken off) those flights as though they were such Very Important Persons that they didn't have to worry (or, couldn't waste time worrying?), because they were Too Important. So that now (no matter how frightened he could be if he

49

let himself think about it) . . . at least he wasn't so bored with life anyway!

"Very well! So Kulik was waiting for me. But so was the Arab. And he took out Ted Sinclair, believing he was me. So why Kulik, then — ? If he was just bait?"

Mitchell shrugged. "So maybe they double-crossed him." Another shrug. "The mouse springs the trap — who cares about the cheese? Not the Russians!"

"No." Elizabeth shifted uneasily. "It doesn't fit."

Mitchell looked at her in surprise. "What doesn't fit, Lizzie?"

"It doesn't fit the Russians, Dr Mitchell."

"No? Everything's sweetness and light now, is it? *Glasnost* and *Perestroika*, and all that jazz?" He cocked his head at her. "And nice Mr Gorbachev off to New York to announce missile cuts — and army cuts, too? Is that what you've been working on, Lizzie: doing Jack Butler's sums for him? Don't kid yourself, *Miss* Loftus —"

"I'm not kidding myself." Elizabeth allowed herself to be provoked at last. "You've been too long in Ireland, Paul."

That was probably true, thought Audley critically. (And, typically for Research and Development, they each had a shrewd idea of what the other had been doing. So much for departmental security!)

"That may very well be, my dear Elizabeth." Mitchell rolled loosely for a moment as he took her measure. "And . . . you may have a point with nice Mr Gorbachev, even . . . seeing how he hasn't really any choice, the way the wind's blowing." He nodded again. "But not everyone in the Kremlin has got the message yet — let alone in Dzerzhinsky Street and Arbatskaya Ploshchad." This time he grinned. "Apart from which, if Comrade Kulik could still have had something to sell . . . And *he* was on the level . . . even nice Mr Gorbachev wouldn't think twice about putting him down, for the good of *Glasnost* — eh?"

"With a hired assassin?"

"Why not?"

"An *incompetent* assassin?"

They were both volleying at the net now —

50

"He wasn't all that incompetent, Lizzie —"

"He didn't recognize David." She looked at Audley: she'd had enough of this exchange. But he wasn't yet ready to intervene.

"So he had a contract for one large male Caucasian, maybe." Suddenly it was Mitchell who was uneasy. "Or maybe he panicked when it looked like Kulik was being picked up, and simply decided to settle for poor old Ted. It happens, Lizzie. If you panic."

"In Ulster maybe it happens." She came back to Audley again. "I don't know, David. But it just doesn't *feel* right." She frowned at him. "Killing *you*, David . . ."

"Yes." Mitchell wasn't quite ready to quit. "Now *that* would have been a scandal, I grant you." He matched her frown. "Our David is . . . just a bit too *grand* for sudden death — you're right there, Lizzie . . ." He trailed off finally, leaving '*This isn't Ireland*' unsettled between them. "So what have we got then? A bit of rogue KGB–GRU private enterprise, David?"

They were both looking at him.

"Or . . . a third party?" Elizabeth accepted victory diplomatically. "Have the Germans identified the Arab yet? He had this suspect passport — and the Israelis were very helpful over that, Schneider said."

"They were, yes." Mitchell steadied himself.

"What —?"

"I talked to Schneider this morning, while I was waiting for you, David." Mitchell sounded only slightly apologetic. "Minding you . . . I wanted to know who we might be up against, just in case . . . just in case your Arab had friends. That was when he told me all about the gun."

"And the passport?"

"It was a very good one, actually. What they call a 'Bakaa Valley' job — the Israelis do." He watched Audley. "They're experts on Arabs and passports, your old Israeli friends are. And your other old friend, Colonel Benedikt Schneider, is well-in with them. So they obliged him by identifying it for him: it's part of a lot they've picked up examples of elsewhere . . . from Abu Nidal –PFLP distribution.

Which doesn't mean much precisely, because any of those splinter groups will provide a hit-man if the deal is right, Schneider says. Complete with a one-way ticket, even." He paused. "Which fits Berlin rather uncomfortably, I'm afraid, David. Because whoever hired that Ay-rab must have known you'd have protection. So two shots were the most he'd expect to manage before the *Verfassungsschutz* took him out. But he knew he was going to paradise afterwards. So he didn't care."

No wonder Mitchell was twitchy, thought Audley.

Then Mitchell made a face at him. "Which doesn't get us much further, if you really don't know why you've suddenly become so unpopular all of a sudden. Which . . . I take it you don't? Otherwise —?" He turned away almost casually. "Lovely view, eh Miss Loftus — Sorrento . . . Capri? And our own transport, too!"

Otherwise you wouldn't be here hung between them for an instant, before the sea-breeze blew it away.

"It's a smuggler's boat." To Audley's surprise she let herself be diverted.

"Is it, indeed?" Mitchell looked up and down the craft. "Or *ex*-smuggler's boat, presumably?" He fixed finally on the low wheelhouse. "Although your *Guardia* friends are certainly dressed for the part, Lizzie. Is that to help us mix with the locals, just to be unobtrusive, then —?"

They were playing with him. But, they were both scared, he decided. So, in spite of the past and the insuperable present of their relationship, they had suddenly come to an unspoken agreement. Because fear, like politics, made for strange alliances.

Or, anyway, what Elizabeth said next would confirm that —

"Not *Guardia*, Paul." She leaned over the paint-flaked gunwale, pretending to study the still-indistinct loom of Capri through the haze. "Captain Cuccaro is Intelligence, not *Guardia* . . . Although I don't know about the crew, such as it is . . ."

"They look like a bunch of pirates, whatever they are." Failing to get any reaction from Audley, Mitchell was forced to prolong the exchange. "Are we being met, in Capri?"

"I expect so." Elizabeth wasn't so good at playing games: she couldn't think what to say next.

"You haven't told them where we're going?" Mitchell began to be stretched, in turn.

"No." Elizabeth leaned further. And Audley found himself watching Mitchell study the stretch of her skirt across her hips, never mind whatever else was visible from their different viewpoints. Because, although Miss Loftus was cursed with the Loftus-face — the Loftus-jaw, particularly . . . her figure was all her own.

"No." She straightened up, and looked directly at him. "Captain Cuccaro doesn't yet know where we're going. Because I wanted your instructions about that, David. But . . . he's not very happy. He wants to talk to you about . . ." She almost blundered too far ". . . about Peter Richardson."

"Yes." Mitchell nodded, suddenly hard-faced. "And so do I, by God! Because there's damn all in the records about him since he left us and went back to the army. And then he retired very shortly after that, anyway."

"I don't see how he could have been a double." Elizabeth shook her head. "If he had been he'd never have left us. They'd never have let him go, once he was inside."

"So it's more likely something from the old days." Mitchell watched Audley. "Something he knows that maybe didn't seem important at the time . . . And you're the expert on that, David."

"Yes." It was no good denying what Jack Butler himself had thought. "Whatever Richardson knows — about Kulik, or anyone else . . . any*thing* else — he's no traitor."

"What makes you so certain? He was Fred Clinton's man, not yours, surely?"

"Wrong profile." What he wasn't about to do was to discuss the instincts of the late — and, in his time, *great* also — Frederick J. Clinton in the small matter of recruitment, let alone that of

53

treachery: Mitchell had hardly known Fred, and never in his heyday — and Elizabeth hadn't known him at all. And neither of them, anyway, had lived through treason's own heyday, as Fred had done: those infamous years when everyone had been hag-ridden by doubts, which Fred had once dubbed 'the Cambridge Age' to put his star recruit from Cambridge in his place.

"'Profiling' went out with the ark." Mitchell hadn't finished, and wasn't going to let go. "It went out with Clinton."

"He was thoroughly vetted." He hated to hear Fred consigned to history so crudely.

"But not by you, David. Fred Clinton's man — and an old-school-tie recruit, right?"

"Army, actually." Mitchell knew too much, again. But not quite everything.

"Okay — old-*regimental*-tie, then." Mitchell was implacable. "Failed the old regiment — and then failed *us*, the way I heard it."

Elizabeth was frowning at him again. But he had to settle with Mitchell now. "Then you heard it wrong." The trouble was, in a perverse way the fellow had it right, all the same. He could even remember Neville Macready summing up Richardson when the news of his departure was announced: "*Yes . . . well, they can't say I didn't warn them . . . Clever fellow, of course — total recall, and all that. And plenty of style with it. But . . . 'Tiggers don't like honey', I said to Fred. 'And they don't like acorns'. And they don't like thistles — you'll see'. But, of course, our Fred's never read 'Winnie-the-Pooh' — wrong generation — he simply didn't understand what I was talking about.*"

"How should I have heard it, then?"

Where Mitchell had been much more importantly right, however, was that guess about 'the old days'. But that was where he kept coming up against the blank wall in the records, and the equally blank wall of his memory (which was more reliable than any record). So it couldn't — it damn-well *couldn't* — be anything that they'd shared, he and Richardson, that had made Kulik bracket their names in his last breath.

54

"He was a very talented man." He eyed Mitchell reflectively. "In some respects he was maybe even better than you, Mitchell."

"Oh aye?" Having goaded Audley into starting to answer, Mitchell wasn't offended by the comparison. "But I got his job nevertheless, didn't I?" He even grinned knowingly at Elizabeth. "We're both Audley-recruits, aren't we, Lizzie? So . . . we may not be as talented. But we're not quitters, are we?"

Elizabeth, who hated being knowingly-grinned-at by anyone, but particularly by Dr Paul Mitchell, became even more Loftus-faced. "Why did he resign, David? From Research and Development? And then the army, too? If he was so good —?"

That had been the question which had hurt Fred Clinton, when his potential star-pupil had graduated *cum laude*, and then turned his back on the service. But, if he hadn't read A. A. Milne, he had known his Dryden —

"I can't say that I'm not disappointed, David. Not to say surprised, too . . . Although Neville says he warned me, with some rubbish about acorns and thistles."

"Yes . . . but, then, it's the difference between 'cold' war and 'hot' war, Fred — isn't it?" (That had been the first time he'd had to face what he already knew, but hadn't faced: that Fred was getting old now, and that the generation-gap between those who had felt the heat, and never wanted to feel it again, and those who hadn't, but who wondered endlessly about what it had been like, was becoming a problem to him.) *"It's like it was with my late unlamented father-in-law, Fred: so long as the guns were firing, he was a hero. But once they stopped, he began to get bored. And then he got up to all sorts of mischief —*

'A daring pilot in extremity . . .

'. . . but for calm unfit . . .'

— so it's probably just as well. Because he'd have got up to all sorts of mischief, if he'd stayed with us."

"Haven't we got enough mischief for him?"

55

"More than enough — I agree!" (But that had been exactly the right moment to hit Fred with what he'd been worried about himself, at that time so long ago: that memory was still sharp, by God!) *"But he's the sort of chap who might get involved with politics, Fred. And . . . de-stabilizing the Government isn't what we're into — is it?"*

"He isn't into that."

"No." (Fred wasn't over the hill yet. But he was no longer sitting on the top of it quite, either.) *"But some of the people he knows are . . . or, let's say, I'm not sure about them, anyway. And . . . I have rather got the impression that intelligence research bores him — when we have to advise others when to risk their necks out there —?"*

That was it: whatever Mitchell might question as unlikely, he wouldn't argue with that. Because Mitchell and Richardson were brothers-under-the-skin; only Richardson had been flawed, and Mitchell wasn't. "He wasn't a research man, at heart." And, also, there was that other difference — which would wound Mitchell deeply. But it would also stop his mouth, too. "He was a soldier, you might say. And we didn't have a proper war for him. So that's why he resigned — from the army, as well as from R and D, Paul."

"Yes. He resigned." Unexpectedly, Elizabeth hit him from the flank. "But he also *retired*, David — from everything? Just like that — from everything?"

"Uh-huh?" Once the man had left R and D, that had been the end of him, was all he could recall. Fred had helped him back, of course: it had been Fred's influence which had promoted him from captain to major . . . if not to keep him on his career-track, then maybe not to discourage their next recruit. So that had been merely prudent, never mind keeping faith with Richardson himself.

He shrugged. "Well . . . that was afterwards." All he could recall from afterwards was the office gossip in which he hadn't been interested. Peter Richardson — *Major* Richardson now — back with his regiment had been of no consequence whatsoever: he had smashed up one of his sports cars (and been smashed up in it, with it . . . but that was no great surprise!); and then his adored Italian mother had died, on whom he had doted. (And that had been sad, maybe . . . but that was the way the world was: kings and queens and chimney-sweepers all had to die sometime; and so did mothers: mothers, and kings and queens and chimney-sweepers were dying all the time. And, anyway, the *Principessa* had died loaded with *lire*, to pay for a great big Italian hearse, drawn by four black horses through Amalfi, to solace her loving son in his grief in his inherited *palazzo*.)

"That was when he retired — resigned?" It was Elizabeth again, not Mitchell. But, where Mitchell had merely questioned him about the sequence of events, Elizabeth was frowning at the events themselves.

So now he wasn't so sure of himself. But what he remembered wasn't in doubt, nevertheless. "That was when he sent in his papers — yes. Because then he had all his inheritance to manage. All the family estates, up and down the coast, Elizabeth — " What made that doubly-sure was that one of Fred Clinton's criteria had been money, always: a man's politics and his sexual weaknesses were two things which mattered most, in those old days. But if he already had money, at least that ruled out arguments about his expenses allowance, when the budget was tight " — so . . . that was old money, anyway." And that was what Fred had liked best: *old* money. Apart from which, Peter Richardson had always loved his other country, as well as his mother: he had been almost as patriotic about the ancient Republic of Amalfi, which was more than half-a-thousand years older than Italy itself, than about his other Land-of-Hope-and-Glory.

But Elizabeth was still frowning at him. "What's the matter, Elizabeth?"

She was still frowning. And so much so that even Paul Mitchell wanted to know what the matter was, also —

"Lizzie — ?"

"I think you should talk to Captain Cuccaro, David."

Now they both looked at her. But Mitchell cracked first. "Uh-huh? And . . . what did Cuccaro say, Lizzie? Does he want to talk to the elusive Major, then? On his own account —? Does he? Never mind the Russians?"

But she shook off Mitchell and all his questions then, together with her frown. "It's the Mafia who want to talk to Major Richardson, Cuccaro says. And . . . and, I think that's what he wants to talk to you about, David —"

IV

THE ITALIANS HAD not sent a boy to do a man's job: Audley had concluded that already from his brief meeting with Captain Cuccaro when he'd come aboard. But that, in view of what was surely in their records, was hardly surprising. Only close-up it was even more evident.

"Professore."

"Captain." Additionally, Cuccaro was what Mrs Faith Audley would have called 'a fine-looking man', as well as an elegant one in his immaculate designer-jeans and expensive shirt (complete with a curious bronze medallion on a chain round his neck). All of which made Audley himself feel even more crumpled and unprepossessing. "Thank you for joining us, Captain. Your assistance is much appreciated."

Cuccaro rolled easily with the boat's motion. "I am here to facilitate your mission, Professore." He gestured gracefully. "And, of course, to ensure your safety as well as your success."

There was no reason why the Italians should connect him with events in far-off Berlin. But there was now the extraordinary Mafia intrusion to be explained. "My safety?" He let himself almost lose his balance.

Cuccaro grinned suddenly. "I am also grateful to you for this —" He swept a hand over the boat "— these days, I command only a desk, you understand. So this is a most pleasant change — to be at sea again, Professore."

Small talk, was what Audley understood, even as he grabbed the nearest stanchion in order to keep his feet: if this was the way the game had to be played . . . then the boat first. And that curious

59

medallion . . . which that last lurch had brought close enough for him to be able to make out a bearded head on it, surmounted not by a crown, but what looked like a German *pickelhaub*.

"Is that so?" He managed to find an Audley-smile from somewhere. "I wouldn't have thought this is your sort of boat, Captain." He waved as best he could with his free hand to include the tattered awning and the flaking paint, glancing quickly at Elizabeth (whose expression still bore the remains of the impact of Cuccaro's grin: being dazzlingly smiled-at by handsome men was for her an outrage only a little short of being actually touched by any man, handsome or not). "'A smuggler's boat', Miss Loftus said —?"

"Yes." Cuccaro grinned again. But this time it was a different smile. "Or, it was until very recently." He held up his hand, with a single brown finger raised, "Do you hear that?"

The only thing Audley could hear was the engine. Which was just an engine, in the same way that the boat was just a boat. But evidently not to Captain Cuccaro.

"Beautiful!" Cuccaro focused suddenly on Audley again, and was himself. "It is . . . an appropriate boat, let us say, Professore."

Audley listened to the engine again. All he could say for it was that it wasn't making much noise. But if it was a smuggler's boat, that was to be expected. "You mean . . . it's unobtrusive, Captain?"

"That also." Cuccaro nodded, but seemed only half to agree. "The *Guardia* seized it up the coast, a few days back." The faint American origins of his otherwise perfect English intruded. "There are many such, in these waters — 'unobtrusive', as you say." Another nod. "And very fast, when speed is required." He stared at Audley for a moment. "Most of the time, they hire out to the tourists . . . with maybe a little fishing, also. And then, one day — one night, they meet a bigger boat, by appointment."

"Uh-huh?" If Cuccaro wanted him to be interested in smuggling as a prelude to their own business, then he would be. "Drugs, presumably?"

"Drugs . . . or what you will." The medallion swung in its nest. "Cigarettes are still very popular with the smaller fry. And, of course, there are the local exports — the ancient artefacts . . . Roman and Greek from Campania and the south. Etruscan from the tombs in the north — they are much sought-after by foreign collectors. It is good steady business, Professore. If one is not too greedy."

Audley nodded politely. "That's very interesting." But two could play at this small-talk-game. "That medal of yours, Captain — is that an ancient artefact?" He leaned forward, keeping tight hold of his stanchion, but couldn't quite make out the inscription. "What does it say —?"

"My good luck piece?" Cuccaro looked down for an instant. "'*Wilhelm der Grosse Deutscher Kaiser*', Professore. '*Koenig von Preussen*'." He took the medal in his hand and turned it over. "'*Zum Andenken an den hundersten Geburtstaf des grossen Kaisers Wilhelm I, 1797–22 Maerz–1897*'." He looked up at Audley. "Not so very ancient. My grandfather picked it up on the Piave in 1918. My father wore it in his war. And now I wear it — for good luck, also."

"I see." Audley had had his own smile ready and waiting. "And you think we'll need good luck today, Captain? Or is it Major Richardson who needs the luck now?"

No smile this time. "He has been lucky so far. Now . . . perhaps you are right."

"With the Mafia after him?"

"Among others." Cuccaro turned towards Capri for a second, as though to judge its proximity. "What is it that you want from him, Professore Audley?"

"I merely want to ask him a few questions."

"About what?"

"I wish I knew." But the truth wouldn't do, Audley could see. "About the old days, when he worked for us. Nothing to concern you, Captain — or Italy." And that was also true. But as Kulik had had nothing to do with Germany, he'd best hedge that piece of truth. "What is it that your Mafia wants with him, Captain?"

"You do not know?" Cuccaro glanced at Elizabeth.

"As it happens . . . I don't." The trouble with the truth was that, with his Italian record, it was quite simply unbelievable. But it was all he had. "The fact is, Captain Cuccaro, he resigned from our service years ago. And then he went back to the army. But then he resigned from that . . . You might say that he was having *bad* luck then."

"Bad luck?"

Audley dredged his memory for what, in its time, had been of no more than passing interest on the *'Heard about poor old Peter?'* level. "He had a nasty road accident. Not his fault." But memory, as always, came to his rescue: *'Poor old Peter! Ran into a dirty great big lorry, right outside his flat. Smashed himself up properly, apparently — and his new Jag, too'*; to which he had said *'Is that so?'* (and thought, from experience and with unfeeling disinterest, *driving too fast, as usual — serve him right!*). "Not his fault . . . and then his mother died. So then he retired here, in Italy!"

But Cuccaro was watching him. "You knew him well, though, Professore?"

"I worked with him only once or twice." He felt a vague irritation swelling up in his throat. "I have not set eyes on him for fifteen years, Captain. And you have not yet answered my question: why is the Mafia interested in him?"

Cuccaro looked away for a second, then back at him. "He has a boat like this one. And an organization to go with it. Only . . . his is an even better boat. And his organization, it would seem, is as good as his boat." The stare became frankly disbelieving. "And this . . . you did not know?"

For a moment Audley could only stare back at him. "Peter Richardson —?" He couldn't quite keep the incredulity out of his voice. "You're saying —?"

"'Wrong profile'?" Mitchell raised an innocent eyebrow.

The trouble was, it wasn't so utterly unthinkable, the next moment, as he thought about it — not, anyway, when he added premature retirement (and in comfort) to Richardson's restless spirit. It had been plain corrosive boredom more than anything else which had in the end

62

parted him from R and D all those years ago, in spite of that wild special aptitude of his which had so captivated Fred Clinton. And boredom, as he well knew himself, was the father of mischief.

But he still wanted more time to think. "Is smuggling your business then, Captain?" He pretended to study the boat as he spoke, as though that was expected of him.

Smuggling —?

"No."

If smuggling wasn't the connection with Kulik, it was nothing, really — or, it needn't be, need it? Half the world's travellers, who filled the duty-free shops in every airport and chanced their arms with that extra bottle, were petty smugglers at heart —

> *Brandy for the parson,*
> *'Baccy for the clerk*

— and if Richardson had merely been supplying that ancient demand —?

"Neither is the Mafia my business." Having waited in vain for him to come back, Cuccaro spoke more sharply. "But Major Richardson interests them now. That is what the word in Naples is, the *Guardia* informants say. And that, perhaps, is why he has become . . . unavailable?"

The cosy picture in Audley's mind dissolved. Brandy and 'baccy . . . or, up-dated, *Lucky Strikes* in exchange for the odd Greek vase or Etruscan funeral pot . . . that was one thing. But the Mafia ——

"What's he in to?" Mitchell could contain himself no longer. "Drugs are where the money is, aren't they?" And, once uncontained, he was irrepressible. "And now what's it? 'Crack' —? Isn't that raising the stakes?"

Money! That was what was wrong, damn it! That damn-well *was* the 'wrong profile' — wasn't it? Except . . . that fifteen years made a nonsense of that cosy picture, too — did they?"

"He's run out of money, has he?" He snapped himself back between them.

Cuccaro frowned at him once more. "He never had any money."

Now they were really at odds. "He had plenty of money, Captain." The gleaming Richardson-cars and the West Central flat were there in memory to support him. "He had money from his mother." Money had always been a huge plus in Fred Clinton's preferences, even before the aptitude tests: if you were heterosexual and well-heeled (and, for choice, not Cambridge!), then with Fred you were over the first fences, they always said. "And she was rich."

"And then dead, too." This time Mitchell was with him. Because, in his time, Paul Mitchell had been over those same fences, and knew them. And despised what he knew, too. "With a *palazzo* all of his very own — right, David?"

Cuccaro shook his head. "There was no money."

"No money?" Mitchell accepted the turnabout more readily. "No *palazzo* — ?"

Cuccaro's lip curled. "There is a . . . 'palazzo', as you call it. But it was . . . how do you say? Mort-gaged, is it?" He nodded. "And the Principessa was a great lady. So there was also credit. And bank loans, too." The nod became a shake. "He had no money. He had only her debts. And some of them were debts of honour." He stared at Audley, not Mitchell. "He had . . . 'bad luck', you said, Professore — ?"

There was more. "What else?"

"She died. And she was a great lady, as I have said. So there was not too much inquiry then. But . . . it seems now that all her little problems had suddenly become big ones, you see." Cuccaro swayed and rolled with the boat's motion, so that his shrug was almost lost with it. "There was perhaps a certain delicacy in asking questions which could only have made for greater sadness at the time, about her death . . . you understand, Professore?"

"Yes." From his own tangled childhood Audley understood far better than the man could imagine. But the hell with that! (And, for that matter, the hell also with whoever hadn't done his job properly, back in the early seventies, on Peter Richardson for Fred Clinton — at least for the time being!).

"Yes." Mitchell looked sidelong at him, and then back at Cuccaro. "But . . . hold on a moment. The *palazzo* —"

The damn palace seemed to have become an obsession. "For God's sake, Mitchell —"

"No." Mitchell shook him off. "It was mortgaged . . . and all the rest. But he never lost it — *Palazzo Castellamare di San Lorenzo* —" He fixed on the Italian "— he never lost it, in spite of everything . . . So he's been cruising these waters from the start, has he? Paying off the interest —? And then the capital, too? And then more —?" He rounded on Audley suddenly. "It's a bloody showpiece, David — the *Palazzo Castellamare di Major Peter Richardson*: that's what Rome Station said. The ruddy guides on the tourist coaches point it out. Blue-water swimming pool, big white yacht by the private jetty — nothing like *this* in view, of course." He swept a hand over the smuggler's boat. "But he must have been at it for years, to turn his hard luck into all that!" He returned to the Italian. "How long have they known about it? Or suspected it, even?"

Not long, thought Audley quickly, watching Cuccaro's face. But then, why should they have suspected anything? There had been no black marks against Major Richardson, he would have passed simply as a rich expatriate Englishman bringing his own money to restore his Italian family fortune.

Cuccaro sighed, and gestured eloquently as only an Italian or a Frenchman could, to gloss over his *Guardia* colleagues' failure. "Not long since, it seems."

"Only when the Mafia got interested in his act?" Mitchell wasn't letting go. "Uh-huh?"

Cuccaro's expression hardened. "It is possible that he has become greedy, after many years of keeping out of their way. But . . . there was no official inquiry into him until recently — that is true. And that is how the matter of his mother's death came to light. But that will not be pursued further now, I am informed."

'The great lady' was safe, if not her son. But that, Cuccaro was informing them, was none of either his business or theirs, anyway. The business in hand was to take Richardson while making sure that

65

Professore Audley neither came to grief nor caused any, as he had done in the past.

"Of course." They were agreed there, actually. What Butler expected of him was results, double quick. But results diplomatically achieved, also. "I am grateful for your frankness, Captain. You have clarified certain . . . aspects of our mission which disturbed us — Sir Jack Butler and Mr Henry Jaggard." He threw the names in for respectability. But when they failed to melt Captain Cuccaro he decided to go for broke. "And the Foreign and Commonwealth Office, representing Her Majesty's Government." Only that still didn't seem to work. And if neither Her Majesty nor Mrs Thatcher could blot out his record after all these years, then he must resort to desperate extremes, with Capri altogether too close for comfort now. "So, if I may, I will take you into our confidence — ?"

"Professore." With Capri looming up, Cuccaro was under the whip too. So, in spite of all his doubts and the lurch of the boat as it cut through the wake of another Capri–Napoli water-bus, he sketched a bow.

"You have not traced Major Richardson yet?" He allowed only two seconds for agreement. "And neither have we. And that disturbed us. Because we didn't know why he's suddenly become so . . . unavailable?" He smiled. "But now we know. Thanks to you."

Cuccaro reached across his chest to take hold of his Kaiser Wilhelm good luck piece. "But you have rendezvous, I am told — ?"

That was what he wanted, of course.

"Not exactly," said Mitchell. But then he looked at Audley. "Only in a general sort of way — " Then he looked past Audley, towards Capri " — a general locality, I mean, David."

"And where is that, sir?" The oddly-Americanized 'Sir' betrayed the Italian's dislike: technically, Mitchell also rated 'professore'. But Mitchell and Cuccaro were Anglo-Italian chalk-and-cheese.

"Please!" Audley held up his hand. "You . . . or . . . the authorities . . . want to talk to Major Richardson, I take it — ?"

66

Cuccaro eyed him warily. "There are questions to be asked. And to be answered."

"About his smuggling activities?"

"If that is what they are." The Italian paused. "Then — yes, Professore."

That was it, of course. Until that sudden Mafia interest had given his game away, Richardson had had everything going for him: his pre-retirement career had not only given him all the requisite smuggling skills to add to his blue-blooded local connections, but it had also endowed him with a certain respectability, as an ex-Intelligence officer. But then, when the balloon finally had gone up, the Italians must at once have thought more than twice about him, with the American Sixth Fleet so often swinging at anchor across this bay, in NATO's main base in the Central Mediterranean: that perfect cover for smuggling — or even the smuggling itself — might cover other enterprises, eh?

He ought to have thought of that. And, by God, it still beckoned him now, as he thought about it! At least it was something Captain Cuccaro would believe — *Perfidious Albion!* — he would believe that, if nothing else!

"Question-and-answer?" Mitchell moved into his silence, just as warily. "Or arrest?"

That was going too fast. "Please, Dr Mitchell —"

"Not arrest —" Cuccaro spread his hands "— say . . . 'protective custody' rather, sir." He switched back to Audley. "We do not desire . . . difficulties, Professore. But there are other matters — other *considerations* . . . which, at present, are not clear to us . . . at this moment, you understand?"

This time Audley didn't quite understand. "What other 'considerations'?"

Such innocence seemed to surprise the captain. "You saw the airport? And the precautions there?"

Audley nodded, remembering Heathrow as well as Naples. "A man in a tank pointed a cannon at me — yes?"

"Then you know that there is an anti-terrorist emergency."

"An exercise, I thought. There was a similar one at Heathrow when I was there a few hours ago." For once he didn't have to pretend innocence. "An exercise? Or — ?"

"*'Sure'*," murmured Mitchell. "That's what they told me."

"What?"

"'Scheduled Unspecific Routine Exercise' — 'SURE' for short, David. They have 'em all the time these days." But then Mitchell cocked an eye at the Italian. "Are you telling us that this time they're not so . . . 'sure', maybe?"

Cuccaro studied each of them for a moment. "There is a great deal of . . . activity, in many different quarters. Very disturbing activity, Professore."

The engine-note beneath them changed from a controlled drone almost to silence, as though it were no longer propelling the boat. The harbour lay just ahead of them, with the island towering up above on each side of the crowded anchorage.

"What sort of activity?" snapped Audley.

"Your Major Richardson is not the only person who has become hard to find." Cuccaro lifted one shoulder dismissively. "He has not been my concern, until now, as I have already told you. But there are others . . ." He stared at Audley ". . . whose sudden absence makes for nervousness."

That, at least, Audley understood. Cuccaro must be an anti-terrorist man, among other things. And one of the first suspicious signs of any impending terrorist operation was the departure of the representatives of suspected terrorist-front agencies to safer climes beyond European jurisdiction.

But where the devil did that leave Elizabeth's Arab?

"I see." That Arab was a damnable coincidence, more likely than not. Because, whatever Kulik had been offering them, the Russians weren't into terrorism in these heady *Glasnost* days — if anything, quite the opposite . . . except that, neither were they into bad-publicity assassinations, by the same token. Yet, in the meantime, the last thing he wanted in the immediate future was Cuccaro breathing down his neck. "Well, that's really rather reassuring."

"It is?" It was Mitchell who spoke. But then, in his present post-Dublin twitchy state, he was another candidate for reassurance.

"Oh yes." He forced himself to brighten. "Major Richardson may be a . . . smuggler." He attempted an Italian gesture, half apologetic, half-cynical, as he turned back to Cuccaro. "And, if he is, my Government would deeply regret that . . . which, quite frankly, comes as much as a surprise—a most embarrassing surprise—to us as it would appear to have come to your people, Captain." Not even Jack Butler could find fault with such diplomatic language. But he had to harden it, nevertheless. "And you can rest assured that after we have spoken with him we will place him at your disposal. And then the law must take its course, naturally."

They were all looking at him now. But the boat was wallowing in the swell outside the harbour, so they were all also finding it difficult to keep their feet as they did so, even the Italian himself.

"After —?" Cuccaro managed to steady himself. Then he looked uneasily towards the harbour. "Are you saying that you wish for no protection, Professore?"

"Protection from whom?" Securely anchored to his stanchion, Audley could concentrate on asserting himself. "The Mafia is none of my business. And I am none of theirs. They do not know me — they do not know *of* me. Why should they?" He shrugged. "And, in any case, since Major Richardson has arranged this rendezvous with Dr Mitchell I think we may reasonably confide that they will not be attending it." He smiled at Cuccaro. 'Confide' was an admirably diplomatic word, with its nuances of smugness and self-importance — a very Henry-Jaggard-word. And that encouraged him to go further. "I am simply visiting an old friend-and-colleague, to discuss matters from long ago, Captain. The fact that my old friend-and-colleague happens to have a problem of his own relating to certain — ah — certain unwise activities in which he has engaged . . . that is a mere coincidence." But now he must sugar the pill. "But he, of course, may not regard it as any such thing. More likely, he will have assumed that my appearance relates to those . . . alleged activities. In which case he will be expecting advice. And my advice will be that he must give himself up immediately." No smile now: magisterial disapproval now! "Indeed, I shall insist that he does that. And I will tell him that there is an unmarked craft waiting for him, to ensure his safety." He nodded the words home. "I trust that such an undertaking meets your requirements, Captain?"

"Hmmm . . ." Mitchell emitted an uneasy sound.

"Yes, Dr Mitchell?" 'Protection from whom?' was what was exercising Mitchell's mind. And it might be as well to deal with the problem of Mitchell here and now, while he was inhibited by Cucarro's presence. "I take it you agree with me?"

"Mmm — yes, of course." Mitchell gave him an old-fashioned look, but then brightened falsely as he turned to Cuccaro. "We can perhaps leave Miss Loftus with you, Captain. We should be able to handle the Major between us, I don't doubt — yes."

"Not 'we', Dr Mitchell." Audley shook his head. "You will both remain here, of course."

Mitchell opened his mouth, then closed it. Then opened it again. "My instructions, Dr Audley — "

"*My* instructions are to meet with Major Richardson, Dr Mitchell." The only problem was that Mitchell had not been very precise. But Captain Cuccaro's presence could be helpful there, too. "Where did you say the meeting-place was — ?" He nodded politely to the Captain. "We appreciate your co-operation in this matter, sir. So there shall be no secrets between us." He extended the politeness to Mitchell. "Yes, Dr Mitchell — ?"

Mitchell was ambushed — horse, foot and guns. And there was nothing he could do about it. "The Villa Jovis."

"And where is that?" He beamed at Captain Cuccaro co-operatively. "The Villa San Michele I have heard of, Captain . . . but I am afraid that I am not conversant with the geography of Capri . . . as, no doubt, both you and Major Richardson are — ?"

Cuccaro, equally ambushed, stared at him for a moment. And then pointed. "It is on the other — " he searched for the right word "— the other mountain, Professore, from San Michele. It is on Monte Tiberio — "

70

"Monte Tiberio?" Audley ducked under the awning to follow the line of Cuccaro's finger, to the left. "And . . . the Villa Jovis — what is that?"

"It is the palace of Tiberius."

"Of Tiberius?" All he could see was what looked like a statue on the high point of the peak, above a fringe of trees, with a scatter of white houses below. So, presumably, the old emperor had been reinstated (probably by Mussolini, in his bid to re-establish the Roman Empire?), to look down on his special island. Which was a nice thought: old Wimpy, in his most memorable Latin lessons, had been a great Tiberius-admirer, disdainful of Tacitus and Suetonius as 'mere gossipers' who had libelled a good man in his old age.

"It is a ruin." Cuccaro was also staring. "It is . . . a maze? How do you say —? There are many walls, and staircases . . . and arches . . . on many levels, on the hillside. A maze?"

"A labyrinth?" All he could see was a hint of a platform among the trees.

"A labyrinth — yes!" Cuccaro welcomed the word. "And . . . it is a long walk up there, by a narrow path between the houses. A path not for cars, you understand —? The cars — the taxis . . . they go only from the Marina Grande to Capri town, below. Then you must walk, between the houses and their gardens to reach the . . . excavations." He turned to Audley, as though questioning his ability to make such a journey. "It is a long walk, Professore."

But maybe that wasn't what he was thinking about at all. And quite rightly, too! Even, in all these new circumstances, quite predictably?

"Well . . . that's good, then." He nodded from Cuccaro to Mitchell.

"Good?" Mitchell frowned at him. "How is it 'good', David?"

"Good for a rendezvous." Audley nodded, pursing his lips. "Only one way in — one way out . . . that's usually bad. But a *long* way in — then you can sit down somewhere, and see who's coming. And decide accordingly?" He cocked his head at them both. "The Major has a bad conscience, maybe? And, although I'm an old colleague —

71

an old *friend* . . . I could be setting him up — for the *Guardia di Finanza*, if not the Mafia?" He concluded with Mitchell. "And we trained him — remember?" He gave Mitchell a thin smile, even as his own personal memories of Richardson increased his own doubts. "What would you do, if you thought the roof was falling in on you, Dr Mitchell?"

Mitchell stared at him. Because what Mitchell would do in that event was to be somewhere else, far away from trouble and even further away from old friends and colleagues. But he couldn't admit that in front of the Italian.

"So Major Richardson will be watching out up there, and waiting." Audley nodded, home at last. And then nodded towards Monte Tiberio. "But if I turn up with someone he doesn't know . . . if Captain Cuccaro accompanies me, or gives me an escort . . . then, if he has been up to no good all these years, he'll sit tight, wherever he is. And he'll walk off, eventually, when he knows the coast is clear — right?"

"Is that what you really think, David?" Elizabeth unwound suddenly.

"What I really think, Miss Loftus, is that we don't really have any choice in the matter. Because, if I take a long walk, up there . . . with you and Dr Mitchell in attendance, never mind whatever quite unnecessary protection the Italian authorities may have imagined is appropriate . . . if that's what we do, then we'll all have wasted our valuable time. Because the Major is waiting for me, and no one else. And I haven't come this far to waste my time, Miss Loftus."

They all hated that: they were agreed on that. But they also couldn't argue with its logic effectively, in front of each other, without aborting the mission, never mind questioning his authority. Which put them all on the line.

"So that's agreed, then." He chose to accept their silent hate as agreement. It was only like it always was, after all: they weren't about to reward him with their approval, any more than he ever applauded Jack Butler for making logical decisions with which he couldn't argue, however much he disliked the profit-and-loss calculation involved.

And, anyway, what was agreeable was that it was like the old days, when there wasn't always a car and a driver in attendance, and another talkative committee meeting at the other end: *it wasn't boring.*

"Well — let's get on with it, then." He pointed at Capri.

V

HE WAS JUST getting into the taxi when Paul Mitchell appeared out of nowhere, pushing his way through the late-season tourists who thronged the quayside of the Marina Grande.

Audley decided not to frown, although that was his first inclination. For he had half-expected Mitchell to try something like this, he realized. So he merely raised his eyebrows instead.

"What is it now?" He had to concede that it had been Mitchell, at the very last moment before he disembarked, who had remembered to supply him with a wad of Italian Monopoly-money, without which he could probably not have penetrated the Villa Jovis ancient monument itself, let alone hired transport to get him near it. "What else have I forgotten?"

Mitchell gave the taxi-driver a friendly grin. "Speak English? No? Well then . . . *momento per favore?*" He turned to Audley. "Give me your coat, David."

"Why?" Audley saw that Mitchell was carrying some sort of alternative garment.

"You don't look like a tourist." Mitchell eyed his crumpled second-best suit with distaste. "You look like a businessman who's slept in his suit. And that won't do." He thrust the garment at Audley. "Take off your jacket."

"F——" But then he decided to give in gracefully while he still seemed to be winning. "Oh — very well!"

He peeled off his jacket. And then remembered to rescue his passport, warrant card, credit cards and Eurocheques, without all of which he never felt he really existed when he was far from home.

Mitchell accepted the jacket in return for what seemed to be some sort of lightweight windcheater, and fretted as Audley bestowed the proofs of his real existence in its breast-pockets. "Now the tie, David."

"The tie?" But, of course, tourists didn't wear West Sussex Yeomanry ties.

"Get in the taxi."

That, at least, was sensible: in the taxi he was out of sight, if there were any prying eyes hereabouts. But then Mitchell held the door so that he couldn't close it, and leaned into the gap.

"This isn't one of your very best ideas, David. Aren't you getting a bit long in the tooth for fun-and-games?"

Audley gave up trying to wrestle the door closed. Arguably, the substitution of the jackets might be sensible. But that had simply been Mitchell's excuse to Captain Cuccaro, rather than another belated bit of sense. "You are supposed to be making polite conversation with Cuccaro, Mitchell. So that he doesn't queer my pitch."

Mitchell screwed up his second-best jacket. "Your pitch is already too bloody queer for my liking, David. What the hell are you up to?"

"I'm not 'up' to anything. I'm obeying orders. Just as you are."

"Oh yes?" Mitchell held the door rock-firm. "I thought my orders were to watch your back. And yours were not to take any unnecessary risks."

"Your orders were to obey *my* orders." The real trouble with Paul Mitchell was that he'd never been a soldier. But the immediate problem was to get the taxi-door closed. "I'm not taking an unnecessary risk, Paul — I'm taking a calculated one. Because everything I said on the boat is true. Or . . . everything I said about Peter, anyway. And I know him better than you do: I know how he was trained to think. So I know what he'll do if he's running scared."

"That was a long time ago." Mitchell's face was like his hold on the door.

"It was — yes." He slackened his own hold deliberately. "But he won't have forgotten. And he'll know that I haven't, either."

A muscle on the corner of Mitchell's mouth twitched. "But we still don't know what's really going on, David. So . . . you're going in blind." He glanced uneasily at the taxi-driver, who had settled down with a tattered newspaper. "After what happened in . . . to Elizabeth, David?"

"This is different."

"Damn right, it is! It's a bloody-sight riskier —" Mitchell stopped as his anger roused the taxi-driver from his sports page.

"Signor —?" The man looked questioningly from Mitchell to Audley as though he feared they were about to come to blows. "Avanti, huh?"

"Avanti." Audley agreed, and then transferred his nod to Mitchell as he felt the door move. "No one else is expecting me up there. I don't exist — remember. So just hold Cuccaro for one hour, Paul. And that's an order. Then you can all come up and admire the view with me. *Understood?*"

Another twitch. "You know . . . I wouldn't mind so much if I didn't think you were enjoying yourself, David —" The final *click* of the door, and then the thickness of the window and the sound of the engine drowned the rest of Mitchell's considered judgement, so that Audley was spared it.

Then the taxi began to nose its way through the crowd.

Mitchell wasn't stupid, of course: his last shot had been a bull, right in the centre of the target. And his previous shot had been an inner, too close to the bull for comfort maybe.

But then he had been on-target all along, towards the end of the exchange: the whole thing had been a cock-up, from start to now, from London-and-Berlin to London-and-Capri —

There was a map in a plastic folder, prudently attached to a piece of string, on the back seat. And, translating kilometres into miles, Capri wasn't very big, mercifully.

"Villa Jovis?" He inquired politely.

The taxi-driver shrugged. "Piazza, signor."

Audley found the Piazza on the map. Cuccaro had said it was 'a long walk' to the ruins, hadn't he? But it was no more than a mile-and-a-bit, maybe even less. And distances on land always confused naval men.

Or had it been Mitchell who had said that? But it didn't matter, anyway. Because he no longer wanted to think about either Mitchell or Cuccaro —

He paid the driver off eventually, with what seemed a lot of Mitchell's Monopoly-money. But presumably the clock had been ticking down there, in the Marina Grande, far below.

It was no good looking round: he wouldn't spot anyone if he'd miscalculated, or if Mitchell hadn't held Cuccaro. And it wasn't because the place was too crowded, the narrow streets and tiny squares, because they weren't and it wasn't — not this late in the season, and in the middle of the day — the *mezzogiorno* so beloved of all Mediterranean peoples (and maybe Richardson had calculated that, too?). It was, simply, that he was in the middle of his own calculated risk now, so that there was no one he would know, friend or foe, to be able to spot, in any case. Except Peter himself. And it was Peter's job to spot him now, not the other way round.

Peter Richardson —

The truth was that he hadn't really known the man very well, all those years ago, whatever Butler and everyone else might think from the record, either from what Fred Clinton might have chosen to add to it by way of footnotes, or because of his established reputation for never-forgetting. But he could feel his memory expanding under pressure (as it always did) . . . and he knew more now, of course — however surprising Cuccaro's information had been —

Mitchell had said it would be a long walk. But that hadn't meant anything: he could walk anyone off their feet, any time. And it was a

77

small island, with small (but mercifully well-signposted!) paths directing him to the Villa Jovis, with anything like an actual road soon left far behind — narrow paths winding among desirable holiday residences tucked behind walls and gardens, or separated by tiny hillside vineyards —

But it *was* a long walk, by God!

Maybe not surprising, at that . . . Or, trying to imagine Richardson short of cash was the first challenge: with Peter the money had always been evident if not just short of flashy — not just the always-new car (and the always new, but never serious, girl), but also the throwaway asides (that first time he had known more about Cheltenham race-course than Cheltenham GCHQ). And it had been old money too, everyone had assumed (of the sort old Fred Clinton notoriously preferred in his recruits): old blue-blooded maternal money, derived from the legendary *principessa* and her *palazzo* inheritance. Fred had been almost as happy with that as with the alpha-plus results from the aptitude tests . . . although, as it had transpired, someone had blundered there too, in not discerning that there had been no true inclination towards scholarship, let alone the happy drudgery of research, to go with those special aptitudes —

There were blue flowers here, trailing in wild profusion in an overgrown hedge beside a vineyard, with the harbour below like a mill-pond full of toy boats. But in fact . . . they weren't flowers at all: they were weeds — he could remember them from the distant past of long-ago Italian holidays, festooning the farm hedgerows on the approaches to Paestum. And they had stirred his pale Protestant English gardener's soul with a curious mixture of admiration and envy and disapproval then, that mere weeds could be so spectacular: weeds were entitled to be both rare and beautiful, but had no right to be so outrageously colourful. But then, of course, they had been *Italian* weeds —

Richardson was half-Italian, that was what he must take account of.

And wasn't it always said of Anglo-Italians that they could be the very devil?

He was getting close to the Villa Jovis now: he could even make out what might be the ruins among the trees on the skyline, surmounted by the statue of Tiberius which he had first seen from far below. And the landscape around him had changed: he had left the cosy holiday homes, with their gardens, behind him. Now there was only one path under the shoulder of the ridge, with secluded houses hidden among the trees on his right and a rock-strewn hillside on his left. And no more blue flowers: the hillside was spotted with what looked like English buttercups among the boulders.

He stopped trying to make excuses for Peter Richardson. Very devil or not, the man had made devilish complications out of what should have been a simple mission — made them with his smuggling enterprise, certainly; but, had he become involved in more than that?

He stopped for a moment, as another fact registered: in all this long walk in the sun he hadn't passed anyone, either going up or going down, since he had left the lowest region of shops and hotels. But now there were two people coming towards him . . . and . . . there was no one at all behind him.

He took them in with another glance, and then admired the view again. They were just boy-and-girl, dressed in uni-sex sweat-shirt and very short shorts, the girl with a camera bouncing between her little no-bra breasts, the boy with an old haversack hanging on his shoulder, from which a bottle-top protruded.

As they passed him, he smiled at them. And got an answering smile from the girl, and a blank look from the boy.

But now there was someone else coming down. And still no one behind him, coming up —

This was the only way up: this was the way the old Emperor Tiberius must have come up to his great marble palace on the island where he'd spent so many years, from which he'd ruled his empire in those first *Anno Domini* years . . . and, for sure, every plunderer and invader afterwards had come the same way, to that look-out point up there — from Arabs and Normans and Spaniards, to Napoleon's Frenchmen and the sweating British redcoats who had also bid for possession — to reduce his palace to rubble between them all.

But now it was Peter Richardson's territory. And, by design and from experience, he appeared to have calculated exactly that there would be no throngs of tourists here at midday in late October, so that the sorting of possible goats from undoubted sheep would be thereby simplified.

After youth came age: this time it was an ancient black-garbed Caprese grandmother, with thick bowed legs and a wicker basket over her arm. And she didn't react to his smile, either: she didn't even look at him.

The last lap was among pine trees, which led him to the guardian's ticket-office, which appeared to be combined with a grubby little café.

Eventually a somnolent guardian materialized at the window.

"Uno?" He regarded Audley incuriously for a moment, then peered round into the emptiness as though to reassure himself that, if there was one idiot abroad when all sensible people were eating, drinking and resting, there weren't others trying to slip past behind him.

"Yes — si." Audley was aware suddenly that his mouth was dry — that, in fact, he was extremely thirsty. "Uno — ah — un*a* bottiglia di birra, per favore?"

The guardian sighed, and then wearily indicated the dirty white tables on the terrace of the café.

At least it wasn't like Berlin, thought Audley. Neither Richardson nor anyone else awaited him on the terrace, it was reassuringly empty of both *Mafiosi* and Arabs as well as tourists, *bona fide* or otherwise. Which was just as well, because it was otherwise an altogether most suitable place for an assassination, with a sheer cliff offering convenient disposal of the body simultaneously: wasn't that how old Tiberius was said to have got rid of those who had offended him?

He sipped his beer gratefully, peering over the cliff down to the wrinkled blue sea far below. Somehow, and in spite of everything, he felt reassured himself, that he had calculated correctly. Or, rather, that Richardson had got it right, after all these years, in remembering that the two preferable extremes for any rendezvous were, respectively, crowds (where there might be safety in numbers, if nothing else!) or solitary places (where anyone who had no very good cause to be there stuck out like a sore thumb — as he himself did now), in spite of . . .

He took another sip. And then found, to his chagrin, that two English sips almost equalled one Italian *bottiglia*, effectively.

But . . . actually, it was possible that Richardson had got it more than right, with any luck at all. Because, in any perfectly reasonable analysis of the events, it was like old Fred always said: that the elements of any situation were seldom neatly inter-locking, with everyone (on each side — or, often, on more than two sides) pursuing related objectives.

He drained the last drops of *birra*, and added his glass to the detritus of the table's previous occupants.

If it was like that now — *if* . . . it was at least reasonably likely that whoever had been gunning for *Audley* and (apparently) *Kulik* in Berlin, might not know about Peter Richardson's private problems (about which even the Italians themselves hadn't known until very recently) in Italy. In which happy case Richardson's present 'unavailability' might have equally caught *them* — whoever? — by surprise . . . as it had also caught the British and the Italians . . . and the *Mafia* too — ?

But now he was making pictures. And even pictures of pictures, maybe?

But now it was time to find out, anyway!

It was like a labyrinth, just as Cuccaro had said —

But a labyrinth on different levels (not like a two-dimensional garden maze of evergreen hedges, in the English style: it was a labyrinthine maze of ruins in brick and stone on different levels . . . brick and stone from which the painted wall-plaster had long fallen away, and the marble had long been plundered and crushed for the lime-kilns of the ignorant plunderers).

Instinctively, he climbed *up*, away from the trees at the lower levels: he was here to be seen . . . either immediately, from some higher level, if Richardson was already here . . . or (which was much more likely) to be followed from behind, if Richardson had watched him pass from some safe vantage along the way, among the gardens and vineyards and walled houses.

What was it that they shared, from the old days? Or . . . if they didn't share it (as he increasingly suspected; because, if they'd shared it . . . then why had he no slightest clue to what it might be—?) . . . no, if they didn't share it . . . what had Fred Clinton given Peter Richardson to do, about which David Audley had had no inkling . . . but which was a good and sufficient reason for David Audley and the man Kulik to die, in Berlin —?

He reached the statue at last, coming out on the highest point—on to a wide stretch of gravel low-walled on its cliff-side and with white ornamental railings above the tiers of ruins on the island-side, with the whole of Capri beyond, and an ugly little chapel at his back. But it wasn't a statue of the Emperor Tiberius at all, presiding over the tremendous wreck of his palace, as it ought to have been by right and by reason. He'd been quite wrong in his assumption —

Wrong?

Even as he frowned up at the statue he was aware that he wasn't alone on the top of the Villa Jovis (and, if he'd thought more about it, he'd have placed Jupiter himself up there, if not Tiberius. But he would have been wrong there, too, wouldn't he!)

Wrong!

So now there were two men away to his left, over by the railings, admiring their view of Capri from peak to peak.

But . . . two men in suits? (*'That won't do!'* Mitchell had said.)

But, anyway, neither of them was Peter Richardson —

He realized, as he stared at them, that one of them was returning his stare: a stocky, almost chunky, man. Whereas the other man was still admiring the view, quite unconcerned. But then he moved slightly, away from his chunky friend, no more than two or three steps, running his hand along the top rail lightly as he did so, yet still not turning full-face towards Audley.

But those steps were enough, even without full-face. Even the steps weren't necessary. What was necessary now was to decide what he himself was going to do. Except that decisions predicated choice. And he really didn't have any choice now.

He walked towards the railings, listening to the sound of his shoes on the gravel, crunch by crunch, and not looking at the chunky man any more.

"Beautiful view." This close his last hope evaporated. But it had never really been a hope, anyway. Because, with some people, recognition had to be face-to-face (and, anyway, he wasn't good with faces). But with others it was how they stood that was unforgettable, with each part of their weight always distributed ready for action, even when they were at rest.

"Very beautiful." The man turned to him.

The movement was fluidly casual. Zimin had been a soldier, and a good one — a trainer as well as an honours graduate of *Spetsnaz*. But he would also have made a damn good rugby player in the three-quarter line of the club lucky enough to recruit him: that was what Audley had thought, that one and only other time.

"We were admiring the view last time we met, I seem to remember, Colonel." For the life of him, he couldn't smile this time. But then Zimin wasn't smiling now, either. "New Zealand House — the sixteenth floor?" Zimin definitely wasn't smiling: he looked tired and drawn under his tan, as he had not done that evening, when they'd watched the lights of London go on together. "What was it? The Wool Secretariat reception —?" Indeed, it was perhaps time to react innocently to such lack of friendliness. "It *is* Colonel Zimin, isn't it?"

"Yes, Dr Audley." The man was almost frowning at him. "It *is* Dr Audley, isn't it? The . . . celebrated Dr Audley?"

That voice was also memorable, with its curiously Germanic inflection. And, of course, he had discovered the reason for that in his subsequent check: Zimin was on record as having the gift of tongues, but German was his second language, just as Germany had been his *Spetsnaz* speciality. And he had learned his English as a German-speaker for that reason, no doubt. And probably his Italian and all the rest, too. That was how *Spetsnaz* worked.

"Not very celebrated at the moment." He felt a trickle of sweat run down his face near his ear, which could have been caused by the un-English October sun, but which was more likely the muck-sweat of fear. "The over-heated Dr Audley, Colonel." He managed to produce some sort of smile at last, even in the knowledge that Zimin's chunky minder was now almost out of view behind him. "I have very poor temperature control. Typical Anglo-Saxon — or North-West European, maybe . . . Although, of course, my other Norman ancestors did rather well in these parts, actually. So maybe it's just me."

"Is that so?" On the surface, Zimin was humiliatingly cool-and-calm, just as the rest of him still seemed to hang loose. But Audley sensed that inside he was dancing on his toes and wound up clockwork-tight: the whole joke — *no joke!* — might be that he must be assuming 'the celebrated Dr Audley' would be even-better-protected here, so far from home.

"Oh yes!" After that chance meeting at the New Zealand House reception Zimin would have done his homework too, if he hadn't done it before (and, indeed, if it had been such a chance meeting on his part, also). And that was what he himself must hold on to now — if only to stop this embarrassing sweat-of-fear which was running off him: that the Russian must be putting two-and-two together logically, when the real mathematics of the situation were such a hopeless mess. "All these parts — from here to Sicily — were once Norman territory, long ago. And they made a better job of running them than anyone has since." *Smile, Audley!* "And long after that, in

84

Nelson's time or thereabouts . . . there was a British garrison here. Only, then the French threw us off. But we got the better of them, eventually . . . with some help from the Russians, as well as the Germans." *This time — grin!* "We always end up on the winning side, Colonel."

"I see." The disadvantage of such crude time-buying was that it bought them both time. "And is it history which brings you here now, Dr Audley? Or are you on holiday —? Is Mrs Audley down there, in the town? And Miss Audley with her, perhaps?"

Audley watched the Russian take in the view again, from the ruins directly below them to far-off Capri-town, and even more distant Anacapri on its mountain beyond, before he finally came back to the ruins and Audley himself.

"No." There was one bonus to all this, among all these hideous new uncertainties: Peter Richardson would not be joining this meeting, as it was at present constituted in full view of wherever he was down there below. With Zimin here — and, even more, with the chunky man in attendance — that was certain. So, with Peter out of mind, he could afford to strengthen his position by dismissing all the small talk. "I'm working. And . . . although it's a pleasure to meet you again . . . I must admit that I'm also surprised to see you here, Colonel."

Zimin studied him for a moment. Then he drew a deep breath. But, before he could speak, Chunky snapped something in Russian, far too quickly and urgently for Audley to understand.

Zimin grunted, and then reached forward, first to touch Audley's arm, and then to hold it, pulling him gently away from the white railings — at least, pulling him gently because he surrendered to the pressure. "Dr Audley — if you please?"

Audley let himself be led, away round the squat chapel and into the shadow of what was very obviously not the statue of the Emperor Tiberius, Ruler of the World, but of the Virgin Mary, Queen of Heaven.

"Thank you." Zimin glanced past him for a second, and then at him. "I am also surprised, Dr Audley — that you are here."

85

They were now infinitely past small talk. "You're surprised that I'm alive — is that it?"

Zimin drew a breath. "I am . . . relieved that you are alive."

The rules hadn't changed. It was simply that there were new rules, apparently. "Then . . . that makes us both relieved, Colonel Zimin. As well as surprised."

Zimin took another look past him, presumably to make sure that Chunky was still doing his job. "You are here to meet with the man Peter Richardson, I take it?" Then he nodded, and it wasn't a question. "He is a former colleague, of course — yes?"

Berlin still could have been the Russians, in theory. And, by the same theory, Capri could still be Audley as well as Richardson, just as Berlin ought to have been Audley and Kulik. Only that wasn't the way Capri felt, somehow.

"He is." No use denying what they knew. But that was no reason for admitting more too readily yet, even though Zimin knew more than he did. "And supposing I am here to meet him?"

"Then we have a common interest."

Audley considered the cards he had in his hand unhappily, and almost with despair. His only trump was his belief that Richardson would be lying low, if not gone already. But that was the one card he couldn't safely play while Zimin had all the others.

"A common interest?" Suddenly he had another certainty, which lifted the huge weight of fear off his back almost magically as it also clarified Berlin. If the Russians had simply been concerned to kill Richardson — with or without the aid of another surrogate Arab assassin — then a man of Zimin's seniority would never be in attendance, even as an observer. Not even in the bad old days, let alone now (when appearances mattered), would that have been KGB/GRU style so to compromise men for whom diplomatic status was routinely required across the world.

So he was safe!

"A common interest?" He realized that Zimin had been waiting for something better than that. And . . . and now that he was safe, he could see more clearly that there was only one reason why Colonel

Zimin should have come to Capri, dropping all his other important duties . . . just as 'the celebrated Dr Audley' had been forced to do.

"You'd like a word with him too, Colonel?"

The happy thought expanded. Because, if the Russians knew better what was happening than he did (and they could hardly know worse), it was now at least possible that they didn't know *everything*, if they had sent Zimin to bring in Richardson.

"We would not like any harm to come to him." Zimin ducked the question smoothly. "Our first concern, naturally, is for his safety. As I am sure yours is, Dr Audley. So you have also taken other precautions, of course — as we have?"

God — that put him on the line! Because that meant Zimin and Chunky weren't the only KGB tourists admiring the ruins of the Villa Jovis right now: Chunky was simply Colonel Zimin's private minder, with other 'tourists' down below, among the passages and stairways and in the trees. And that was the other reason why Zimin had tightened up on seeing him: he had only been an unexpected ghost for that half-second which the Colonel had needed to remember that he didn't believe in ghosts. But, after that, he had been consumed by the fear that there must be British tourists down there too, sniffing his own men suspiciously.

There was no help for it. With the Russians as twitchy as this, the possibility of appalling accidents multiplied, involving innocent people. And, for Jack Butler's sake, he couldn't take that risk —

"I am here alone, Colonel Zimin. I have help . . . further down."

That actually raised the Russian's eyebrows slightly. Then he snapped an order at Chunky, in fast Russian vernacular.

Chunky vanished behind Our Lady's statue, and Audley was left with his familiar problem with modern languages, in which the difference between the written and the spoken word was always a source of humiliation.

Or maybe it was because he couldn't believe his ears — ?

"What was that, Colonel — ?" It was the verb which eluded him, among the rest. But, after having guessed at it, he still couldn't believe it.

"You are either very brave, Dr Audley. Or you are very stupid." Zimin considered him dispassionately for an instant. "After what happened in Berlin." Then he seemed to decide to give Audley the benefit of the doubt, as from one genuine soldier to one temporary one (but one from a real war before the Colonel's time nevertheless, which therefore demanded recognition).

"Oh — yes?" In less pressing circumstances Zimin's wrong choice from those alternatives would have been as interesting as it was wounding to his already damaged self-esteem. But meanwhile the sense of that command, if he understood it correctly, had to be resolved. "That order of yours, Colonel Zimin — to your man . . . I'd be obliged if you would explain it to me, nevertheless."

"Obliged?" The word seemed to throw the Russian.

"Yes." Audley realized that the word wasn't to blame: Zimin was waiting now for his instruction to be carried out, and until it had been then even the celebrated Dr Audley could not hold his attention absolutely. "Obliged, Colonel."

Zimin's lips tightened. "It was not for your former colleague, Dr Audley."

"I know that." The man's waiting was infectious. "Or . . . I gathered that."

"Then you also know that he is in great danger."

If the Russian had been concentrating on him fully he would be amending 'brave' to 'stupid' now. But he was boxed in by his own doubt, just as Audley himself was by his own stupidity. "Indeed? But not from you?"

Almost as though against his will, Zimin forced himself to attend to Audley. "We do not want him dead, Dr Audley. As others do."

Audley held his face steady. *Tell them to kill the Arab* was undoubtedly what Zimin had said, although 'kill' hadn't been the word he'd used: what he had just said made that certain, never mind the untidy events in Berlin.

"And we do not want you dead, either, Dr Audley. We do not want any . . . unnecessary violence in this matter. All we want is Major Richardson."

88

So Berlin had been as much a disaster for the Russians as for the British, albeit a different sort of disaster: in so far as that made sense, it made much better sense. Only he mustn't let his relief show, any more than his ignorance: anger was what he must show now. "The correct word is 'kidnap', I believe, Colonel."

"He will not be harmed. Nor will he be held very long."

"But he will have been kidnapped. And my Government —"

The scream took them by surprise equally, with its throaty mixture of mortal agony and terror: he saw Zimin's eyes widen as the sound rose from below to their left, among the trees, only to be cut off instantly, as though by a switch, leaving them staring at each other.

Then Zimin's mouth opened in a silent swear-word, that something which should have been accomplished equally silently had been bungled so noisily.

For a moment there was no sound at all: the very lack of sound mocked them both. Then it was shattered by another scream — but a very different one: a high-pitched cry punctuated by breath, ululating unstoppably.

That was a woman's scream! The certainty raced through Audley's brain as he thought also of Elizabeth disobeying him. But then the scream hiccoughed into hysterics; and . . . *Elizabeth wouldn't scream — wouldn't have hysterics . . . and, anyway, it wouldn't be Elizabeth who disobeyed him —*

Zimin was staring at him, ready-tensed as though the sound had tightened up his spring.

Audley relaxed himself slowly and deliberately. Once upon a time, maybe, he might have chanced a forward's weight against a three-quarter's speed at this distance. But that time was long gone, and the Russian had far too many years' youthful advantage. So all he had now, to steady his fear, was the echo of the man's words — *no unnecessary violence?* — and his own wits.

The scream ran out of breath at last, degenerating into sobs. But now a man was shouting, somewhere down among the ruins.

He drew a deep breath. "I rather think —" Embarrassingly, he had to clear his throat "— I rather think your men have queered both our pitches now, Colonel . . . I'm afraid." He spread his hands as eloquently as he could, and shook his head.

Zimin frowned, but didn't unwind.

"Richardson won't come now." He shook his head again. "God only knows what he'll be thinking!" That certainly was true. "But he'll know he's been betrayed, anyway." That was also true. So why not more truth? "He's not stupid." But now the important half-truth. "So I'm afraid we've both lost him. And he won't be so easy to find next time —" He could hear the sound of footsteps on the stone steps at the back "— if we ever find him now, that is, Colonel." He could feel the hairs on the back of his neck rise. But he gave the Russian his ugliest scowl, and nodded towards the railing beside which they'd met, in full view of the whole of Capri. "And what *rather* pisses me off, Colonel Zimin, is that . . . if, by any chance, he saw us exchanging pleasantries just now, before your idiots dealt with that Arab so incompetently . . . then he may very well think we're in this together. And that sort of *glasnost* won't be to his taste, seeing as how the Mafia and the Italian police also want to nail his hide to the nearest tree as it is."

Zimin shook his head suddenly. But he was no longer looking at Audley.

Audley turned, just in time to observe Chunky straightening his ill-fitting suit-jacket.

"Goodbye, Dr Audley."

The words and Zimin himself passed him together.

"Goodbye, Colonel —"

When they had gone he was ashamed to discover that his hands were shaking. So he grasped the railings and admired the Bay of Naples far below him. It would have been a very long drop. But the first outcrop of cliff below him would have silenced whatever sound he might have made.

Then he started thinking about Peter Richardson again.

Between the Russians and the Mafia, Peter had been betrayed

somehow. But maybe that wasn't so very surprising. And it was what Peter would do next that mattered now, anyway.

He began to think about the old days: it was in his memory of them that his only hope now lay.

PART TWO

Just like the Old Days

I

"I AM NOT . . ." he had carefully told Elizabeth *". . . as young as I once was."* So, as they approached the centre of London, she wasn't surprised when he appeared to doze off. He had been through a lot, after all. And that made it easy, when a red light caught them in the Bayswater Road, to be out of the car before either Elizabeth or the driver knew what was happening: it was just like the old days!

"David! What on earth are you doing?" She threw herself across the seats, her consternation emphasized by the mixture of fatigue and the unnatural light of the street lamps which dawn hadn't quite cancelled, which together gave her a three-day corpse look. "Where are you going —?"

"Sir!" The driver added his pennyworth of desperation to hers, all too aware that he was trapped by the lights in the outer lane. "We're to go directly —"

"It's all right." He closed the door on them both as the lights changed, flattening himself against the side of the car to let a delivery van pass on the inside lane. "Don't worry."

A muffled sound from within turned into words as she tried to open the door again, only to have it shut again on her as an early-morning taxi hooted angrily behind. But other vehicles were following the van — damn!

"David!" She had the window down. But there was a gap coming up —

"It's all right." He judged the approaching gap carefully. It would never do to push his luck again so soon after Capri. "Tell Sir Jack that I won't be long — don't worry, my dear."

Just like the old days! And no shortness of breath — only relief at being

95

able to stretch his legs again. (Don't run! Never run, unless you have to!)

Just like the old days, of course: not many pedestrians around, as yet; but the good morning smell of London — London with its streets not yet fully charged with carbon monoxide: he could breath it in gratefully, with his country-boy's memory of it going all the way back to exciting recollections of even older days — even to childhood forays, from steam-trains into Waterloo and on to Hamley's and a museum before lunch.

But now he was safe enough, anyway — safer after that last turning, after having re-crossed the road, and done all the necessary things which would have been no damn good at all in less advantageous circumstances: poor Miss Loftus and her driver had been not so much out-smarted as out-ranked, and Jack wasn't the man to penalize them for that, anyway. So he didn't have to worry about them . . . only about his own chickens properly coming home to roost.

Now he actually knew where he was, too: he'd jinked to reach Cato Street, which he'd imprinted in his memory long ago because of its famous conspirators . . . so a quick *right* down and across the Edgware Road, and then *left* into Kendal Street . . . and then he'd be close to Matthew — ?

Always supposing Matthew was at home today — and this early? And one difference between the *old* days and *these* days was that he wasn't absolutely sure which day of the week it was, after so many *alarms* and *excursions*, from one continent across another, and back: did Matthew still keep an eye on his bank mid-week (give or take a day), now that his sons and grandsons and nephews ran it?

He pressed the *Fattorini* button: *now he was going to find out.*

"Hullo there! Who is that?"

Audley turned his back on Hyde Park. "It's David Audley. Can I come up please?" He felt himself relax. "Please?"

96

"*David* —?" From having been slightly foreign, and more than slightly outraged at so early an intrusion, the voice welcomed him immediately, and the door clicked. "David!"

"David!" As always (or, since he had never called on her at dawn, as he had always imagined her, anyway), Marie-Louise had stepped out of one of her French magazines. "You have come for breakfast — at last!"

"Lady Fattorini — Marie-Louise!" For the first time since Washington, Audley felt safe. "Whatever's on the menu, you look good enough to eat." Safe, but smelly, he thought belatedly as she advanced to embrace him. "But don't hug me, darling: I'm jet-lagged and unfit for civilized company."

"Mmm . . ." The years had augmented Marie-Louise not too much, just comfortably ". . . *mmm* . . . I agree! But Matthew is just coming out of the bathroom, I think —"

"Matthew has come out of his bath — prematurely." The chairman of Armstrong Fattorini Brothers materialized behind his wife, clad in thick grey-black hair and a towel. "So you can have my bath, like in the old days. Or you can run another . . . because you're not going to get my breakfast."

"Hullo, Matt." He extricated himself unwillingly from Marie-Louise: more even than the sight of her, her smell was of safety from an outside world which promised nothing but danger now. "I don't want your bath — or your damn breakfast. I just want to make a couple of phone-calls, that's all."

"Oh yes?" Sir Matthew Fattorini lifted up one fold of his towel to rub his hairy chest. "You're in trouble, then?"

"In trouble?" It was no good lying to Matthew. "Of course I'm in trouble." Then something more than old acquaintance spiked him. "Why should I be in trouble — more than usually?"

Matt considered him briefly. "Get the man his breakfast, dear." The look focused on Marie-Louise. "Put the door on the chain, and don't answer any more callers." The look came back to Audley. "And lock up your jewellery and the silver." The re-directed look concentrated. "Or . . . on second thoughts, my dear . . . phone up Sands, and tell him to bring the car round to the back. *Then* lock up the silver — *bien entendu?*"

"Yes, dear." Marie-Louise had been a child in Normandy long ago, when Audley's tank had passed five miles from her family home. So, while she didn't believe all her husband was telling her, she believed some of it. "Matthew is enjoying his fish day, because it is Friday, David. But would you prefer bacon-and-eggs, not kippers —?"

"Give him the bacon." Matthew dismissed her sharply, waiting until she'd gone before continuing. "'Jet-lag', you said —?"

Audley had been thinking hard through Matthew's warning signals, of which there were altogether too many to take lightly. "I've been in America, Matt. So what's the matter?"

Matthew Fattorini's expression hardened. "You just dropped in for breakfast — after all these years —?" Matthew frowned at his own questions. "Well . . . I suppose, if I must give you the benefit of the doubt — though God only knows why . . ." He shook his head. "But . . . there's this major terrorist alert out, David. Isn't that up your street — the safety of the realm?"

"Uh-huh?" The non-commital grunt came naturally now.

"Didn't you see the soldiers at the airport? If you're jet-lagged —?" Matthew looked at him suspiciously. "One of our fellows coming back from Brussels said they had tanks at Heathrow."

"I came in through RAF Brize Norton." He bought time with a lie. "It's probably just an exercise, Matt."

Matthew nodded. "Yes — that is the official explanation: a 'Scheduled Unspecific Routine Exercise'. '*SURE*' for short. The newspapers are full of it."

"So it's just an exercise then." But the suspicion was still there, that he could see. "So what's new?"

"What's new?" Incredulity displaced suspicion. "Doesn't the Russian bit of it count as new? What that idiot on TV described as '*double*-SURE' last night — anti-terrorist co-operation being just another bit of Glasnost?" Matthew shook his head. "The word in the City yesterday was that they'd started cracking down on all their ports and airfields hours before anything happened in the West. Not 'co-operation' — more like cause-and-effect . . . But you don't know anything about this? You're just in one of your own fifty-seven varieties of trouble?"

"I don't." Being able to answer the first question quickly and fairly honestly gave Audley five seconds' rest on what had suddenly become a slippery rock-face before he tackled the second. "As regards my present predicament, Matt . . . I wasn't looking for information, just for a nice safe telephone, that's all."

"Of course, my dear fellow!" Matthew hitched up his towel with one hand and pointed with the other. "In my study there. No scrambler, of course. But I think it's safe enough . . . And then breakfast?" He produced his merchant banker's smile. "And my driver will then take you wherever you want to go after that — within reason. Go on, then."

"Thanks, Matt." Neither that interest nor those suspicions were surprising: Matt knew too much about the old days, *via* the adventures of his brother Fred as well as because of friendship and certain mutual favours traded in those days. And he was himself an unashamed operator in a business where the smallest piece of reliable inside information could always be made to pay handsomely somehow. What was surprising was that neither Jack nor Paul had mentioned the Russian dimension of the supposed emergency.

He picked up the receiver and pressed the buttons. (Maybe Paul hadn't known. But Jack surely would have done — wouldn't he?)

He heard the ringing note —

(Captain Cuccaro would have now. And so had Zimin!)

Cover story first, just in case, though.

"Hullo?" Faith answered properly for once, neither giving her name nor her number. "Who is that?"

"It's me, love." Also he simply wanted to hear her voice.

"David! Are you in trouble?"

"What?" Everyone seemed to know too-bloody-much: he hadn't

even had time to lie — and as far as she knew he was still safe in Washington. "What do you mean — am I in trouble?" All the half-truths he'd marshalled turned their backs on him mutinously, looking for escape. But he grabbed the slowest of them. "I was just phoning to say I'm back."

"Yes. I know you're back. And now you're going to tell me that you won't be coming home just yet."

"What? How do you know?"

"I've just put the phone down on Jack Butler. He told me to tell you — to tell you *if* you phoned me — to come in at once."

The rest of the half-truths were running for cover now, having thrown away their shields and spears. "Oh?"

"And he didn't sound too pleased."

And Faith herself didn't sound too pleased, either. "No?"

"No. And I've been given protection, David. *If* you're interested." No one transmitted displeasure down the phone better than Mrs Audley. "A very nice young man. Who thinks the world of you. Although I can't think why."

"No?" There was a set of Low cartoon originals on the wall of Matthew's study. But it didn't include the famous 1940 one, in which an embattled British Tommy shook his fist against the dark clouds of impending defeat, facing it alone. And that omission switched his own control from *Defence* to *Offence*. "Well, don't forget to get his name, love — he's obviously ready for promotion. But meanwhile . . . give me some bad news: tell me something awful."

"What?" The tables were turned on that word.

"Tell me something awful." What was awful? "Mrs Mills is pregnant again — and the washing-up machine has gone wrong . . . And Cathy's fallen in love with the boy who delivers the papers — *anything!*"

"*What* —?" Suddenly her voice changed. "You mean it — don't you!"

"I mean it — yes!" There was just an outside chance that all this was going on tape somewhere. But, as Jack wasn't the man to squander his resources eavesdropping on someone he trusted, it was on the far outside.

Several seconds ticked away. "Cathy wants to go to India for her year off before University as a nursing auxiliary. And I've said no."

Audley agreed with her. "Change your mind — say yes."

"What d'you mean? They catch the most awful diseases —"

"I know. But 'yes' will buy us time. 'No' will only make her more determined. Just leave it to me." He began to feel guilty. But then the genuine awfulness registered, and he didn't. "Goodbye, love! I'll call you again . . . when I can —"

He put the phone down, and then picked it up again and punched in the well-remembered numbers of the Saracen's Head public house by the river.

"Saracen."

Teenage female voice. "Get the boss, dear."

"Dad's 'avin' 'is breakfast. You'd better call back later."

There had been a child in the background at the Saracen's Head long ago, he remembered. "Just tell him it's a friend of Mr Lee's, dear."

"'E won't like it —"

"He won't like it if you don't tell him. Go on! A friend of Mr Lee's."

There was a moment's silence. "Oh—all right! But 'e won't like it."

Audley waited. It had been a very small child, his memory corrected him. But it had also been a long time ago — the old days indeed!

"Saracen." Dad's tone bore out the ex-small child's warning. "'Ullo."

"I'd like a word with Mr Lee." Audley crossed his fingers.

"'Oo wants 'im?"

So far, so good. "A friend of his."

"Oh yus? Well, 'e 'ain't 'ere.

Audley relaxed. It was like fitting a key into the rusty old lock of a long-disused room and finding that it still turned easily, as though newly-oiled. "Mr Lee owes me three favours, for services rendered." Over the years, those numbers had gradually decreased, as those Anglo-Israeli debts had been called in one by one. Although, of course, it wouldn't be Jake himself, now. So it all depended on how well his successors had been briefed. "I want to speak to him, nevertheless."

"Oh yus?" The landlord of the Saracen's Head might also be struggling with his memories of long-disused procedures, as between 'Mr Lee' and his 'friend'. But when you worked for the Israelis once, you worked for them always, was the rule. "An' this would be an emergency, like — as per usual?" The phlegm rattled in the man's throat as he chuckled. "Naow — don't tell me! Face-to-face — or you got a number?"

Audley estimated Butler's orders against his own need. With the trouble he was already in — the *new* Russian trouble as well as the Berlin-Capri trouble — he was already in for a penny, in for a pound; and he could easily (and probably safely) encode Matthew's number with the very private and unforgettable formula which he and Jake had decided so long ago, after they had agreed that the one set of figures which no soldier ever forgot was his old army number. But he had always hated the telephone, and the hothouse temperature of Matt's flat was stifling him. "Face-to-face." Everything came together as he spoke: perhaps because he felt suddenly starved he imagined he could smell Marie-Louise's bacon, and her coffee too . . . and this side of Heaven there would be nothing to equal a thoroughly-Anglicized Frenchwoman's coffee-and-bacon. And also he must allow 'Mr Lee' time to make a rendezvous. So the lines on the map converged as he drew breath: ten minutes from here, in Sir Matthew Fattorini's Rolls-Royce, plus five for him from there to Jack Butler's fastness on the Embankment . . . plus fifteen to demolish the bacon and the coffee before that . . . finally offering 'Mr Lee' maybe twenty minutes —? "Fifty minutes. By the statue of General Abercrombie, in Abercrombie Gardens. One hour, maximum. Then I'll be gone. Have you got that?"

"Yuss." The phone clicked and died. Time — seconds, rather than minutes — was always of the essence on the phone, when you didn't know you were on a safe line, they would have taught him.

He looked at his watch. Fifty minutes from now.

"And how is that beautiful daughter of yours, David? I am told that she takes after her mother — yes?"

His mouth was full of bacon. And the bacon carried with it a hint — the merest paradisal hint — of kidney-fat, did it — ? "Cathy?"

"She must be working for her examinations, surely —? Always, now, they are in the midst of examinations!"

A major anti-terrorist alert? (Matthew, still only half-dressed, had been silenced by his wife: 'Let the poor man eat his breakfast, chéri! Is the car ready? Do something useful!')

"She has exams, yes." *Not co-operation — more like cause-and-effect*: but what cause could produce this effect? The irony was that he needed to know the answer to that much more urgently than Matthew himself, who only had his stocks and shares at risk. "But now she wants to go to India, before university. So Faith's worried sick."

"Ah! India — yes!" Marie-Louise nodded sympathetically. "She is too young for India. The women there are wonderful — they hold the country together. But the men . . . they are *not* to be trusted with young unmarried girls." Then she brightened. "But India . . . that will be Christian India, yes? To do mission work — that is what the young people do now . . . That could be worse, you know."

"Worse?" The more he thought about Cathy in India, the worse it genuinely became.

"It is not *political.* One of my nieces wished to go to Nicaragua, from where the dreadful coffee comes, to help the revolution. Matthew had to arrange a more suitable enterprise for her — where was it, chéri? Perhaps you could do the same for David's Catherine —?"

India, damn it!

"Round again, sir?" The voice of Matthew's driver sounded cool and distant over the intercom of the Rolls as they turned into Abercrombie Gardens once more, past the statue of the old general who was one of Jack Butler's special idols.

Audley looked at his watch. The Israelis were almost out of time now, and his bright idea was beginning to look more than ever like the desperate long-shot it had always been, with the temperature of Anglo-Israeli intelligence relations so chilly these days.

"Yes — *no!* Hold on — slow down!" Where there had been nobody on the last circuit, there was now a young man loitering, although he looked far too young to be 'Mr Lee'. But then everyone was young now — not just police constables but police superintendents and the Mr Lees of this world. "Stop here, please."

The Rolls drew up with its usual silent good manners. "Shall I come back, sir?"

"Ah . . ." Audley felt crumpled and disreputable in his creased suit and three-day shirt: all he could hope for, if anyone was peeking through their curtains on the other side of the street, was that he might pass for an eccentric millionaire taking his morning constitutional. "Yes." *Damn Butler! Damn India — and damn Berlin and Capri, most of all!* "Ten minutes —" *Damn the whole bloody-lot-of-them!* "— and then keep coming round. Right?"

The Rolls slid away, as though powered by thought rather than anything so vulgar as an internal-combustion engine, and the London October-chill hit him immediately. So . . . he was grasping at a straw, then. But there was a newspaper kiosk at the other end of the crescent of trees. So he would grasp the straw nonchalantly, as though he had all the time in the world, even though he suspected he'd already lost the game, and was into injury-time.

"*Daily Telegraph*, please." For a moment he was embarrassed then, in the sudden knowledge that he had no Queen's coinage in his pocket, having nearly had no lire to purchase his Villa Jovis ticket. But then he thought again, re-estimating the odds that there might yet be some of the Queen's coins among the foreign detritus in his palm. "How much is that — ?"

The old woman in the kiosk goggled at him for an instant, not so much as at an eccentric millionaire as at an idiot, while keeping tight hold of the *Daily Telegraph* she'd been about to surrender.

Audley squinted at his small change. "Yes — ?"

"'Ere —" On second thought, she decided that he was a Martian who had made his historic landfall inadequately prepared; but, if she could, she would sell him a paper; so she leaned across to finger his coins. "Thirty-p . . . that's twenty — that's forty —" she pinched the appropriate coins "— an' eight-p change — right?"

"Right." Audley accepted his *Telegraph* gratefully. When it came to newspapers, he knew his business in content, if not in price: the subs on the *Telegraph* weren't into clever design on the news pages, even under the new Max Hastings editorial management; but they still picked up all those unconsidered trifles of news, local and international, for their fillers —

He opened the paper up. (Let the very-young-man wait — if he was a Mossad very-young-man he still had three minutes of waiting-time!) Cuccaro's cover story was just the sort the *Telegraph* liked —

Virus kills tiger —

That wasn't it . . . even though it was a vintage *Telegraph* heading —

Pushchair snatch
foiled by nannie

Another good one. But it was not the one he wanted.

He turned the page to foreign news —

Mafia shoot-out
on holiday isle —

Elizabeth's handsome captain had done his work well, even allowing for all his advantages —

A man fell to his death and two more were shot in a Mafia-style execution on the holiday island of Capri yesterday, visited by thousands of British tourists every year —

The grammar was maybe a bit rocky. But the facts were nearly right, as reported, even though absolutely wrong —

Holiday-makers scattered as gangsters opened fire on their rivals without warning —

That was also pretty close to the facts, give-or-take the truth —

The Italian police have taken a fourth man into custody, who is believed to have taken part in the shoot-out. A fifth man and a woman are also helping the police with their inquiries —

Even that was good, in its acceptance of what any uncontrollable eye-witnesses might have seen in the aftermath, when half of Capri had appeared out of nowhere, even before Cuccaro had arrived with Paul and Elizabeth, and the situation had become decidedly messy.

He re-folded his *Telegraph* quickly and untidily, shivering slightly as he set out for General Abercrombie's statue — even remembering, as he did so, why Jack Butler so admired the old soldier —

The trees above were dripping early-morning moisture, and the pavement was pock-marked by all sorts of filth — pigeon-shit and dog-shit, and general all-sorts-of-litter-lout shit, from take-away plastic containers to beer-cans and last night's evening newspapers. And the need to avoid this different mess took his attention until he reached the corner of the gardens, where the old General stood, sword-in-hand and bare-headed, looking blindly out over the London traffic, as he would surely not have looked over the Egyptian desert when he'd beaten the French.

There was nobody there — *sod it!*

He looked half-around. And then at the blackened panel below the statue: the old General, mortally-wounded, had still worried about the soldier's blanket in which they'd covered him. Because every soldier needed his blanket, just as he himself would have liked one now in the morning chill.

"Hullo, David." Jake Shapiro appeared from behind the statue. "You travel in style these days!"

If the old General had stepped down and offered him another blanket, Audley knew he'd not have been more dumb-struck. "Jake —?"

"Let's go and walk among the trees." Jake kept well behind the statue, away from the road. "Come on!"

The seconds of his minutes were ticking, Audley remembered. "For God's sake — I thought you'd retired, Jake!" But he stepped out automatically: Jake had not only retired — he ought to be even more out-of-favour now, as an Arab-lover, with his present government. "What the hell are you doing here?"

"You asked for 'Mr Lee' —" Jake pushed him towards the central path, between the trees "— and now you are complaining ?" Audley disciplined himself. "I'm not complaining. I'm just thinking . . . maybe I should have retired, too. But then . . . by the same token . . . I suppose I might still be here, mightn't I? Taken out of mothballs?"

"Ah . . . well, as to that, I can't say." Jake grinned at him. "But maybe with us it's like the old music-hall jokes: the old ones are still the best ones?"

"Uh-huh?" Matthew's Rolls-Royce was cruising out there somewhere, like a stop-watch ticking silently. "Unfortunately, I haven't time for jokes, Jake. Why are you here — in London?"

"Because this is where the action is. Isn't it?" The Israeli stepped delicately around a nameless mess on the path. "I was back home. And you were in Washington, and you were not in Berlin. But now you are here, where the action is? So now we are both here —?"

The Israelis didn't know about Capri. Or, if they did, Jake wasn't ready to admit it yet. But if they *didn't* . . . then they might not know about Richardson. But what they did know had to be substantial indeed, to force the new generation of Mossad to swallow its pride and re-enlist Jake Shapiro? *Yes!*

"You're here because of me?" The Israelis had been very helpful in Berlin, of course. But Jake's presence in London now put a different gloss on that, taken with the present terrorist alert. So whatever they knew must be frightening them. "Because of our old 'special relationship', would that be?" There was no time for finesse. "You need a friend at court?"

"'The Court of Queen Margaret'?" Jake slowed down as they approached the end of the trees. "Ah . . . well, we never did have many friends here, even in the old days. Your Foreign Office was full of Arab-lovers — unrequited lovers, of course." He smiled at Audley. "Sure — okay! Well . . . you, at least, were pragmatic,

David. You were willing to do business in the old Yorkshire manner: 'Owt for nowt' — ?"

"What do you want, Jake?" He could see the very young man standing on guard at the far end of the gardens, apparently engrossed in his *Guardian*.

Jake gestured to turn them round into the trees again. "I thought it was you who wanted something, David?"

Audley glimpsed a large car through the trees. But it couldn't be the Rolls yet. "I just want to know what the Russians are doing."

"Only that? Where do you want me to begin?"

"Don't piss me around." In the old days Jake had usually got what he wanted by indirect means, he recalled: for Jake, an Audley question was as good as an answer. "I've been minding my own business in Washington, working up our submission on the new Secrets Bill for Jack Butler. As I'm sure you know."

"Yes." The Israeli nodded. "The worthy Sir Jack has heretical views on Freedom of Information and the Public Interest — he believes in them! *That* I know — yes! The worthy Sir Jack! Yes?"

And the not-so-clever Jake Shapiro, thought Audley. But then half Jack's strength was that no one really believed in his sincerity. "Yes. But now I want some information — in *my* interest, Colonel Shapiro."

"Yes?" Jake peered into the trees on his left, pretending to be nervous.

"What's the matter?" Suddenly Audley actually became nervous.

"Don't worry. We are well-protected, old friend." The reassurance came quickly. "You lost someone in Berlin, didn't you?"

"Tell me something I don't know." He decided not to hide his fear. "Answer the question. My time is running out. And maybe in more ways than one, *old friend*."

The Israeli faced him. "Correction. You lost *two* people in Berlin: you lost a man named Kulik also."

"How d'you know his name?"

"I know all three names. But only one of them matters now."

Audley held his tongue without difficulty. No more questions!

Jake held up three fingers. "Kulik is dead in Berlin." One finger went down. "That was very careless of you — what my old boss would have called 'unnecessary carelessness'. But perhaps understandable at that stage."

Audley concentrated on the remaining two fingers — blunt, serviceable fingers, rising from a work-calloused hand. In retirement, Jake had become a working farmer. But soft fruit looked like hard work, judging by those hands.

"And now Prusakov is also dead, as of two days since." The second finger went down. "But your people cannot be blamed for that."

Something out in the furthest corner of Audley's peripheral vision diverted him from the last finger: the shape of Sir Matthew Fattorini's Rolls flicked through trees on the inner side of Abercrombie Gardens. But the Rolls didn't matter now: *Who-the-hell-was 'Prusakov'?*

"So that leaves Lukianov at large." The third finger seemed to get larger as Audley stared at it. "The luckiest — or the cleverest . . . yes?"

So there had been *three* runners. And although he dearly wanted to know who *Prusakov* was — and *where* and *how* and *why* Prusakov had run out of luck and cleverness 'two days since', that would have to wait. "At large where, Jake? Lukianov?"

Jake shrugged. "That, I don't know. And neither do the Russians, evidently." The shrug became a shake. "They are tearing their hair — but that also is common knowledge . . . What was it Cohen used to say, in the Saracen? 'Screaming blue murder, like Auntie Vi did when she caught her tits in the mangle'?" The shake stopped and the bushy eyebrows lifted. "All the way from Finland to the Black Sea — how many perfectly innocent criminals have been caught? And honest smugglers, who reckoned they'd bribed the border-guards sufficiently, too —?" The eyebrows came down. "The first plus-side is that the KGB is pushing all its contacts so hard that *we* are picking up people we never suspected, who are sticking out their necks. But the minus is that we're also losing valued middle-men who never knew who they were working for." Quite terrifyingly,

Jake began to become incredulous at his own revelations. "If they were moving their tank divisions and dispersing their SS-20s as well, then we'd be battening-down for the Third World War — just as you are, David!" But then the incredulity steadied itself. "Only you've gone off half-cock. Because they haven't shifted a mobile army-cookhouse." The shake came back, but more disbelievingly. "Just all their bloody *spies* . . . and their sleepers . . . and even some of their *Spetsnaz* sleepers — which is even more outrageous . . . the handful that we know, here in England — " Jake Shapiro actually bit his lip, under his moustache, on that " — and that's strictly between you and me, as of now, David: if you want more on *Spetsnaz*, then you've got to trade at the very highest level — not you, but Jack Butler and his Minister. And it will involve a public pronouncement on your Government's attitude to the PLO." He nodded. "This is big business now, David."

Audley felt almost as disembodied as he had also so recently felt on Capri when the screaming had started, half-aware that his features must have become as wooden as Jake Shapiro's suddenly were. Because Jake knew what he was saying: it had all been agreed — and bloody-quickly agreed, too — at his own very highest-level, in the few minutes which had elapsed between his 'Mr Lee' call to the Saracen's Head and their joint-arrival under General Abercrombie's statue. Or (what was more likely, actually — and what was certainly worse, therefore) it had been agreed before? Which meant that the Israelis were so worried that they were desperate to co-operate at any price, in spite of Jake's pretended arrogance.

"I can't promise that, Jake." Suddenly he felt greedy: having got so much · so easily, he wanted more. And, anyway, however interesting that *Spetsnaz* information sounded — and in exchange only for some half-arsed ministerial statement, which could be made to sound like something-and-nothing — it was just a sprat to catch a mackerel. "I'm not even supposed to be talking to you now."

"I can remedy that." Jake gave him a bleak look. "If you hadn't called me this morning, I would have called you this afternoon. Because I am empowered to do business with you, old friend."

"With me?"

"With you to start with. And to show good faith I will give you Prusakov: they took him in Italy, in a house outside Rome. But, unfortunately he swallowed a pill, so that is the end of him. However, they also took the Arab who was with him. And they will have squeezed *him* for sure. But that has not given them Lukianov. And he is the most dangerous of the three, we believe. Because he was the one who approached the various terrorist organizations in the first place, seeking the highest bidder for his merchandise — we know that."

"What merchandise, Jake?"

Shapiro shook his head. "That we do not know." He looked at Audley sidelong. "And you do not know —?"

He must give the Israeli something. "You've heard about Capri?"

"Capri —?" Jake frowned.

Audley unfolded his *Telegraph* and offered the right page. He had to allow that the stage might have lost a great actor when Jake's parents had illegally emigrated. But his surprise looked genuine.

"You were there?" The Israeli crumpled the newspaper as he looked up from it. "This was . . . *yesterday* —?"

"Yes." Whatever else Mossad knew, Capri didn't fit in with it. "Tell me about it."

Audley shook his head. "The Russians killed two Arabs. And they lost one of their own men, doing it. That's what we believe. But the man wasn't Lukianov, anyway. At least, I don't think so."

The Israeli drew a deep breath. "It can't have been 'Lucky' Lukianov. Because the Russians wanted all three of them back alive, from the start. And as of last night — as of this morning, too . . . they still wanted him." He lifted the crumpled *Telegraph*. "So if this is kosher, then it could be a terrorist squabble to decide who's going to attend the auction. The fewer the bidders, the lower the price, maybe? Not that they can't all afford to pay . . . But Abu Nidal certainly isn't going to let Ahmed Jebril get it, if he can stop him." He sighed. "Whatever it is . . ."

Audley let out his own breath slowly. It was probable that Jake knew more than he was telling. But he didn't know about Peter Richardson yet.

"Okay, Jake." If he risked more, then he might betray how little he'd known. Because Jake was smart. "Tell me about this fellow Lukianov."

II

"Good morning, Mrs Harlin." Audley could always gauge how far he was into the doghouse from the expression on the face of Jack's PA. And one glance this morning was enough. "Any messages for me?"

"Good morning, Dr Audley." All the years of their acquaintance made not the slightest difference: with Mrs Harlin it was Jack Butler *contra mundum* now, just as she had once given her whole loyalty to Fred Clinton before him. "There are no messages for you. But Sir Jack is waiting for you in the conference room."

"In the conference room?" It was still her loyalty to Jack which allowed her to warn him that they already had visitors. And she had no need to elaborate on her encoded message: a conference before 10 o'clock in the morning always meant trouble. "Thank you, Mrs Harlin. Would you tell him I'm here, then?"

"I have already told him of your arrival, Dr Audley." The arrow on her disapproval-dial moved up into the red as he failed to move. "He is w ——" Her features relaxed suddenly "—— ah, Sir Jack! Dr Audley ——"

"Yes." Butler's voice came from behind him.

"Hullo, Jack." Audley glanced over his shoulder, but then returned to Mrs Harlin. "Just one thing, Mrs Harlin. Would you phone my wife and tell her that I've had a talk with Matthew Fattorini, and that he's going to fix up a trip to America for Cathy." He shook his head at her. "She'll understand . . . We've got this problem of Cathy wanting to swan off to India for a year, to do her Christian duty. But she's still much too young for India." He gave Butler half a shrug. "And if this doesn't work I shall call on you, Jack. She's your god-daughter after all."

Butler considered him dispassionately for a moment, as though weighing his anger with this flimsy alibi against other more pressing matters. Then he looked down at his PA. "And while you're about it, Mrs Harlin, you may reassure Mrs Audley that her husband has found time to attend to his duties. So she is not to worry about him."

"Oh — ?" Audley decided then to cut his losses also, for the same reason. "We have company, I gather?"

Butler pointed towards the passage.

"Who —" He found himself addressing Butler's back "— who have we got, Jack?"

"Henry Jaggard." Butler stopped suddenly, indicating the door to a side-office. "In there, David."

The office was empty. "Who else, Jack?"

"Your friend Renshaw, from the Cabinet Office. Leonard Aston. Commander Pitt." Butler stared at him. "And a woman named Franklin. You know her?"

"I've heard tell of her." Jaggard evidently meant business. "Isn't she Henry's new secret weapon?" He cocked his head at Butler. "Is she targeted on us this morning — not the enemy?"

Another hard stare. "Is there anything I should know before we go in, David?"

Not yet there wasn't. "Have they seen Mitchell's report, on the Italian debacle?"

"Of course."

Of course — yes! Because Kulik had been Henry Jaggard's business, and they had just been 'helping out' — eh? "Uh-huh? So now I'm getting the blame for losing Peter Richardson — is that it?"

"You didn't lose him. He didn't turn up." Butler's jaw set firm. "And with the Russians there too, as well as those Arabs, that was just as well."

Good old Jack! "He's still loose, is he? Old Peter —?" That was the real worry. "The Italians were locking all the gates when I left."

Butler drew a breath. "They think he's off their patch now."

Audley relaxed. Richardson under Italian lock-and-key might

114

have made things easier. But Richardson still free strengthened his own position right now. "Why do you think that?"

"Someone answering his description chartered a plane at Rome late yesterday afternoon, just before they closed things up. An American businessman, with a good American passport. Name of Dalingridge." Butler frowned slightly at him. "The Americans don't know anyone of that name . . . Do you?"

The name had caught him so much by surprise that he'd let his face show it. "Where was he heading?"

"You know the name?"

It was too late to deny it. But, also, it was altogether too good to be true . . . unless Richardson had intended it to be exactly that. "I might — yes."

"From where?" Butler was past doubting that Mr Dalingridge was Major Richardson. So now it was far too late to deny it.

"Christian name . . . 'Richard', by any chance?" And it was fair enough, anyway: old Jack had given his orders and had taken all the responsibility for what he'd done (and not done), with no recriminations. So he deserved a bit of good news. "'Richard Dalingridge', Jack?"

Butler nodded. "That's a name he would have used, is it?" Then he nodded the question away as superfluous. "And he'd expect you to know that, would he?"

Old Jack was smart, and quick with it, as well as loyal, the new question reminded Audley. But that, of course, was why he deserved to be where he was, as well as accounting for it. "He would — yes. Where did he go?"

"Mmm . . ." Butler was doing his arithmetic. "He went to Lyons. And that's all we've got so far."

It was enough, anyway. By high-speed train 'Mr Richard Dalingridge' could have been soon enough in Paris. And then it would have been time for another passport, from his professional smuggler's stock, prudently acquired for such a rainy day. And what would that name be? 'Hugh Saxon', maybe . . . because 'Hugh Dallingford' would sound a bit too much like 'Dalingridge' —? Or . . . maybe

115

he'd reckon that one signal from Italy, where it would be sure to be picked up, would be enough.

He grinned at Butler. Once the shock of that retirement criminality was assimilated, it came as no surprise that Peter hadn't forgotten any of his lessons — or anything else from the old days. *Yes . . . Peter, of all people, by God!*

But his grin wasn't being returned. "Is there something I should know now, David?" Butler glanced towards the door. "I can't keep them waiting much longer."

Audley disciplined his face. There really wasn't any reason to keep grinning, anyway. Not in view of all he still *didn't* know . . . which, apart from Peter's most likely intention . . . included almost everything else that mattered. "Not really." He hardened his heart against Butler in his own interest. "We've still got the inside track on Richardson . . . But then there's this terrorist business." He looked at his feudal lord accusingly. "You didn't exactly come clean about that yesterday." But he mustn't know too much about that. And, anyway, it was more than likely that it had been Henry Jaggard who hadn't come clean with Butler. "Or didn't you know that, Jack?" Better to let old Jack off the hook altogether. So he shrugged. "The Italians seemed to think there was a connection. Even after Comrade Zimin appeared on the scene. But they weren't very forthcoming after that. They just wanted to get shot of me as quickly as possible after they'd decided that I wasn't going to be helpful." He cocked his head at Butler. "There is a connection, I take it?"

Butler's lips tightened. "I think you'd better hear what Jaggard has to say. Then we can decide what to do."

So that was the way the land lay. This was Jaggard's business, not theirs — they had merely been 'helping out'. And, whoever was to blame (or, as the case might be, whoever finally carried the can, justly or not) for Berlin and Capri, Butler wasn't going to be caught twice.

But that wouldn't do at all — not now! "I don't see that we have any choice in the matter, Jack." He took a step towards the door.

"Choice?" Butler didn't move. "It isn't your job to run Henry Jaggard's errands. And it isn't my job to waste your time."

In another moment Butler would be telling him he was also 'a bit long in the tooth'. But it wouldn't do to get angry: if there was one thing he'd learnt during his long years with Fred Clinton it was that a good salesman tailored his sales pitch to the customer. "No, of course. But . . . I'm the only person with whom Peter Richardson is likely to make contact." He gave Butler a sly look. "'Mr Dalingridge' — remember?"

"You're also a three-time loser." Butler held his ground. "You can be de-briefed this morning. And back in Washington this evening."

He had to try another line. "Richardson was our man, Jack — "

"He was Sir Frederick Clinton's man." Butler cut him off brutally. "And only briefly. And then he resigned."

He could try 'the National Interest'. But, coming from him, that would be no more convincing than ancient departmental loyalty. So all that was left was for him to act in character. "I'm too far in to want to stop now, Jack. And, if anyone wants me dead, I'll be damned if I stop — I'll be damned if I'll leave what concerns me to Henry Jaggard. Apart from all of which . . . he'll fuck it up for sure."

Butler winced at the obscenity, as he always did at Audley's deliberate lapses, in spite of all his army years. But then he drew a deep resigned breath. "Very well. We'll wait and see."

The woman Franklin would be the one to watch. So he mustn't look at her first —

"Ah, David!" Even on Sir Jack Butler's own ground, and in his own conference room, Henry Jaggard had to assert himself as though it all belonged to him. "Good of you to join us."

"Henry." Audley ignored him, nodding first and second to Len Aston and Billy Pitt, then grinning at the Honourable Charles Renshaw. "Hullo, Charlie. Sorry to get you out of bed so early." Now the woman. "Miss Franklin, I presume —?" Well, well! She was damn-well worth looking at, never mind watching! "Sorry I'm late, Henry. But . . . I gather you all know what's happened. And if you must give us the tricky jobs that your chaps aren't up to, then what can you expect?"

"That's unjust. The man Kulik asked for you, David." Jaggard rolled easily with the punch.

"But, fortunately, he didn't get me."

"You can say that again!" Charlie Renshaw made a face. "You go along with the received wisdom, do you, David — that they were gunning for you?"

"It certainly looks that way now, yes."

"You were lucky." Jaggard nodded.

"Not lucky. Jack just made the right decision, that's all. As usual."

"And that was lucky." Jaggard stuck to his guns. "I would have sent you — to Berlin, anyway."

"And I would have gone. I've always liked Berlin." Audley nodded back. "Maybe you're right at that — I'm lucky to have Jack to save me from myself. And from you, Henry."

"On the other hand, you might not have conducted matters there quite as insouciantly as did Miss Loftus." Jaggard pursed his lips. "In which case we might not be in our present quandary." He stared around before returning to Audley. "Because Sir Jack has informed us that Kulik's confidence in you was misplaced — that you don't know what is going on?"

"I don't know what it is I'm supposed to know — not yet . . . that's true." Audley looked at each of them in turn, with the exception of Butler. "I know a lot of things, about a lot of people —"

"Including Major Richardson?" Miss Franklin interrupted him more gently than he deserved, he thought. "We were hoping he would narrow the field for us, Dr Audley."

She had a pleasant voice, the thought expanded: received Queen's/BBC/Oxbridge accent, but with the merest hint of Welsh somewhere in its background.

"Well . . . yes, he does . . . or he *may*, Miss Franklin." He must stop thinking how pretty she was, and remember only that she was reputed to be formidably intelligent. "Although I'm afraid I didn't know him as well as everyone assumes, Kulik included. He was one of Sir Frederick Clinton's Queen's-shilling men . . . And old Fred always played his cards close to his chest." He smiled at her. "But Peter Richardson didn't turn out to be quite the trump he expected. However, given more time, I shall do better —" He completed the smile, and then erased it before catching Commander Pitt's eye "— although I could do the best of all if you could produce him, Commander."

"Oh aye?" Pitt seemed ready for him. "You think he's coming here, do you?"

"You think he's still alive?" Jaggard offered the alternative quickly.

"I think . . . I think that if Fred Clinton fancied him, then he's a downy bird, Henry. So . . . yes, I think he's still alive." He nodded at Jaggard. "He certainly wasn't on the Capri casualty list, anyway. And it looks as though he's heading for home now."

"But his home is in Italy, Dr Audley." Miss Franklin was just as quick. "Isn't he half-Italian? And more than half-Italian in some respects?"

That was true. But it hadn't been in the file. So Miss Franklin had done her homework. "Yes. But his Italian home may not be too homely for him at the moment." Now he included them all. "It isn't just that all the various parties who are involved in this are after him now — not just the Italians and the Arabs and the Mafia, but also Colonel Zimin . . . It's that they knew where to look for him — both Zimin and the Arabs. Which means that his own organization has gone sour on him. So, as there's no one he can trust out there now, his best bet is to cut-and-run back." He decided to reward Miss Franklin for doing her homework properly. "That's what I'd do in his place, Miss Franklin. Because he'll have friends here still. And even some family, if I remember correctly." Then he looked at Commander Pitt again. "You're watching out for him, are you, Billy?"

Pitt grimaced. "Yes — well, Dr Audley . . . we're doing our best. And, because we happen to have a SURE-exercise in place, our best isn't too bad." But then one honesty collided with another. "Only, if he used to work for Sir Frederick Clinton, then he'll know the ropes. So our best may still not be quite good enough, if he keeps his head."

"But that doesn't matter." Charlie Renshaw stirred again. "Because once he's here he'll be a darn-sight safer. And we stand a darn-sight better chance of picking him up too, I should hope — once he's here, Commander?" Having delivered a Cabinet Office-eye-view of What Ought to Happen, Charlie dropped the unfortunate Commander in favour of Audley. "You'll be advising how we should go about that, I take it, David?"

"Uh-huh." Audley temporized. "I think my best advice is to let him come to us — whether he's here or not, Charlie."

Charlie brightened. "You think he will?"

"After Capri, I think he *must* — sooner or later." It was always a pleasure to do business with the Honourable Charles Renshaw. "If I'm even halfways right about what happened on Capri, then he'll be in even more of a — ah — a quandary than we are, I shouldn't wonder —"

"Scared shitless, you mean?" Charlie swung quickly towards Miss Franklin. "I *do* beg your pardon, Miss Franklin — scared witless, I meant to say."

"Please don't worry, Mr Renshaw. 'Scared shitless' would seem to be an accurate description of everyone's condition at this moment — even Mr Aston's friends in the Russian Embassy, apparently —" She drew the FCO man into the conversation "— you were just saying, Leonard — ?"

Leonard Aston gave a dry little cough, and then touched his lips with a very white handkerchief. "There is a certain nervousness, it seems. And there have been comings and goings."

"More comings than goings." Charlie Renshaw nodded towards Audley. "They're exchanging old Brunovski for a hard-faced character named Voyshinski — Boris Voyshinski. Do you know of him, David? Wasn't he on that list of yours?"

"Uh-huh." No intelligence report ever passed Charlie unread. "One of the new promotions. Upped from colonel to general in the KGB in the spring."

120

"With a St Mikhail label on his underpants?" Renshaw glanced at Jaggard. "Told you so, Henry. That makes us the operational centre, eh?"

"And it also rather confirms what Dr Audley has just said about Major Richardson," Miss Franklin added her nod to Renshaw's, but then turned to Audley. "And . . . since you are the expert on the New Order, Dr Audley . . . isn't your old friend Colonel Zimin an associate of General Voyshinski? Or an old army comrade, anyway?"

"Yes, Miss Franklin." She knew her stuff, quite evidently. But, more immediately, the appearance of Boris Voyshinski in London raised the stakes of whatever game the Russians were playing enormously — almost outrageously. "Will someone kindly tell me what is happening?"

"We were rather hoping you were going to enlighten us there, David." Henry Jaggard leaned forward slightly to emphasize the order beneath this superficially polite request. "We have learnt the bare details of what appears to have occurred on Capri. But we have not yet had an account of your — ah — your conversation with Colonel Zimin."

Audley met Charlie Renshaw's eyes. "Are you going to tell me, Charlie?"

"No." But then Renshaw grinned. "You tell him, Billy."

That put the unfortunate Commander Pitt midway between the Cabinet Office and its Intelligence Service, and in something of a quandary as to which of those two awkward masters to obey.

"Oh, for Christ's sake!" Renshaw produced one of his controlled explosions of irritation. "It's exactly as Jack Butler's just been telling us: we drag David back from Washington when we don't know what's happening — and now, but for the grace of God, we might have been bringing him back from Berlin in a coffin, too . . . and then we throw him in the deep end in Italy, on the assumption that he'll pull our chestnuts out of the fire — eh?" he looked around the table.

Charlie had always been a great one for mixed metaphors, thought Audley. And they usually came in threes.

"But for once he hasn't — okay?" Renshaw fixed his eye on Jaggard. "And now he objects to playing pig-in-the-middle, with himself always cast as the pig. And I don't blame him." He dropped Jaggard for Commander Pitt. "Tell him, Billy. And then we'll see what he can make of it. Which I bloody well hope is more than I can. *Okay?*"

"Of course —" Jaggard moved smoothly into the fractional instant of silence before Commander Pitt caved in "— you're quite right, Charles. And I had taken Sir Jack's point —" The smoothness oozed over Butler and Audley as well "— when he defended your actions in Italy . . . not to say your courage, in going in like that by yourself, after what happened in Berlin. You were, after all, only obeying orders — I do agree!"

Nobody was better at putting the boot in than Jaggard. And now he had very skilfully left everyone with the impression that either Butler had given a defective order, which had then been incompetently obeyed, or (which they were more likely to be thinking) he had unwisely left the decision to Audley himself, who had then cocked things up. And there was just enough truth in each of those alternatives to render any explanations self-defeating.

"Yes — well, it never pays to keep people in ignorance, Henry." Hugging Jake Shapiro's information to himself helped him to smile pleasantly. "But ignorance is no excuse, you're also quite right . . . So, Billy, everywhere I go, there seem to be soldiers . . . as well, presumably, as your well-armed heavies. And now I gather from the media that you are co-operating with our gallant Russian allies in some sort of anti-terrorist operations? Which I nevertheless assume is not quite the case, eh?"

"No, Dr Audley, it isn't." Commander Pitt seemed almost relieved to be able to speak at last. "We had an exercise planned — a short-notice SURE. But it wasn't actually scheduled until next month. But then the Americans tipped us off that something was up."

Renshaw nodded. "And they got it from the Israelis, David. And then the plot really thickened — sorry, Billy!"

"Yes, sir." Pitt had decided that, if it came to the crunch, it was Charlie who had the edge. "First, it was the usual form: certain individuals we've been watching — or, other people have been watching, anyway . . . dropping out of circulation."

"Arabs?" Up to now the Arabs had been doing the dirty work. "Or who else?"

Billy Pitt looked at Jaggard, and Jaggard nodded to Miss Franklin. "Mary —?"

"There's been a close-down in Eastern Europe, Dr Audley." In turn, Miss Franklin also seemed relieved, to her credit. "And in the Soviet Union."

"When, Miss Franklin? In relation to Kulik's arrival in Berlin, I mean."

"The same day. But perhaps a few hours afterwards." She took the point. "But Commander Pitt's information preceded our information by a full twenty-four hours."

"I see." At least events had been occurring in the right sequence, both to allow Kulik to get out and (though for reasons unknown) the Arabs to be ready for the Berlin ambush. "And this was all to catch Kulik?"

"No." Mary Franklin shifted to Jaggard doubtfully "— Henry?"

All the while, Audley had been aware of Henry Jaggard more than anyone else, even though Mary Franklin was infinitely easier on the eye.

Jaggard drew a deep breath, to match his final decision. (Which was, thought Audley cynically, that with General Voyshinski here, and Colonel Zimin *somewhere*, he needed Major Richardson more than ever. So, however unhappily, he also still needed Lieutenant (demobbed/retired) Audley.) "It seems that there were three of them, David: Kulik, Prusakov and Lukianov." Having committed himself, he watched Audley like a hawk. "Kulik, I gather, you don't know. But what about the other two?"

Getting so much so quickly posed a pretty problem, in view of both Jake's information and his loss of face on Capri. So perhaps it would be advisable to compromise. "Prusakov . . . don't know."

123

Prusakov was a dead duck, anyway, according to Jake. "But Lukianov . . ." He frowned, but encouragingly. Names, after all, were supposed to be his stock-in-trade.

"Leonid S. Lukianov," Charlie regarded him hopefully. "Come on, David!"

He mustn't disappoint Charlie, who had supported him in his hour-of-need. "Soldier. Originally soldier, anyway — *Spetsnaz*, too. Maybe GRU once, but then KGB. Colonel . . . but maybe General Lukianov now. Served in Afghanistan . . . And — " He frowned at Jaggard " — wasn't he a friend of Brezhnev's son-in-law? The one they've just sent down the river, Henry?"

But Jaggard was frowning at Jack Butler.

"That's very good, Dr Audley," said Mary Franklin, with a hint of misplaced admiration. "Especially as he isn't in our records — or yours."

Ouch! "Isn't he?" That would teach him to underrate her! "Well . . . no, I suppose he wouldn't be, at that." He looked into the space above her head for a moment, playing for time. "Or . . ." *Lukianov had to be in the records, somewhere!* ". . . or, are you sure?" Neville Macready came to his rescue: dear old Neville was safely dead. "It was Neville Macready who mentioned him to me, a couple of years back." All he had to do was to imagine how Lukianov's career might have gone downhill since then. "I think he'd just been posted out of Moscow to Kabul, or something like that." He shrugged at her. "But I'm only interested in the coming men, not the ones who backed the wrong horse, Miss Franklin." That would do for the time being. So he could return to Jaggard. "Where did you get these names, Henry?" (And at least Charlie looked satisfied.)

Henry Jaggard slid a picture across the table for an answer. "Have a look."

"Is this him?" It was irritating that he'd missed Lukianov somehow. "Good-looking chap. But I still don't know him."

Another picture came across the table.

"Prusakov?" Less irritating. But still irritating. "Ugly bugger."

He shook his head. "Don't know him either." But now curiosity was in order. "Where did you get these pictures?"

"Huh!" exclaimed Charlie. "Where indeed! They've been hawked right across Europe, my dear chap — like 'Most Wanted' posters, if not pop star pin-ups." He twisted a ghost of his usual cheerful grin at Audley. "The Kulik one has now been withdrawn: he's no longer in the Top Ten . . . or Top Three, in this instance."

So the Russians had been so shit-scared of these three defectors that they'd flooded the market, regardless of consequences, only interested in quick results. Just as, in another age and with the aid of better technology, the British would have transmitted mug-shots of Burgess and Maclean, among others, once upon a time.

"So what else is known about them —?" He addressed Mary Franklin in order to stop her thinking more about his remarkable special knowledge of General Lukianov. "Kulik was a military intelligence computer-man, I gather." He made a face at her. "According to Sir Jack, anyway."

"He was only a technician, Dr Audley." She accepted that, anyway. "He was perhaps a whizz-kid, technically . . . we're not sure, though."

"And Prusakov?" It was Lukianov, the action-man — *Lucky* Lukianov — who really mattered now. But he must be interested in Prusakov first. "What was he?"

"He was also in computers. But he was much higher up, and into politics too." But she seemed to be accepting this, also. "Only . . . he wasn't one of your 'coming men' either, Dr Audley." She didn't smile. "He was a 'going man'."

"And now he's gone," murmured Charlie.

And gone in more ways than one, too. But Mary Franklin was watching him, and he had to keep Jake Shapiro under wraps for the time being still. So he pushed the photos back towards Jaggard and looked at Billy Pitt. "And you haven't had a sight of him?"

"We're on the look-out for him, as well as Major Richardson. And Lukianov, of course." Pitt nodded.

"And so is everyone else." Renshaw also nodded. "According to

Henry these pictures have been scattered around like confetti by every KGB station in Europe. So they'll know we've got them by now, David."

"Yes." Mary Franklin claimed his attention. "What I was wondering, Dr Audley, was whether you'd had sight of either Prusakov or Lukianov in Italy. But obviously not."

"Why should they be in Italy, Miss Franklin?" inquired Renshaw. "Do you mean . . . one of them was going to be bait for Richardson, the way Kulik was the bait for David here?"

"Something like that, Mr Renshaw." She still watched Audley. "What do you think, Dr Audley?"

"I think . . . I'd like to know more about General Lukianov, Miss Franklin." He was tempted to smile at her, but decided against it. "Then I'll tell you what I think. For what it's worth."

"Very well." She accepted his serious face at face-value. "But I'm afraid we don't know much more than you do. He was a *Spetsnaz* specialist, as you know. And the Americans say he was a European expert originally — they think he made a special study of our own Special Forces, too. But then he may have transferred to the GRU or the KGB, they're not sure. But after that he did a tour in the Middle East, they believe, in the late 1970s."

That would be the Israelis feeding the Americans most likely. "So he could have had contacts with the terrorist groups? As a trainer, maybe?"

"It's possible." She was properly cautious of guesses tacked on to nebulous second-hand information. "Then he was posted to Afghanistan. And he was with *Spetsnaz* there — that's certain, Dr Audley."

Audley nodded. It was certain because the Americans had worked hard on analysing the Soviet Army's personnel, as well as its performance, in its first hot war since '45. But there was something more, he could see. "Yes, Miss Franklin —?"

"There's a story about him." She paused for a moment. "He went on a raid into the mountains with one of his units — a unit he'd once served with. They were dropped by helicopter, to block a

126

Mujahadeen escape route. But then the weather closed in, and the main attack was delayed. So they had to hold out for a week, instead of three days. There were only three survivors, all of them wounded. And two of them died afterwards. The youngest one died in his arms, apparently."

'Lucky' Lukianov, indeed! But also a real front-line general, thought Audley.

"*Beau Geste* stuff!" Charlie Renshaw frowned at Jaggard suddenly. "And this Lukianov is now a defector, you say, Henry? He doesn't damn-well sound like one — if that isn't just a propaganda story, anyway." He took the frown to Audley. "Eh, David?"

Leonard Aston emitted one of his dry little coughs. "Defeat, Charles, does strange things to heroes. Especially humiliating defeat."

Audley saw Charlie's eyebrows lift, and realized that his own had also gone up. Coming from little Len, who was as dry as his cough, such an insight was surprising.

"I have had no first-hand experience, of course." Aston touched his lips with his ever-ready handkerchief, aware of their astonishment but quite unembarrassed by it. "I am not a military man, and never could be. But . . . I was in our embassy in Washington during the last days of Vietnam, and for two years afterwards." He gazed from Renshaw to Audley and back like a tutor with two rather thick undergraduates. "And during that period I observed some very strange behaviour among some senior officers, as well as a predictable disorientation among those beneath them." Aston's voice became more pedantic as he spoke. "It was no surprise. For a long time they believed they were invincible . . . in the knowledge that they had never been defeated, or in any real danger of final defeat . . . at least, not since 1814. But then, long before the final debacle, the senior officers knew better — knew better that it was a matter of political will, anyway. So then they knew that defeat was inevitable, and all their men had died for nothing." He nodded at them. "It was more a long corrosion of the spirit. And it happened among some of the very best and bravest of them, who had fought hardest. One or two behaved quite irrationally, even though their actual careers were still assured." Now he dropped them both, turning to Henry Jaggard. "And, in General Lukianov's case, I believe you indicated that his career-future is *not* assured, Henry?" Finally he embraced them all. "We need to know a great deal more about him, I would think. Because while he may not have been the moving spirit behind whatever plot the three of them have hatched, he will be the action-man." He even managed a thin smile for Mary Franklin. "I do not know what the motto of the Russian *Spetsnaz* force is. But for our own SAS it is 'Who dares, wins', I believe? And I would guess that General Lukianov is daring now. So it is up to us to see that he does not also win." He settled on Audley himself. "Is it possible that, while he was working for you . . . or, rather, for the late Sir Frederick Clinton . . . your Major Richardson may have encountered this man Lukianov?"

Butler cleared his throat. "We have been through everything in the record, Mr Aston — several times. And there's nothing to indicate any connection between Richardson and any living Russian, or even any foreign or suspect contact, who isn't fully accounted for."

"Apart from which, he wasn't with us very long." Audley came in without hesitation. Because, when Jack Butler did a job, then it would be well done. "And he was only a beginner."

"All of which doesn't mean a thing nevertheless," snapped Butler. "It's the man himself we need. Nothing else will do."

"But the man himself is missing," Renshaw looked at Audley. "And you think he's coming home, David?"

He had to put his mouth where his money was. "After Capri — yes, Charlie."

"Interpret Capri for us, Dr Audley." Aston was also looking at him. They were all looking at him. "We know only the bare details, remember." The handkerchief came up again. "Or, perhaps you may prefer to start in Berlin?"

"He wasn't there," Jaggard put the boot in again neatly, like a Welsh forward in a loose scrum on his own line. "More's the pity."

"Fortunately, rather." Aston was hiding that thin smile behind his handkerchief. "But Berlin will have concentrated his mind, I would think."

It was Leonard Aston who was concentrating his mind right now. With a little help from Colonel Zimin and General Voyshinski, among the others (*four others: two down, but two missing — and the important two, by God!*).

"Thank you for reminding me, Len." He had made a balls-up of Capri. And he had underrated Mr Leonard Aston. So he had to get it right now. "There are four sides to this triangle — right, Len?"

Leonard Aston thought about his opening gambit. "Creative geometry, would that be?"

"Us and the Russians." Was it possible that Mr Aston was being measured for Mr Jaggard's job? "We both want Lukianov — and Prusakov . . . or, failing them, Peter Richardson. Because he knows what Lukianov is up to — " He had to be quick now " — or, if what he knows is added to what I am supposed to know . . . and what the Russians already know . . . that's the jackpot."

Charlie Renshaw grunted doubtfully. "Are you saying the Russians don't know what he's up to, David? Lukianov, I mean — ?"

He could probably shrug to that. "Zimin said he wanted Peter alive. And I don't think that was just window-dressing, Charlie."

"Yes." Aston nodded. "With Gorbachev down to address the United Nations, and then to visit the Prime Minister . . . they don't want any scandals they can't handle, Mr Renshaw." The handkerchief came up again. "Remember Khrushchev and the Schwirkmann affair? If they start killing people, or trying to kill them . . . then *she* will have to react to that, just as Chancellor Erhard had to — remember?" He sniffed. "It's a finely-balanced thing, I agree. And . . . I don't doubt you know better than I do. But, if there's any sort of scandal, she'll be able to get much better terms on conventional arms, at the very least. And Gorbachev can't afford that yet — can he?"

"It's all bull-shit — " Charlie started to shrug high politics off. But then pretended to be embarrassed " — I do beg your pardon, Miss Franklin — again! But . . . do go on, David: they want Major

Richardson alive . . . because he will know what Lukianov and Co. are — are trading on the open market?" Then he produced a typically silly-idiot Charlie Renshaw grin to muddy the waters. "Well . . . that's privatization for you: Lukianov *plc* are the third side — is that what you're saying, David? And they're offering shares to International Terrorism *plc* — in this case on the Arab splinter-groups? Not the Mafia, anyway — ?"

The Honourable Charles Renshaw had assimilated those 'bare details' — and had quickly eliminated the accident of Peter Richardson's private life from them, quite rightly: the Mafia was prepared to tangle with anyone in the West, any time. But it wasn't prepared or willing to fight a war on two fronts when there was no profit in the East, as well as no comforting democratic legal process.

"The Mafia is irrelevant, Charlie." Actually, the Mafia had been very useful, in frightening Peter into hiding, quite coincidentally. "There's just Lukianov and his clients, for the other two sides."

"So why did Kulik have to die?" Mary Franklin hit the Berlin problem on the nail. "Are you suggesting that he was double-crossed? That he was just bait for you, D—— Dr Audley?"

She'd almost said 'David'! "I don't know, Miss Franklin — Mary?" He wasn't ashamed with himself for being pleased at attempting her Christian name. "But Zimin didn't deny that Peter Richardson had been betrayed, before he had those two Arabs killed." He blanked out the memory of Zimin's cold-hearted order before it could frighten him too much, with its implication of his own escape, which had been too narrow for easy recollection. "Only he wasn't expecting two of them: he was expecting just one, like in Berlin, not two. And that was why he lost one of his men, when things went wrong." All the same, that might have saved the 'celebrated' Dr Audley. "At least, that's the way it looked — the way the Italians thought it was." He shook his head honestly. "And . . . he said 'Arab', in the singular — I know that." This time he shook his head, just as honestly. "I'm still guessing — or, as Len would put it more diplomatically, 'interpreting' . . . But I think Peter Richardson agreed to see me because things were getting too hot for him, with the Italian authorities and the Mafia both on his tail. And, if the Italians had brought me into the business, he maybe thought he could make a deal with them, through me." He shrugged. "It could even be that Lukianov's Arab friends had also come looking for him. But he might well have mistaken them for Mafia-types, on contract — I don't know . . . Only, whatever he thought, the rendezvous was blown, both to the Arabs and — fortunately for me — to the Russians, too. It's even possible the Mafia helped out with that, with one or other of them."

"The Mafia has links with Abu Nidal," Mary Franklin nodded. "The KGB isn't so keen on either of them these days, though."

"But this was top-priority —" Charlie Renshaw stopped himself. "Go on, David."

"The rest is factual. Zimin wanted Peter alive, to squeeze him. Lukianov's Arabs wanted him dead, to make sure he couldn't be squeezed. And Zimin wasn't going to risk that happening. My arrival put him off his stroke, but as soon as he knew I was by myself he went ahead, and gave the order. But, of course, it wasn't neatly done, because of the second Arab, as I've said." He gave Renshaw a rueful nod. "I am guessing. But the undeniable fact is, Charlie, that everything went wrong for everyone — both in Berlin and Capri. And, in my experience, that's what usually happens when there are too many cooks mixing the broth."

"Mmm . . ." That was Charlie Renshaw's experience too, obviously. "I take it that Zimin has also disappeared from the scene now, like Major Richardson, Henry?"

Jaggard nodded. "The Italians are almost certain that Richardson was the pseudo-American — 'Dalingridge', Charles. So that puts him in France."

"En route here." Renshaw stroked his chin. "But otherwise we're none the wiser as to what Lukianov is offering the Arabs. Except, if Len is right about General Voyshinski's unexpected arrival, here is also where Lukianov intends to transact his business."

Jaggard sat back. "Neutral ground, maybe? Apart from which, if David has interpreted Zimin's words and actions correctly, the

131

Russians themselves don't know what's on offer. So they are in the dark also. But if David is right about Richardson coming home, then we may have the edge on them yet. Because, even if he doesn't contact us . . . or, as the case may be, David himself . . . we should be able to rely on Commander Pitt picking him up in due course. And then we'll know what it is that David has forgotten."

That was neat. Put like that, all they had to do was to wait, and if things went wrong either he or Billy Pitt could take the responsibility, for guessing wrong or incompetence respectively.

"No." Butler grunted explosively.

"Jack — ?" Renshaw looked at Butler expectantly.

"'Due course' won't do." Butler nodded to Billy Pitt. "No disrespect to you or your men — or your organization — Commander. But Major Richardson is a trained man." And that was all Commander Pitt was getting. "The Russians are treating this as an urgent matter —"

"The Russians —" began Jaggard.

"But it is not the Russians who particularly concern me first, Mr Renshaw." Butler ignored Henry Jaggard. "It is the man Lukianov and the Arabs. Because, if they frighten the Russians so much, then by God they also frighten me. And I have no reason to believe that I'm not the only one they are frightening."

"What — ?" Renshaw frowned at Jaggard. "Henry — ?"

"Colonel Jacob Shapiro is in London." Butler got in first. "Right, Mr Jaggard?"

The wily old bugger! thought Audley admiringly. "Jake Shapiro — ?"

"Who is —" Renshaw was torn between the three of them "— Colonel . . . Jake Shapiro?" He settled on Audley. "David?"

"Ex-Mossad." Audley wondered how much Butler had guessed. But meanwhile he allowed himself a grin for Charlie Renshaw. "An old mate of mine, from prehistoric times, Charlie. But . . . back in London?" He looked innocently to Jaggard. "He was always a good friend of ours, Henry. When we gave him the chance to be, anyway."

"Yes." Jaggard had to swallow that. "He is supposed to be on holiday, Charles. We know about him."

"Holiday my foot!" Audley shook his head. "He's someone we can do business with, Charlie. And, when it comes to Arab terrorism, the Israelis have forgotten more than we're ever likely to know. So . . . if Jack's right, they could be waving old Jake like an olive branch, hoping that we'll accept him."

"I see." Renshaw shifted to Butler. "Would you be prepared to release David for a few more days, to open negotiations with his 'old mate', Sir Jack? Assisting Henry of course —" He acknowledged Jaggard a little belatedly "— Henry?"

"If Dr Audley is agreeable." Again Butler got in first. When he wanted to be first, he usually was. "I think we should regard the matter as urgent."

"Hold on, there!" In this transformed situation Audley had to think quickly.

"You don't want to —?" Renshaw frowned "— what, David?"

"I'd like fine to meet Jake again, in — ah — in due course. But I'm not an expert on terrorism, Charlie."

"What are you driving at?" Renshaw was surprised. In fact, they were all surprised. And, additionally, Henry Jaggard was also consumed with suspicion.

"I think Peter Richardson is still my priority." He could make contact with Jake any time. But he didn't want Jaggard breathing down his neck when he did. "I want to have a look at the old files first. And then later today I think I'll saunter through some of Peter's old haunts in the country, just in case." He gave Charlie his most serious face. "It would be much better if Henry here and Commander Pitt asked for a meeting with Jake, at top level. To get whatever he's got on Comrades Lukianov and Prusakov, and their Arab associates. And on Russian intentions in general too. And, meanwhile, if I can come up with anything, I'll let them know, of course."

"That sounds eminently sensible." Len Aston spoke out of nowhere, having effaced himself since his own surprising contribution to the conference. "I would agree with Sir Jack that the matter is urgent. And also . . . I am not convinced that we are 'neutral ground'." He stared at Charlie Renshaw. "And, finally, I would prefer someone of Mr Jaggard's seniority to negotiate with the Israelis. Because our present relations with them are . . . shall we say . . . cool, if not unfriendly?"

Nobody trusted him, when the Israelis were involved, thought Audley — even after all these years. But for once that was to his advantage. Because Henry Jaggard was now even more suspicious. But there wasn't one damn thing he could do about it.

"Right." Renshaw sat up very straight. "Then I will inform my masters to that effect." But once more he settled on Audley. "What we want is *no trouble*, David. That may prove impossible in the case of Lukianov and his Arabs, I grant you. But Henry and Commander Pitt will handle that. So, what I mean is, no trouble with the Russians, in view of the meeting scheduled between the PM and Gorbachev next month. Do you understand, David?"

"Yes, Charlie." But it wasn't easy to keep a straight face, all the same, now that Jack was off the hook, and Henry Jaggard was in the barrel. And he himself was . . . a lot more free than he'd expected, anyway. "That suits me."

III

As the car dropped down into the great motorway cutting through the Chilterns escarpment, and the panorama of the Oxfordshire plain below opened up in front of him, Audley debated with himself whether or not he ought to be frightened, and finally voted against it.

"Goodbye, Charlie." Where the others only rated nods, Charlie had deserved more, for his help. "Thanks for the support."

"Oh yes? And you'll wear it always?" Renshaw had given him an old-fashioned look (as, also, had the flawless Mary Franklin from the doorway). "Don't forget what I said, eh? No trouble, David?"

"No trouble, Charlie." He had lingered beside Mrs Harlin's desk. "Did you get through to my wife, Mrs Harlin?" He had seen Butler hovering outside his own door, watching him almost as suspiciously as Jaggard had done.

"Yes, Dr Audley. She said for me to thank you. And she will phone Sir Matthew herself now."

"That's fine." Now for the Headmaster's study, Audley. "Coming, Jack." He'd have to get his act together now, too! "Well . . . that's one worry off my mind . . . yes, Jack?"

"You knew Shapiro was here, didn't you?" Butler opened a file on his desk and extracted a print-out from it. "And you've already talked to him."

No matter how hard he tried not to underrate Jack Butler, he always failed. "I didn't know he was here. But I have talked to him — yes, Jack." But even this truth failed to set him free. "When it comes to Arabs, they always know more than we do. And . . . after losing Richardson I wanted to have something in the bag, just in case. And . . . well, they've never been unfriendly to me, have they?

Because of the old times." He still wasn't helping himself much. "How did you know?"

Butler looked up from the print-out. "What did he tell you?"

It must have been because he'd passed up the chance of meeting Jake with official blessing. "He thinks Prusakov is dead, like Kulik. Something seems to have happened in Rome. Either the Russians spotted him, and he bit on his happy pill. Or maybe his Arab minder made sure he wasn't taken prisoner — Jake wasn't too sure."

"How did the Russians get on to Richardson? Did he know that?"

"He didn't know about Richardson. I don't know, Jack. The Russians may not know what it is that Lukianov is offering the Arabs, but they must know more than we do, for God's sake. Because we know fuck-all, it seems to me."

'Fuck-all' closed Butler's face up again in momentary distaste, but then he came to terms with the truth of it. "What else?"

"Nothing else, much. We were just sounding each other out, really. He'll give Jaggard enough to keep him busy. And then I'll see him again, pretty soon." He wanted to get Butler off his back too, he realized. "But we'd better get our skates on, Jack. Because the Israelis are scared."

"Even though they don't know what Lukianov is up to?"

"They're scared because the Russians are scared — like us. And for the same reason, too: knowing . . . *not* knowing anything isn't to their taste, much." His best bet was to frighten Jack a bit too. "If what Lukianov is offering is worth enough for Abu Nidal or whoever to lend him manpower — *two* hit-squads, Jack — to slow us up . . . I don't know . . . but it could be that he's afraid his former masters may even be preparing to make a deal with us, to pool what they may know with whatever it is Richardson and I know, between us. And then we'd be able to pre-empt his game, maybe. So he had to try to take us out, and he was ready to sacrifice Kulik and Prusakov to do it . . . It's possible that he didn't take them into his confidence about that, is the way it rather looks . . . But, I really don't know, Jack. So that's why 'Mr Dalingridge' is my priority, anyway." And, of course, he had one card Butler couldn't trump. "And those are my orders now, in any case."

136

Butler looked at the clock on the wall over the door. "Mitchell will be back this afternoon. You can have him."

What Butler was doing was assessing the risk now. "I'll be leaving after lunch, Jack. He can catch me up — I'll phone in, don't worry!"

"Where are you going?"

"Oh . . . I think I'll take a drive in the Cotswolds —"

The vote was against danger, by an easy majority. Because, after Berlin and Capri (and with Colonel Zimin loose and on his track), Lukianov and his Arabs wouldn't know where he was. And by now they must have other more important fish to fry, anyway.

And he knew Peter Richardson better than they did. And better even than what was on file and record: the bald facts of that damnable computer memory on which they all depended, and which Henry Jaggard shared at the touch of a few beastly little keys. Henry had access to everything that was known to the computer as of right, with a Master Word probably possessed only by himself and God (or maybe not God), on which lesser breeds could only draw by arrangement and agreement, with every withdrawal recorded for posterity; so that now (for all the good it would do her!) the enchanting Mary Franklin was probably studying the same useless stuff he himself had dutifully skimmed through an hour ago — what a waste!

Where is he?

With the Chiltern Hills behind him and the featureless Oxford-shire plain sliding past all round he was able to think of Peter Richardson again, and the old times of fifteen years back, flexing his memory to double-check his reasoning —

Really, Peter wasn't the *old* times — the good old, bad old times of the Clinton heyday of the late fifties and swinging sixties, when the trick had been to try and hold things together when everything was coming apart at the seams, and the truth of Fred's two-hundred-year Rise and Fall of the British Empire thesis had been evident. No . . . Peter had been very much towards the end of that period,

137

anyway . . . when Fred had been beginning to lose his grip and flying more and more by the seat of his pants. In fact, in retrospect and with hindsight, Peter himself had been a sure sign of the Decline and Fall of Fred's own empire: a clever young barbarian *foederatus* who had grown up in those locust years and worshipped different gods from those of Fred, who had recruited him in a vain attempt to keep up with the times — was that it?

It was. But——

(Was there anything behind him? But then, if there was, it would be well behind, and quite out of his view; and anyway, having thought about it, he really didn't much care after all —)

It probably was right, that interpretation of Richardson's recruitment. But even if it wasn't . . . and though in the end Fred's seat-of-the-pants had turned out wrong, undeniably . . . the young man had still been quite something, in his way —

"Richardson, David — Peter Richardson. Hobson of King's put me on to him. You'll like him." *(That morning in Fred's office, it had been)* "Oh aye? Fresh from university, you mean?" *(In peacetime, as Sir Frederick was often wont to complain, recruitment was a sore trial.)*

"Yes and no. He's a soldier, actually."

"Another damn redcoat?" *(Not least of Fred's complaints was that even Solomon might have baulked at judging between the military misfits and the graduates still-wet-behind-the-ears who were offered him.)*

"Well, at least Major Butler will approve of him, then."

"I don't think he will. This is a new breed, David. They've let him take a degree, and now regimental duty is no longer to his taste. So they've let us have him on secondment for a year. With the usual mutual option after that. And, as I say, I think you'll like him. So will your wife."

"Oh aye?" *(That was when people behind his back had not yet given up referring to Faith as 'a much younger woman'.)* "What makes you think they'll ever meet?"

"I want you to have him to dinner — to one of your dinner-parties."

"Why should I do that? Other than because it's an order, I mean?"

"A little experiment. You should enjoy it —"

Had he enjoyed it, though?

The westering sun was trying to get through the clouds ahead, but not quite succeeding. He had spent longer among the records than he had intended, he realized. But it had been necessary to make sure that neither Butler nor Jaggard had missed anything, for his own peace of mind . . . even though, of course, they hadn't. So . . . whatever it was, whatever it had been, that he shared (or half-shared?) with Peter Richardson was *off* the record and unimportant (so it had seemed, anyway): some unconsidered trifle . . . like Fred's 'little experiment' of long ago —

Had he enjoyed it, though?

But that didn't really matter: what mattered was that he remembered it. And — for sure, among so many uncertainties — Peter Richardson had naturally remembered it too: *that* was one absolute certainty which Richardson himself had conveniently and deliberately established, taking the only chance he had with 'Mr Dalingridge', after he had spotted both Audley and the Russians (if not the Arabs too) from some observation point along that long hot path up to the Villa Jovis —

Faith had probably enjoyed it (that was a near-certainty, although an unimportant one): she had admired both Richardson's car (long and low and sporty, Jaguar or Triumph or whatever was in vogue then) and Richardson himself (dark and handsome, like some Roman military tribune in one of the more fashionable Legions, far from home but good with senior officers' wives automatically, especially when their husbands were somewhat older?) —

Memory expanded under pressure. (He had driven along this very road . . . or along the old A40 to Oxford and the West, which had preceded this motorway . . . except that he was off the motorway now, and back on the old A40 again, circling Oxford itself: but . . .

he had driven westwards with Peter Richardson himself that time, towards GCHQ at Cheltenham in its earlier days, anyway.

But that was the key in the lock. And he could feel it turning in his memory, between Fred's 'little experiment' and its unrecorded sequel. And the experiment and its sequel were so beautifully bridged now, after all these years, by 'Mr Dalingridge', that there could be no mistake: he could even remember Richardson himself directing him off the main road, up on the higher ground of the Cotswolds, into a maze of stone walls and sleeping villages untouched by time since the days of sheep which had built the tall churches and the manor house —

"Just a little detour, David. To meet a friend of mine for lunch . . . Someone only you know about, eh?"

It all came down to memory. And not to damned computer-memory, which was no better than common coinage in the pockets of anyone who had access to it, but to *private* memory, which he alone possessed now (although which Zimin had aspired to, in attempting to take Peter on Capri, by God! That was the memory which really counted now, by God — *by God!*) —

But Peter couldn't come first, now. (The digital clock on Jack Butler's 'Buy British' Rover advised him that, as well as the setting sun, which had given up its attempt to shine before dark: he had delayed too long among those records to attempt Peter first: he had to keep another rendezvous before that. And, because of Peter's importance rather than despite it, better so, perhaps?)

There was still nothing behind him, when he took the Burford turn-off. But then, if there had been (as before), it would have been well-back, and he wouldn't have been able to spot it. And it didn't matter now, anyway.

And, also, it was late enough in the day, as well as out of the high tourist-season (as on Capri!) for there to be no crowds and plenty of room to park, right outside the appointed place.

"Do you have a Mr Lee staying with you?"

The girl in reception had evidently been warned that Mr Lee was expecting a visitor. "Yes, sir. Number Three — just up the stairs there, and on your left."

He knocked on Number Three. But then had to wait, because Mr Lee had locked his door.

"Hullo, old friend." Jake locked the door again, leaving the key in the lock. "You're early — or are you late? Your message was rather vague." He wiped his moustache and grinned. "Would you like a beer?"

There was an unopened suitcase on the bed and a very much opened crate of beer on the floor beside it: it had had twelve bottles, but there were fewer now — and another one fewer as Jake himself removed it.

"This is good beer, too." Jake opened the bottle, then inverted a glass on top of it, and handed both to Audley. "We passed a local off-licence and they offered me a local brew. And it isn't half-bad, I tell you."

'We' added itself to the emptiness of the crate. "You're not by yourself then, Jake?"

"Lord, no!" Jake replenished his own glass. "I'm much too old to be let out on my own in these dangerous times." He glanced at Audley almost casually over the froth. "What about you?"

"Just me." He felt thirsty suddenly. "So far as I know."

Jake raised his glass in salute. "Not to worry." He drank deeply and appreciatively. "My *custodes* will let me know who are *custodieting* you, old friend." He smiled at Audley. "Your Mr Jaggard said you were working for him. And . . . I suspect he trusts you even less than I do."

So Jake had been well-briefed, then. Or had drawn the right conclusions, anyway. "You've met my Mr Jaggard, then?"

"I have indeed." Another drink. Then another smile. "A very cautious gentleman." The smile was a smile-of-many-colours. "And I have told him everything I know. Or . . . some of everything I know,

141

anyway. And he is very grateful. And . . . I am to see him again later tonight. Or, failing that, early tomorrow morning. And then he will be very grateful again." But no smile now. "You look rather pleased with yourself, David. And that worries me."

"I am pleased with myself." He wasn't such an expert on English beer as Jake had once been. But it tasted good because he was thirsty.

"I see." Jake nodded over his glass. "So that will be because you are hoping to meet your old colleague Major Richardson? For whom you people are all looking — as well as for General Lukianov?"

Everybody knew about everyone everybody was looking for now, evidently. "I might be, Jake." With everybody looking, that was hardly surprising: Jake had merely chosen the more likely of the two.

"But Mr Jaggard doesn't know this yet?"

Jake was another one like Paul Mitchell: he was too clever for his own good. "What have you got for me that you haven't given Henry Jaggard? On Prusakov and Kulik, as well as Lukianov, Jake?" He looked at his watch ostentatiously, and then at the remaining daylight outside.

"You're in a hurry?"

"Not particularly — if you've got a lot to tell."

"You ought to be in a hurry. And . . . I do not have a great deal. But what I have is good." Jake paused. "It is also sensitive, David."

"Sensitive?"

Jake hid behind his glass for a moment. "I must ask that it goes no further, from you, for the time being. It will surely come from other sources eventually."

It was the source, not the information itself, which was sensitive. "Don't insult me, Jake. When have I ever blabbed?" But he saw at once that injured reliability was not enough. "Very well. You have my word."

"Fine. Your word I will take." Jake nodded. "We have a Kremlin source, David. But we do not want it put at the slightest risk, you understand. Even for something which worries us as much as this." He made a face suddenly. "Also . . . there are those on my side who are not so convinced that we should be frank with you. They believe that terrorist operations always weaken the credibility of the PLO itself. And that suits them — whatever the cost to others."

Jake had always been a moderate. "I understand."

"Good. Well . . . Prusakov was the brains. Kulik was a useful idiot — a very necessary idiot. It is even possible that he thought he was about to ake a genuine deal with you in Berlin, when actually he was setting you up. And himself, of course. At least, that is what the Russians believe now, anyway."

"But Kulik was a computer expert. He can't have been that stupid."

"He can. But . . . they were both computer scientists, he and Prusakov. And they were both in severe personal difficulties. Sex and money in Kulik's case. Money and politics in Prusakov's. With Lukianov . . . he is more complex." Jake cocked an eye at him. "You know about computers, David?"

"Not a lot." Audley was only too-well-aware of his Luddite tendencies where computers were concerned. But it wasn't just that they so easily could out-perform him in his own special field (though not, as it happened, in the case of Peter Richardson, by God!). It was that computers had passwords which could be broken, and no words-of-honour, he told himself. "Try me."

"Computer viruses? How about them?"

"No." It was no good pretending, even though he rather liked the idea of computers catching the common cold. "Make it simple, Jake."

The Israeli nodded. "What it looks like is that Prusakov found out about Kulik's problems. And that gave him an idea, which he sold to Kulik. And then they studied the form together, and came up with General Lukianov, who was angry and disaffected with life in general. And with the result of defective tactics in Afghanistan — defeat and the planned evacuation — in particular." He nodded again. "And who, additionally, was up for the chop, professionally if not personally . . . Only, with his Middle Eastern contacts from the old days, he then came up with a variation of Prusakov's idea, it seems."

"Which was?"

Jake sighed. "Well . . . that's what the Russians don't know, exactly. But it was selling something to Abu Nidal, we're pretty sure. Which, of course, isn't the same as doing business with you and the Americans, or anyone in the West — that would have been treason, to Lukianov's way of thinking." He gazed at Audley in silence for a moment. "But, unfortunately, they don't know what it is that he's selling. Because Prusakov and Kulik between them have sabotaged the collective KGB/GRU memory bank, erasing whole sections of it —" He shook his head quickly "— don't ask me how. It wasn't supposed to be possible, with all the fail-safes and back-ups . . . And then there were the old-fashioned files —"

"Files?" Audley knew about such old-fashioned things. Files were what he had once browsed through at leisure like a contented herbivore, and almost without let or hindrance in the days of Sir Frederick Clinton, who had come to take a relaxed view of his omnivorous habits. He had even done a bit of browsing that very morning, like in those halcyon days.

"They've gone, too. Shredded, presumably. And that was General Lukianov, for sure. Because Kulik and Prusakov wouldn't have had access rights to them." Jake nodded again. "Their job was to fix the computers, however that could be done . . . Which I frankly don't understand — whether they simply did some sort of demolition job, or left triggers behind to be activated by the right inquiry — I don't know. Because all this new information technology is way over my head now."

"I see." It was Audley's turn to nod. The technology didn't matter: in this context computers were only glorified files. But files were the beginning of everything — they were any organization's collective memory, and they were sacrosanct. "No wonder they're desperate — never mind what Lukianov himself is up to."

"The Russians?" The Israeli grimaced at him. "They've been running around in circles, trying to find what's been wiped out. Because they can't start trying to reconstruct what's gone until they find there's a gap. Then — in theory, anyway — they can try to get on to the original sources of the information which might have been in it. But it's one hell of a job, even for the experts. And some of the stuff has probably gone forever — that's what our people reckon." Jake's expression changed, becoming almost quizzical. "The funny thing is . . . or, 'funny' isn't the right word . . . our whizz-kids aren't exactly rubbing their hands — they're as worried as everyone else is. Because they've now got to make damn sure that our secret information retrieval systems are as fail-safe as the missile systems have to be — safe from human mischief as well as human error. Which is near as damn-it impossible, I'd say." He finished his beer, wiped his moustache, and set his glass down. "But which is the least of our problems at the moment, David."

"Yes." It wasn't their problem at all, thought Audley dismissively. "Jaggard doesn't know any of this, you say?"

"Not yet. But he will know soon enough."

"How?"

"The Americans will tell him. We have ensured that one of their sources will pick it up. At . . . his own risk, of course." Jake sighed. "He would have got it soon enough, probably. Because it isn't the sort of thing that can be kept under wraps long — especially as Lukianov will certainly have taken out more than he needed, just to muddy the waters." He spread his hands. "We don't know how much they've managed to reconstruct as of now. But they'll have started with him. And, of course, they know that you and Richardson are involved. So it would seem a reasonable guess that everything that was ever on file about Messrs Lukianov, Audley and Richardson has been consigned to oblivion, whatever else may have gone." One bushy eyebrow lifted mockingly. "You should perhaps thank him for that, even though he did not intend you to enjoy the benefits of it?"

"Uh-huh?" But there were people enough over there who could quickly fill most of that gap, Audley concluded dispassionately. In fact, old Nikolai Panin could probably do the job single-handed from his honourable and well-deserved retirement niche in Kiev University.

"Flattering, too . . . when you think about it." Jake played idly with the bottle-opener, as though tempted again by his remaining stock of Cotswold bitter. "That he wanted to erase you personally, as well as your record — don't you think?"

Audley looked at his watch, and then at the window. It was almost dark enough now — and he had no time to gratify Jake's curiosity about the truth of Berlin. "How bright is General Lukianov, Jake?"

"Bright?"

"I know he's a gambler. But he backed two favourites which didn't stay the course — Afghanistan and Brezhnev's son-in-law. And before that . . . the Middle East? Your home ground."

"That's right." Jake could hardly deny that. "We didn't really overlap, though. My field's Egypt — as you well know . . . Or, it was. But his was Syria and Lebanon. With side trips to Libya and the old Barbary Coast."

"The terrorists' home ground. And he liaised with them?"

Jake thought for a moment. "Nobody *liaises* with them — not in the way you're seeming to imply, anyway." He shook his head sadly. "You British do not understand the nature of terrorism — Ireland, the Middle East . . . the old Empire before that."

This was dangerous ground, which must be skirted now just as it had to be in the old days. "And neither do the Russians?"

"And neither do the Russians — no matter what they think — " Jake also felt the ground quiver beneath him " — Lukianov . . . was perhaps marginally safer there than any of your people, or the Americans, might have been. But that was more because the Russians have a heavier-handed response; no publicity or public muscle-flexing, just an old-fashioned eye-for-an-eye operation, without fuss. So that protected him in his dealings with all sorts of people."

"Some of whom he's dealing with now?"

"That's certainly the way it looks, yes."

"He must have something pretty damn-good to offer them." Audley couldn't help speaking aloud to himself, banal though the thought which everyone had been thinking for days undoubtedly was. But no wonder everyone was scared!

146

"In answer to your question, old friend —" Jake didn't bother to agree with him, he simply succumbed to temptation. But then Jake's capacity for alcohol-without-impairment had always been enviable "— *no*, not ultimately intellectual-bright . . . *Crafty*-bright, like a good soldier." He flipped the metal top off, "Or . . . *tactical*-bright, rather than *strategic*-bright . . . like a good *Spetsnaz* graduate — which he is —" He considered Audley across the top of his Cotswold bottle "— if he hadn't ever got hooked into the Brezhnev nepotism malt-whisky-smoked-salmon-ballerina-girlfriend circuit he might never have got past field-rank. He'd have stayed at the sharp end, with his old *Spetsnaz* comrades, in Afghanistan." He poured slowly, until froth oozed just above the rim of the glass. "He'd have been like your Kipling-characters only on the other side, with his Cossacks instead of Gurkhas and all your other mercenaries . . . You and your 'Great Games'! 'A plague on both your houses' to that, now." He raised his glass mockingly. "But I do not think you can afford to play games now, great or otherwise."

"No." He could see that it was dark enough outside.

"You want to go." Jake observed his glance. "And quite rightly, too. Because what you must bear in mind now is not what Lukianov was, or what he may have been, but what he *is*, old friend. Because, as an old *Spetsnaz* man he was trained for the big show-down — to fight and cause havoc far beyond his own lines, and single-handed if things went wrong. So now perhaps he has guessed that Berlin and Capri did not go quite as he planned. But that will not stop him going ahead, and doing what he planned to do. He will merely move that much quicker, by instinct: he will want to clinch his deal, and then fade away." He grinned suddenly. "It is like my old landlady in Crofton Park used to say, when I was a student here, and I stayed too long in bed. 'You must *bustle*, Mr Shapiro,' she would say. 'You must *bustle*!' So now you must *bustle* old friend. Or you will be too late —" But then he held up a calloused palm warningly "— except that, first, I will make sure that the coast is clear for you, eh?" He put down his glass and picked up the phone beside the bed. "Can I have the bar, please?" He nodded at Audley. "I have minders down there . . . and elsewhere outside, you see."

"Jake —"

"It's all right . . . hullo? Please, you have a red-headed gentleman at the bar, drinking, I think? A Mr Pollard — yes?" He grinned at Audley. "A red-headed Jew? Who would have thought it, eh?" Then he concentrated on the phone again. "Hullo, Angus. Any visitors?" He paused. "Indeed? Is that a fact? Thank you, Angus." He replaced the phone. "And a red-headed Jew named 'Angus', too! A Scottish Jew — *such* a clever boy." He nodded at Audley. "Your also-clever Dr Mitchell has a new girl-friend, he says. And Angus admires his taste, I think . . . Okay, David? The back entrance, is it?"

"No." There was only one way they could have got here so quickly, on his heels. So there was no shaking them off, if the car was bugged (as, when he thought about it, he should have expected, anyway). Or . . . there were two ways, actually. Because Jake would provide a private car. But the other way was better. And, anyway, he wanted to know if there was anything new from London, which fitted in with that way. "No, Jake. I'll go down and talk to them. Don't worry yourself on my behalf."

"Very well. You know best." Jake went to the door, to unlock it. But then he touched Audley's arm, hesitantly yet deliberately all the same. "But don't forget what I said, David old friend — eh? Lukianov . . . I do not think, perhaps, that he is interested in you now . . . or your Major Richardson, for whom all your people are also looking, I hear — yes?" But he didn't wait for an answer to that. "However . . . he is a hard man. And his Arab clients — they do not care for anyone, even themselves . . . at least, those who do their bidding do not care, eh? Remember that the original 'Assassins' — the *Hashasheen* . . . they were one-way ticket holders. You remember?"

"How could I forget." He couldn't bring himself to return the grin. "Just like old times? Thanks, Jake."

Jake patted his arm. "Go with God then . . . as they say."

★

The blast of warmer air rising up the staircase, mixed with the early evening sounds and smells from the bars below, did nothing to dispel the cold which had spread from that uncharacteristic touch. In all the years he could not ever remember Jake touching him deliberately like that — or even touching him at all, since that first original handshake so long ago. Jake wasn't a toucher, he was almost Anglo-Saxon in his fastidiousness. Even, when in the past he had wanted to push his 'old friend' in one direction or another, towards a car or a taxi (or, more often, towards a pub and a bar), he had shepherded like a sheep-dog, blocking off every alternative route. *But this time he had touched, and it had been fear, not any other virtue (and least of all affection) which had been transmitted through his finger-tips —*

He saw them immediately he entered the bar. And a handsome couple they made too, he thought critically, as he passed the red-headed Angus by the door without a second glance. If he had had Faith with him, and they had been strangers, he would have envied their beauty and relative youthfulness while she would have moved on from their good looks to fantasize about their relationship and professions, to no possible purpose.

"Hullo, David." Mitchell betrayed neither relief nor surprise as he stood up. "Can I get you a drink?"

"No." For an instant he wondered what Faith would have made of this pair. Then he shook his head, and concentrated on Mary Franklin.

"You know Miss Franklin, of course," said Mitchell unnecessarily.

Audley sat down. "I haven't got much time, Miss Franklin. Have you any information for me?"

"Dr Audley — " She had taken her cue from Mitchell, to match his neutral expression "— the Russians aren't looking for their man Prusakov anymore. But it looks as though they are definitely concentrating on General Lukianov here in England. The search elsewhere has been either scaled down, or called off altogether."

"And the various terrorist groups — what about them?"

"They've all gone to ground," said Mitchell. "Elsewhere as well as here. But the Israelis have got a maximum alert going. Also especially here." He cocked his head at Audley. "Here's what it's all at, evidently. But we should have guessed that the moment your old buddy Colonel Shapiro buckled on his guns again and rode into town. He used to be the *numero uno* expert on the KGB and the terrorists in Western Europe in the old days, didn't he? Before he switched back to their Egyptian bureau?"

Trust Mitchell to know it all — and to guess that it wasn't just the old Shapiro-Audley relationship which had brought Jake back to England.

"Have you got anything on Major Richardson?"

Mary Franklin didn't beat about the bush. "Is he in this area?"

"He may be, Miss Franklin." He smiled politely at her, but then returned to Mitchell. "What else have you got?"

"What else?" Mitchell gave Mary Franklin a hopeful look. "You've got that CIA stuff on Kulik and Prusakov, Mary?"

So it was 'Mary' already! But then it would be.

"Nothing very definite." She wasn't quite ready to be 'Mary'. "The Americans now think they were both vulnerable to pressure, their Moscow sources say. The sort of pressure General Lukianov may have been able to exert, perhaps — with the access he had to personnel files."

"What about the computer angle?" He had to keep faith with Jake. But, after Prusakov's demise, he needed to ginger up his own side.

"Yes." Mary Franklin let herself be gingered. "Prusakov was the senior. But Kulik was a real whizz-kid, Dr Audley. And he'd most likely met Prusakov at the joint KGB/GRU computer seminars they've been having, with the improved systems they've been putting in." She allowed herself the merest hint of an apologetic smile. Which might be because she incorrectly thought that she was teaching grandfather to suck eggs, but which only made her more beautiful.

"Indeed?" Grandfather nodded encouragingly. But that was as far as Grandfather's word-of-honour would let him go, even in a thousand years — even at the risk of appearing stupid. "Well, I suppose they must have had plenty of access to information too, then." He nodded again, including them both. "And Lukianov?"

"Not a sign of him, David." Mitchell shook his head unhappily. "Kulik and Prusakov were the whizz-kids, like Mary says. And they both had to get out. Although they both also probably wanted to play with more advanced computers as well — ours, but the Americans' even more. And . . . especially Kulik, I'd guess. Prusakov was more into politics and the good life. And he was the older of the two, with a lot of Brezhnev-era friends who were also being weeded out." He shook his head again. "But it's Lukianov who frightens me, David. He sounds like a real tough egg, SAS-style. And I'd feel a lot happier if I knew what sort of deal he's made with the Ay-rabs."

"Yes. So what about Peter Richardson, Dr Audley?" Having given something, Mary Franklin still wanted more in exchange. But then Peter was her priority, after all: he was why she was here, inconveniently on his back.

Only, things had moved on since she had left London on his tail. Most notably, the CIA had moved like lightning after the Israelis' tip-off, evidently scared enough to hazard one of their Moscow insiders.

"'The Americans think' — 'the Americans say'?" He ignored her question. "What do the Israelis say?"

"They gave us the lead on Prusakov's disappearance from the 'Most Wanted' list, David," said Mitchell. "Jaggard's had a meeting with Freyer and Shapiro — a very friendly meeting, by all accounts. And the exchange is 'ongoing', he told Jack. So everybody's buddy-buddy for once." A muscle in his cheek twitched. "They're all being especially nice to us — the CIA as well as Mossad. All of which is scaring the daylights out of poor old Henry. So, apart from putting Mary here on your tail, he's not yet muttering 'What's that bastard Audley up to?'", like he usually does, David. It's just like your favourite poet said it always is —

For it's David this, an' David that, an' 'Chuck 'im out, the brute!'

151

— he knew a thing or two, you're quite right! So whatever you want . . . just say the word, and we're yours to command. Isn't that right, Mary?"

Mary Franklin's face was a picture. But then, however much she might know about them both, she might not know that one of Dr Mitchell's favourite indoor sports was quoting passages from Dr Audley's beloved Kipling at him, preferably in public.

Only this time there was more to it than that, he realized: if Mary Franklin was Henry Jaggard's woman first and last, Paul Mitchell was *his* man still — with or without Jack Butler's full approval: the Kipling lines were also the wrapping for that final message.

"Miss Franklin —" He caught her still in mid-gape at Mitchell "— so . . . what are the Russians doing, then?"

"The Russians?" She frowned at him.

"Dr Mitchell says that everyone is — ah — 'buddy-buddy'." He pronounced the Americanism with pretended distaste. "But I don't think he was including the KGB in that happy condition — were you, Dr Mitchell?"

"No." Mitchell came in happily on cue. "There's been some interesting coming-and-going in the new trade mission, Len Aston reports. But that's all to do with some Anglo-Soviet wooden furniture factory project, allegedly. Which they're thinking of switching from the north-east to the Welsh valleys. Only they could be bringing in some reinforcements perhaps, he thinks. But no *glasnost* of the sort you're suggesting — if that's what you're suggesting?"

"Well, it's about bloody-time that there was, by God! Where are you parked?"

"Round the back." Mitchell frowned. "Why d'you want to know?"

"I want to borrow your car."

"My car? Over my dead body! You've already got ——" Mitchell stopped abruptly.

"The new departmental Rover?" He could see that Mitchell understood. But so too, unfortunately, did Mary Franklin, judging by her obstinate expression. "I don't want to be followed — 'protected' — where I'm going. Either by you, Miss Franklin, or by Mossad."

She hadn't expected that. "Mossad?"

"Colonel Shapiro is upstairs, my dear. I've just been talking to him. And the red-headed fellow at the bar belongs to him. And they'll be watching my car, even if they haven't added one of their bugs to yours." This wasn't betraying Jake: it was merely using him to get her off his back, he reassured himself Jesuitically. "I believe I now know where I can find Peter Richardson — where he is waiting for me. But if I turn up anywhere near his safe-house with anyone on my tail he'll be off again, like on Capri. And I'm not having that."

"David —"

"I shall be perfectly safe this time. Apart from which I have work for you both."

They looked at each other.

"What work?" Mitchell sighed.

"What work, Dr Audley?"

"I want you, Paul, to make sure I'm *not* followed." There wasn't the slightest likelihood that Jake would try anything so stupid. But it would keep Mitchell occupied. "And I want you to contact Henry Jaggard, Miss Franklin. Because I've got work for him, too."

Mary Franklin stared at him even more intently. "What work, Dr Audley?"

"I want him to set up a meeting with the Russians as soon as possible." He met the stare arrogantly. "Because I don't think we've got much time."

"Much time . . . before what?"

"Either before Lukianov clinches his deal. Or before the Russians get him themselves, just as they got Prusakov. Which may be preferable. But which isn't acceptable to me."

She breathed out slowly. "Is this because of what Shapiro has told you?"

"Partly. But partly also because, whatever Lukianov is engaged in, I'd guess that the Russians must be close to him by now, the way they've been pulling out all the stops. Because they've always had the inner track — he was *their* man before he ran . . . as well as a head start after Berlin, even though they were too late with Kulik."

"But . . . they haven't got Richardson, Dr Audley."

"That's exactly right, Miss Franklin: Richardson will be *our* strength. Because he was *our* man once . . . That is, if you don't frighten him off now." He nodded at her. "If I can bring him in, then Henry Jaggard will have something to bargain with tomorrow. You tell him that: tell him to tell General Voyshinski that Dr Audley and Major Richardson have been talking together about the old days. That might spark a bit of much-needed *glasnost* in him."

EVERYTHING DEPENDED ON memory now.

First, there were the old precautions, even though he was tolerably certain that, of all cars, Mitchell's ridiculous pride-and-joy would not be bugged for easy following as the office Rover had been. But here, in the darkness and solitude of this deep Cotswold countryside of tiny roads and rolling hills, he had the advantage, anyway: no vehicle could move in it without lights, and from each crest the undisturbed night behind reassured him.

His only fear was that he wouldn't find the place again, after so many years: here, the darkness was not his friend, forcing him to drive by the map, squinting at every sign-post, noting the mileages he had memorized, and finally counting off the side-roads in the maze until he found the track on its hillside at last.

But then, quite suddenly, he was sure, against all doubt. There were dangers out there — all the old horrors, and the *negotium perambulans in tenebris* — the Foul Fiend himself, if not General Lukianov. But they were far away. And this was the place. Because, in a world of untruth and half-truth, Her Majesty's Ordnance Survey maps and his own memory never lied.

Even . . . although the track was narrower than he remembered, and the hedges higher . . . he was prepared for the unavoidable potholes, including the boggy stretch where the spring on the hillside above oozed out of the bank and crossed the track without the luxury of a culvert —

Everything depended on memory —

The cottage comforted him even more, it was so photographically exact. The years had added a few feet to the slow-growing holly-trees, and to the magnolia which had struggled bravely annually with the English winters and the late spring frosts, just as his own did at home. And the Porsche's fiercely-glaring headlights yellowed the Cotswold stonework and turned the moss black on the slates of the roof while taking out all the colour from the autumn flowers by the porch. Yet every difference served only to confirm his memory of the place.

For a moment after he extinguished the car's lights the darkness engulfed him again, and the newly-loosened knot in his stomach tightened again. Then the porch-light snapped on before he reached the door.

As he stepped into the circle of light he heard a chain jangle on the other side of the door, then the snap of a bolt. Then the door opened as far as the chain would allow.

"Can I help you?"

"I hope so, Mrs Kenyon." She had spoken so softly that he didn't even try to recall the voice. And she was standing at such an angle to the porch-light that he couldn't see her face while she could see his. "Is it Mrs Kenyon?"

"What d'you want?"

The relief which came after certainty was almost an anti-climax. "You remember me, Mrs Kenyon. I came here once, with a friend of yours — one morning long ago. We stayed for lunch. Your husband was in hospital at the time. You were busy planting the garden — begonias and petunias. It was in May . . . My name's Audley — David Audley. You remember me — don't you?"

She breathed out: it was as though she had held her breath as he had re-created his day in May long ago for her. "I remember you, Dr Audley."

"Then you know what I want, Mrs Kenyon. Can I come in?"

Sophie Kenyon chewed on that for a moment. "I remember you. But I'd still like to see your identification."

"Of course." He waited patiently. "Very sensible."

"Thank you." But she remained unmoving. "Is there anyone with you."

"No. I am quite alone, Mrs Kenyon. I have been very careful, I do assure you." He smiled at her. "Quite alone. Quite unarmed. And quite cold."

She unchained the door. One step down, he remembered. And then mind the beams (although that did not call for any special memory-trick: the old English had been a stunted race, and he had learnt to stoop automatically in parts of his own home from his fifteenth year onwards).

The smell of the house refined remembrance further. Every house had its smell, but old-house smells were more individual and distinctive, mostly derived from the working of damp on their building materials. And in this house the damp had been memorable; although now there were hints of wood-smoke and hot cooking added to it, as one might expect in October. And also, just possibly, *dog* (he wrinkled his nose at that: *dog* he couldn't recall from that last time, as he surely ought to if there had been one: it would have barked its way into his memory then; and, as an after-dark visitor *now*, it ought to have barked even louder at his arrival this evening).

"You know where to go?" There was a curious intentness in the question.

"It's this door, isn't it?" There damn-well *was* a dog-paw scratch mark on the lowest corner of the door, all the same — he caught himself staring at it.

"Yes. What's the matter?"

Warmth and more-pronounced wood-smoke greeted him. The curtains and the chair-covers and the carpet were different, but the room and the major things in it were the same.

"Have you got a dog?" In spite of himself, he couldn't resist the question.

"Yes." She stared at him, for a fraction of a second incredulously, but then with a slow smile. "So it *is* true, then."

"What's true?"

"He said you'd come. Would you like a drink?"

What he would like, he thought, was to follow up that cooking smell: it promised something he hadn't had for more days than he cared to think about, never mind since the day before yesterday: a

157

good square English home-cooked dinner—preferably with cabbage.

"Thank you. A very small scotch?" In the full light of her sitting-room he could study her for the first—or, more accurately, the *second* time. "What's true, Mrs Kenyon?"

She poured two very small scotches and handed one of them to him. The years, he thought, had been kind and not-kind to her: she still had her figure and the natural grace to go with it. But fifteen Cotswold winters, at least some of which must have been lavished on her dying husband (and the rest of which had presumably been wasted on loneliness and good works? But now he was making pictures!) . . . those fifteen winters had added Cotswold grey to her.

"He's not here at the moment, Dr Audley," she said simply.

"No?" He took comfort from the lack of emphasis on 'here'. "But not too far away, I hope?"

She considered him and his question together across her small untouched scotch. "You really are alone, Dr Audley?"

"You called me 'David' once—after Peter had introduced me, Mrs Kenyon. And I then called you 'Sophie' over lunch, I remember."

The smile, slow as before but gentler for the memory, returned. "And what did we have for lunch . . . when we were 'David' and 'Sophie' . . . David?"

"I don't remember. Salad, was it?"

"So you're not perfect!" She nodded, nevertheless.

She was not an enemy. But she was something much more worrying than that to a man running out of time. "Not quite perfect. But alone." He felt time at his back. "I do need to see him very badly, though. And the longer you delay our meeting, the less certain I can be that either of us will be able to stay out of trouble."

She raised an eyebrow. "What sort of trouble?"

It was always the same: to get more he had to give more. "He told you what happened on Capri, did he?"

The eyebrow came down. "Yes. But he doesn't know why it happened, he also told me."

"He thinks he doesn't, perhaps." He shook his head at her. "But he does."

158

She stared at him for another over-long moment. "What he thinks . . . is that you are a very dangerous man, David. You were in the old days. And you still are."

Audley sighed. It was not unreasonable on Peter Richardson's part that he should think that — however unjustly. "I don't know about dangerous. More like *endangered*, I would say."

Another long stare. But for that ailing husband and her Catholic scruples she would have been Peter Richardson's woman long ago, not just his friend and his friend's wife. So now she was more than all of that.

"But you get people killed." It was a statement not an accusation.

He had to correct it, nevertheless. "When I make mistakes, people get killed sometimes. Peter was a soldier — he should understand that." He felt the iron entering his soul. "And now, if I don't get to talk to him very soon, more people are going to get killed." He could almost taste the iron: it was because, if he let himself be, he was tired as well as hungry. "Almost certainly, whatever we do, I think that more people are going to get killed. But it may be within our power . . . how many. Or whether they're the innocent ones or the guilty."

She didn't reply. But this time she nodded, and then reached down into the hearth. Audley watched her as she lit a candle with a thin wooden spill and placed the brass candlestick on the ledge of a tiny window to the right of the stone chimney-breast.

Then he met her eyes. "Did he go out as soon as he heard the car?"

"No." She shook her head. "He's been indoors all day—ever since I collected him late last night, in fact."

He must have got his skates on! Audley thought admiringly. But then, in his line of retirement-business and with his training, Peter would have had his contingency plans worked out, right down to passports, spare cash and safe houses.

Which, of course, brought him to the old moment-of-truth, which they had rehearsed together on that unforgettable-unforgotten night, straight out of Kipling, on which they had both relied now: *If one told thee that all had been betrayed, what wouldst thou do? — I would run away. It might be true!*

Now she smiled again at him. "He wanted a breath of air, he said. But . . . he's been watching all day, through John's old field-glasses, out of the attic windows front and back." The smile trembled slightly, and the corner of her unpainted lip turned down. "He said that, if anyone came in daylight, it wouldn't be you. But he didn't think you'd be so quick — or so careless." She looked down at his glass. "Would you like another drink, David?"

He looked down at his glass, which had somehow emptied itself. "Only if I'm not driving — and if you've got enough supper for three —?"

"I always make too much." The smile turned up again. "Although Peter's done most of the cooking: we're having spaghetti bolognese. Only with a lot more meat than is proper, apparently. So there'll be enough, I'm sure."

There was much more whisky in the glass this time. "If I drink this I'll need a bed too, Sophie."

She let him take the glass from her. "There's a camp-bed . . . if you have time —? But you said —?"

"I'll be leaving early." He couldn't risk saying *we*, even now. "But . . . I'm not as young as I was." Let them all worry — the others! From Paul and Jake to General Lukianov and Others (always supposing *they* were still worrying, by God!) "If I don't get a few hours . . . then I won't be able to think straight tomorrow." He felt only slightly guilty at disturbing two middle-aged love-birds (which, under pressure and without any sign or mention of poor old John, to whom they had once been so faithful, they probably were now, at last). "Is it very inconvenient?"

"Not at all, David." She seemed almost relieved. "Peter didn't really expect you tonight. He thought it would be tomorrow night, more likely. If at all." Her mouth tightened suddenly. "No — he didn't say 'if at all' — I did. *He* was almost certain that you'd come." She touched her lips with her glass. "But he was afraid someone else might come with you."

"He thought I'd be careless." That was disappointing.

"No." She closed her eyes for an instant. "He just wasn't quite sure that they'd let you come alone." She sighed. "After what had happened on Capri."

"That's all in the past." He shook his head reassuringly at her. "How long will he be?"

She glanced at the candle. "Not long, I shouldn't think. It all depends on whether he's on top or down below at the moment. He said he was just going to stretch his legs . . . and take Buster for a night-jaunt." She came back to him. "You're quite right: I didn't have a dog, that time you came. I only got one three years ago, when . . . after John died."

The poor devil had lasted all those years! God — small wonder she was grey and stretched! And that, of course, accounted for Peter's own behaviour over the years, taken together with his own problems.

But he had to think of Peter now — out there somewhere. And not just 'stretching his legs and the dog's', either: the dark would be his friend equally. And especially with a dog at his side, for 'Buster' would be both a useful ally in casing the area for strangers and a splendid cover for such an enterprise: a dog was worth several men, day or night — and a man walking a dog at night would pass for a local man, not a stranger.

"Either way, he will have seen the car lights anyway, David."

"Yes." And then he'd be thinking hard, thought Audley. In fact, if he had known near-enough what had happened on Capri, but not *why* . . . and also with the name *David Audley* in the forefront of his mind . . . he'd be thinking very hard indeed —

But she was watching him intently again with that stretched look of hers. Only now that look must have more to do with her living Peter than her dead John. "Don't worry, Sophie. We're both being careful, that's all."

She drew a long breath. "It's easy to say that. But I don't know why you're being careful. And neither does Peter. Except he knows that someone wants him dead — and maybe you, too."

"Uh-huh." Knowing so much, yet so little, no wonder the poor woman was so frightened behind her brave front. "Well, that's why I'm here, my dear: because I don't know either. And that's why we're both in danger. It's like having poison in your bloodstream — not knowing enough, either of us. But together, you see, we may also have the antidote. That's what I'm hoping, anyway."

Another long, almost shuddering breath. "It doesn't make sense."

"Why not?" The heat of the fire and the whisky were getting to him. Only hunger kept him awake.

"It's just . . ." She gestured despairingly " . . . how did you *know* he'd be here, with me? How could you be so *sure*, I mean?"

"He was sure, wasn't he?"

"Yes. But —— "

"Why was he sure?"

She pulled herself together. "He said you'd remember. He said you never forget anything — that you've got a memory like an elephant."

"And so has he. I knew he'd remember — he knew I'd remember. It's the gift the good fairy gave to each of us. Sometimes it's a mixed blessing. But it gives us an advantage."

"Like now."

"Like now maybe. But maybe not. Because when we remember the past we recall the bad things just as vividly as the good ones. The saving grace of ordinary fallible memory is that old unhappiness blurs, and then it often becomes a joke before it's virtually forgotten. But the good times get rosier . . . like, my wife can never remember it raining when she was a child. And she's got crystal-clear recollection of her father looking handsome in his uniform, and bringing her sweets and books and toys, even though she knows she was only a tiny tot, and he only saw her a few times . . . and he was a bit of a rascal — " he caught himself too late, knowing he must go on " — if not actually a villain." He saw from her face that Peter Richardson had come clean with her. So in another moment she would conclude that his *faux pas* had been deliberate. "I know that my *temps perdu* really are the lost good old days . . . But anyway, one reason why Peter and I were first recruited was that we didn't always have to be looking up the files: we remembered what was in them once we'd read them — " Damn! She had made the connection, and was looking even more desolate at the thought of Richardson's rascality.

"How much trouble is Peter in? Apart from . . . this trouble of yours, David?"

"He isn't in any trouble in England, Sophie. Apart from *my* trouble, that is." He half-smiled at her. "What I was going to say was that he and I have a special reason for remembering each other. Or . . . two special reasons, actually. Because he saved my bacon once, in Italy . . . But, before that, there was this little experiment our mutual boss set up, you see."

"What . . . experiment?" She frowned at him.

It was working, his diversion. "He ordered me to invite Peter to dinner — to a dinner-party in my home. He — our esteemed master . . . he implied it was so we could get to know each other. But then, some time afterwards, he offered a crate of champagne to whichever of us could more exactly remember everything that had been said that evening. And the loser was to match the crate with another one —" Unbidden, the image of Sir Frederick Clinton superimposed itself on Sophie Kenyon "— the wicked old devil! He said if I didn't want to take part the crate would be Peter's by default. But he reckoned Peter would win it anyway."

A dog barked joyously outside the house, at the back in the distance.

"Go on, David." She swam back into focus, strangely relaxed now. "Peter has a key — he can let himself in."

The back had been a jumble of out-buildings and greenhouses full of carefully-wintered plants, he remembered, using the picture to obliterate Fred's obnoxious self-satisfaction. But could Peter ever exchange his exotic Amalfi coast for the rigours of even a south-facing Cotswold hillside?

"Go on, David." She was almost serene now that her living man was back under her roof. "But . . . how was it going to be judged, though?"

He could hear other noises now, so that it was hard to concentrate. "He said he would leave us to judge ourselves. But if we didn't agree then we could turn our entries over to the guests."

The noises resolved themselves into a door clattering and the wretched dog scampering and sliding on the flagstones outside before it started removing more paint from the sitting-room door.

And then the door opened and the creature hurtled through the gap, filling the room with furious uninhibited activity — making for its mistress first, and then happily and incorrectly assuming that any friend of hers must be another friend.

"Down, Buster!" She attempted half-heartedly to restrain the animal's enthusiasm for his new pretended friend. "Do you have a dog, David?"

"He hates dogs." Peter Richardson spoke from the doorway. "He has geese to protect him. Although he probably has electronic sensors now . . . Good to see you, David. I never thought I'd say that. But . . . *autres temps, autres moeurs*, eh?"

"I don't actually." The years had greyed Richardson, too: he looked like a distinguished Italian nobleman fancy-dressed in someone's old clothes. (The dead husband's clothes, maybe?) "I am relieved to see you, too, Mr Dalingridge."

"Is that a fact?" The brown well-tanned face and the too-knowing smile on it hadn't changed. "But . . . as a matter of *fact* . . . you've just given me a nasty turn." Richardson spread his hands out towards the fire. "Brrr! I'd forgotten how chilly England can get . . ." He gave Audley a sidelong glance. "The thing outside . . . You always used to drive a sedate Austin . . . not your thing at all, I thought."

The *thing* was the Porsche, of course. "No, Peter. Not my thing at all — you're right." He needed to assert himself. "I borrowed it. Because it doesn't have a bug in it." He managed to smile at Richardson at last. "It belongs to one of your successors actually."

"One of my successors?" Richardson turned to Sophie Kenyon at last, and his face softened. "Give me a drink, Sophie . . . And don't worry, dear: it's like I said, isn't it? It'll be David. And that means someone else should be worrying a lot more than us." He nodded at her, with a half-knowing, half-bitter little smile. Then glanced sidelong again at Audley over his outstretched arm. "One of my successors, eh? Well, he never bought that on his pay — thanks,

Sophie dear — but then, the Department of Intelligence Research and Development always favoured well-heeled young gentry, didn't it?" He sipped his drink. "But it did give me a bit of a turn, I tell you. I saw the lights from the copse by the road — that was fair enough, I just thought you'd been quick off the mark. But then I saw the back of the car . . . very nice, I'd have thought at any other time — like Cardinal Alberoni when he saw Philippe d'Orleans' backside: *Que culo d'angelo* . . . but not *your* sort of car, David. And that worried me for a bit . . . Still, he must trust you, to lend you his Porsche. In fact, if he knows how you drive, he must be a friend indeed!"

There was an edge of bitterness there as well as strain, beneath the old banter: once upon a time Richardson had taken an equally ridiculous car of his own like that for granted. But Audley was not of a mind to soften the contrast by recounting the tale of Mitchell's purchase of the thing second-hand, for cash, after last autumn's Stock Exchange debacle. Instead, he let the thump of Buster's over-worked tail fill the silence between them.

"David was just explaining . . ." Sophie moved loyally to break the deadlock, and then faltered ". . . he was just telling me why he knew you'd be here, Peter . . ." She faltered again.

"Oh yes?" Richardson sank into one of the dog-battered armchairs.

"But I still don't see *how* —?" She waited for him to take up the story. Then when he failed her, she turned back to Audley. "Which of you won the champagne, David?"

Audley watched Richardson. "Peter bought the champagne — the extra crate."

Sophie recognized the unstraightness of his answer, but couldn't make sense of it. "So you lost, Peter —?"

Richardson was watching Audley. "Fred Clinton said I was going to lose."

"He said the same to me," murmured Audley deliberately. But . . . typical Fred, to spur them each in the same way!

"He also told me that David Audley didn't like to lose." Richardson smiled at her suddenly. "He omitted to tell me that David Audley was a dirty player."

"I didn't play dirty." Audley addressed Sophie. "I simply let Peter see my version of the evening, that's all."

"Not all. He advised me that it would be better if I conceded defeat. So I did. But mine would have been the winning entry, if we'd played fair."

Sophie frowned interrogatively at Audley. "I don't understand."

To his surprise he didn't want her to think ill of him. "I did give him Fred's champagne. So the honours were equal in the end."

"You had a bad conscience!" Richardson accused him. "You lost."

"Not at all, my dear fellow! I was your host that night. I couldn't let you be out of pocket."

"I still don't understand —" Sophie accused them both.

They looked at each other, each waiting for the other to speak.

"It's really . . . quite simple." Audley decided that he must break first. "We didn't know about Fred Clinton's game, of course."

"But we played a game of our own, that evening, Sophie. You see." Richardson cut in. "Or . . . it was that tame Member of Parliament of yours — the barrister? Sir Laurie Deacon — it was his idea." He stared at Audley. "But he called it the 'Kipling game'. So it may have been yours originally, David — was it?" He shook his head, as though to clear it. "So —— "

Candlelight.

Faint smell of damp beneath the fading dinner-smells. (Those were the days when Faith hadn't quite defeated the rising damp; and, of course, the cellar-door had been opened, to bring up another bottle.)

Laurie Deacon: *"That fellow you've all been looking for — the one who did a bunk . . . The word is that you've found him, David — right?"*

"Not me, Laurie. Peter here did the finding."

Peter Richardson: *"Not me either. It was Sir Frederick who did the finding — like Sherlock Holmes. He said the chap hadn't really done a bunk — hadn't defected . . . He'd just had a bit of a breakdown. And he wanted to be found . . . only by someone sympathetic, that's all. So it was just psychology."*

Laurie Deacon: *"Ah — yes! He'd be one of Fred's old mates, from the war, of course. So Fred knew all about him, I suppose. But he had a pretty good hidey-hole, all the same — the Special Branch fellows were tearing their hair, I heard tell."*

Peter Richardson: *"He had . . . a friend he could trust. That's all."*

Laurie Deacon: *"That's not all — that's everything, and a bit more, by God! It's just like in that book you gave my daughter, David — when she was little . . . and you ordered me to read it to her at bedtime. I've never forgotten it. Because it could be any of us."*

"What book was that, Laurie? Pippa's had so many birthdays —?"

Laurie Deacon: *"That Kipling book, of course — your favourite, you said . . . And there was this story in it, about these three old Norman knights scheming to prevent another invasion of England. And one of the things they do is to plant a false message on the enemy, across the Channel . . . the sort of thing you chaps do all the time these days, I shouldn't wonder . . . telling 'em that all their plans had been betrayed — remember?"*

"Yes. 'Write to any man that all is betrayed, and even the Pope himself would sleep uneasily', Laurie. That's why you've got a numbered account in Zurich, eh?"

Laurie Deacon: *"Huh! Every sensible man takes precautions. In fact let's play a little game, then. If all was betrayed, have you got a bolt-hole? Is there anyone you'd trust absolutely, life-and-death? Will you play my 'Kipling Game' —?"*

Peter Richardson: *"There's a girl, lives in the Cotswolds . . . Sophie Kenyon. Married my best friend . . . should have married me. But she wouldn't give me up to anyone —"*

"I'll never know why I said it. But I did." Richardson gave Sophie an apologetic look. "I could have bitten off my tongue . . . Too much of David's claret, maybe. And . . . I must have thought I was among friends."

"And so you were." Audley fended off Buster irritably. "I

167

promised him his secret was safe with me, Sophie. And I told him that my word-of-honour was good for a thousand years — like Sir Richard Dalyngridge's — 'Dalyngridge' with a 'y', actually — in the Kipling story. And I have kept my word." And now he really could smile genuinely at her at last: after this, so long as she was present, Richardson could deny him nothing. "Only then, you see, Frederick Clinton challenged us to *his* little game. Or, his 'experiment', as he called it . . . Memory versus memory, Old Dog versus Young Dog, Sophie."

"Why did he do that?" She looked from one to the other.

"Huh!" Richardson got up to pour himself another drink. "He could be a mischievous old sod when he wanted to be. He probably wanted to take David down a peg, at that!"

"Or teach you a thing or two, my lad."

"He certainly did that, by God!" Richardson shook his head at Sophie. "I was his very own new recruit, my love. And in one of their silly aptitude games — one of their less dirty games — I'd scored rather high marks, for memory apparently. So he wanted to show me off, I reckon." He drank. "To show how smart he was by showing how smart *I* was, when it came to 'automatic recall' — 'automatic recall'?" He cocked the jargon at Audley. "But he waited two or three months before he hit us with his 'experiment', didn't he? Yes — it was exactly six months before I went into the field for the first time, playing games for Jack Butler on Hadrian's Wall. Because that was on a ——" He bit the rest off with a scowl, and pushed the dog out of his way to regain his chair. "Get over, you great lump!"

It was on a Monday? Or a Friday? Excitement slightly tinged with envy tightened Audley's chest as Richardson automatically displayed his special aptitude before realizing what he was doing.

He smiled at Sophie again. "I had the pleasure of meeting you that time, because of that, anyway. I wanted to see Peter's paragon of secrecy!"

"And that was his first piece of blackmail." Richardson nodded at his paragon. "The second being that, after Fred Clinton had challenged us both, *he* —" he pointed "— suggested that the crate of champagne was his. Because he was inhibited from providing a full account of the evening by his so-called word-of-honour . . . Otherwise, I would have won — in spite of his plying me with drink, Sophie."

"No. *I* would have won." He *had* plied Captain Peter Richardson, Fred's clever new boy, with drink, Audley remembered guiltily. "Our separate reports are still in the files — do you know that, Peter?" He smiled at Sophie, who was regarding them both with a mixture of comprehension and absolute incredulity. "But without your name, of course." The truth was . . . it might have been smarter to let the clever new boy win, and give Fred his satisfaction. But he had never liked losing, either then or now. "I know what you're thinking: childish games . . . all quite ridiculous, eh?"

Half of her couldn't deny that. But the other half was frightened. So she still stared from one to the other of them.

"And you're right." It was the frightened half he addressed. "But that's what happened. And that's why I'm here, not . . . somebody else." He nodded to the frightened half. "Because we both remembered. And Peter also gave me 'Richard Dalingridge', just in case I'd forgotten." Both halves of her were properly frightened now. But he had to be sure of her. "Because we're not playing silly games now, my dear. We're not playing games at all, now."

That very nearly substituted *gravitas* for ancient silliness. But then a log tumbled on the fire. And the wretched Buster, who had settled into happy oblivion on the hearth, emitted a canine fart so loud that it woke him up, causing him to look round inquiringly.

"Oh, for God's sake, Buster!" Richardson fended the animal off. "Where the hell did you get him, Sophie?"

"From the animal sanctuary. Here, Buster!" She snapped her fingers, and the dog grinned at her. "He was a stray. Like you, Peter."

"Indeed? It's like that, is it?" He stared at her for a moment, then settled back in his armchair. "Okay, Dr Audley! We've played one old game by the old rules — both of us cheating: you wanted to find me all by yourself, to get all the *kudos*. And also because you think I can get you out of another of those awkward predicaments in which you specialize, maybe?"

That was nasty. And nasty not least because it ignored the element of 'keeping faith' which he had so carefully emphasised. But it did have certain other elements of truth, it had to be admitted.

"You were in a bit of a predicament yourself, Major Richardson." If some elements had to be admitted, then so had others. But he would also pretend an element of decency, if only to keep Sophie on his side. "But I don't need to go into that, I think."

But Richardson shook his head. "I have no secrets from Sophie." All the same, he looked at her. "I had debts of honour to settle — she knows that." He came back to Audley. "I used the skills I had. Only then I became greedy. But you wouldn't know what it's like to make a lot of money, David — after you've suddenly discovered that you're poor, when you thought you were rich. Because you've never had to worry about money — never mind the debts!"

Little he knew! But, then, the less he (and the rest of the world) knew, the better. "So then you had the Mafia on your back?" It occurred to him belatedly that maybe Richardson hadn't been such an innocent smuggler after all, but had simply been a more successful one; that, certainly, would account for that hint of reserve in Captain Cuccaro's attitude, not to mention the Mafia's increased interest. "So when strangers came looking for you just recently, you were already hard to find?"

"Yes." Richardson was oblivious to Sophie and the unfragrance of her dog equally: this was the hard side of him which Fred had identified, even before it had been tempted by adversity fifteen years ago. "'Strangers' is right, too: my people didn't know who they were, the other day. Except that they weren't local. But . . . I thought maybe it was hired talent. Only, they don't need to hire anyone."

"And then someone dropped my name?"

"Yes." The shutters came down. "And then I didn't quite know what to expect. Except trouble."

"And the KGB?"

"And the KGB?" The corner of the man's mouth twitched. "For Christ's sake, David! What the hell have they got to do with me? After all these years — ?"

"You don't know?"

"The hell I don't!" Richardson's whole face surrounded his frown. "Do you think I haven't been cudgelling my brains every spare minute, these last twenty-four hours?"

Suddenly, there was something not right. And although Audley didn't know what it was, it was like a knife at his back.

"But David says that you *do* know, Peter." It was as though Sophie had picked up the same vibration.

"He does, does he?" Richardson started to reply almost savagely, but then also registered the doubt in her voice. "Then perhaps he'd also be good enough to give me a clue to what it is. Well, David?"

"Do the names Kulik, Prusakov and Lukianov mean anything to you?"

Richardson's face went blank again. "They sound like a firm of Moscow solicitors." It was almost as though there was a *click* as the three names went into that incomparable memory-bank for checking. "Who have they been soliciting, then?"

"The first two were computer specialists, GRU and KGB respectively —"

"*Were* — ?" Still blank. "And . . . Lukianov?"

"General Lukianov. KGB, ex-GRU . . . ex-Red Army — ex-*Spetsnaz*."

"'Was'? Or 'is'?" Richardson looked at Sophie quickly. "Should she be hearing all this?"

Good question! "You've put her in the middle of it."

"No I haven't. Go and look at my bolognese, Sophie."

"No. What's 'Spets . . . naz', David?" She folded her arms obstinately.

Sophie! thought Audley suddenly. "They're the Russian version of our SAS."

"And none of your business." Richardson turned back to Audley. "I've never heard of any of them. I never had anything to do with computers — ours or theirs. Or with anything that was going on over there, come to that. Christ! You should know — you must have been through my record enough times now! I never did anything — not as a principal operator, anyway — anything that amounted to a row of beans . . . anything that wasn't straightforward, and signed and sealed and *closed*, for God's sake!" He half directed the complaint at Sophie. "Professionally speaking, I was still wet behind the ears — still training and learning. So there was always someone there to hold my hand, more or less." Then he turned fully to her. "And, I told you . . . what I learned wasn't always to my liking, as it turned out. And when Fred Clinton told me what he was really grooming me for —" He shook his head at her "— that just wasn't for me, I had to tell him. So that was when we agreed to cut our losses." He swung back to Audley. "Never heard of any of them. But I take your point, David —"

"What point?" Sophie refused to be dismissed. "What do you mean?"

"It doesn't matter — to you, my darling. *David* —"

"He means that if someone wants him dead then it's because he knows something. So all we have to do is to run his memory back until we find it." Audley smiled at her, and was almost certain — even though he no longer felt like smiling. "And he's just volunteered to help me. Correct, Peter?"

"If I must." Richardson half shrugged, and then made a comic face at Sophie. "The sooner I get out of your hair, the better, Mrs Kenyon. Now that I've become so popular all of a sudden."

"Don't joke ——"

"I'm not joking. Being so popular is no fun. Neither is being recalled to the colours, come to that. But David here will look after me — he'll keep tight hold of my hand, you can be sure of that! Won't you, David?"

And being so clever, but not clever enough, was no fun either, thought Audley grimly to himself. But he had to play Richardson's game now, as a penance for that. "Yes. You are worth more alive than dead at this moment — just like me Peter." But he owed something to her, all the same. "And, of course . . . once we've got the answer between us, then we won't be in danger anymore, Mrs Kenyon — Sophie. It's really as simple as that."

Richardson nodded in support. "As simple as that! Shall I pack my bags now? 'Waste not an hour' — Horatio Nelson? Or, in your case, David . . . 'Fill the unforgiving minute' — Joseph Rudyard Kipling?" He stood up to suit his words, bringing the dog to its feet with him. "No — not you, Buster!"

"David's staying the night," said Sophie.

"Is he?" Richardson looked down at Audley. "Is that wise?" Then he acknowledged Sophie. "Well, we'll have supper first. And then we'll see, eh? So . . . if you'll attend to my over-cooked bolognese, David and I will start unravelling old times — okay?"

Audley watched the man watch his woman obey him. Then waited for the dark eyes to come back to him.

"Go with your mistress, Buster!" Richardson pushed at the animal's hind quarters. "Because, if you break wind like that again, I swear I'll kill you . . . O-U-T!" He thrust the dog out of the room. "'Out' and 'run', are words he understands. But being just a rescued stray, like me, he hasn't learnt 'kill' yet, evidently . . . Would you like another top-up, David? Courtesy of Richard Dalingridge's duty-free allowance."

"No. Thank you." The man was too laid-back. Of course, he had always had style, in the old days: good school, plus Sandhurst and university, multiplied by that deceptively generous allowance from his doting (and doted-on) Italian mother. But those small injections of anger at his situation hadn't really carried conviction. "You got in easily, did you?"

"No problem." Richardson topped up his own glass. "Now, tell me more about this Russian triumvirate of yours. Why am I supposed to have known them? When I know that I may come up with an idea or two — you never know. Then we can get going."

Not just too laid-back, but too unfrightened also.

"Kulik, Prusakov and . . . who was it? The *Spetsnaz* fellow? Lukianov — yes!" Richardson swilled the whisky round in his glass without drinking it. "Sounds like 'Caesar, Pompey and Crassus' . . . and, as there's only one left now, you indicated, that makes Lukianov the Caesar of the three. Right?"

And, finally, too helpful, and altogether too willing. After having been so interested to meet him in the first place, and so concerned to be found so quickly and easily after that.

It was humiliating, really. He had made a picture of Richardson, and on the record it would look as though he'd been exactly right in his prediction, and very clever as usual with it, whatever the outcome. But he hadn't been right at all. And that made him angry.

"Why did you come back, Peter?"

"Why did I —?" Richardson stared at him. "With half Europe after me . . . it seemed the sensible thing, David."

"No." There was no point in admitting his error. Rather, he must still pretend to have been clever. "We trained you. And, with what you've been up to all these years, you must have known your luck would run out eventually. So you would have been well-prepared for the day when 'all was betrayed'."

"I was well-prepared for it." Richardson lifted his chin aggressively. "That's why I'm here."

"No." He could hear distant kitchen sounds. And they confirmed his certainty. "You'd have had a better bolt-hole than this, a lot further away. And, with half Europe after you, you'd never have risked Sophie — even if you did trust my word-of-honour still. So that won't do, Peter."

"No?" Richardson returned to toying with his whisky. "Well . . . let's say I was curious —" The look on Audley's face stopped him. "No . . . and I don't suppose Queen and Country will do any better, eh?" He nodded. And then matched Audley's expression. "I came back to help you, actually. Because that was what I wanted to do."

They were getting closer. "And what else do you want?"

"Just that: to help you. And not to be tucked away in some damned safe-house in the back-of-beyond." Quite suddenly Richardson's lips smiled unnaturally, with no support from his eyes. "But I also want to be in at the kill, with you. That is what I want."

174

Audley was conscious of the warmth of the fire on his face contrasting with what felt like a cold draught on his back. What he had just got from the man was everything and nothing, simultaneously. "Why?"

Mercifully, the lips lost the Borgia smile. "Is your word-of-honour still good, David Audley? Will you take me with you?"

It might be safer to have a man who could smile like that under his own eye than anyone else's, the way things were. But if those terms had been waiting for him ever since Capri, he also had something with which to bargain now. "That's not going to be easy, Peter. There are rules."

"Not for you, there aren't. Or there never used to be . . . in the old days." A ghost of the old Richardson-smile returned. "And it's the old days that you want, isn't it?"

"I'm not in the killing business." They were only haggling now. "I never was."

"No?" It was the old days that the man was remembering — just as Charlie Renshaw had done when he had re-iterated his final order. "Very well. I'll settle for observer-status, to see how things turn out. Okay?"

Buster began to bark somewhere beyond the door.

Richardson nodded. "He's getting his dinner. So we haven't got long. And . . . I don't want Sophie to know more than she already does." He nodded again. "You were quite right: I wouldn't have come back here, and risked her . . . if it hadn't been necessary."

"Necessary for what?"

"Necessary for me." No sort of smile now, either twentieth-century English or sixteenth-century Italian. "Your word, David?"

"All right. My word — if what you've got is worth it, Major Richardson."

"Thank you. It's worth it. If it isn't . . . I agree, Dr Audley."

Now Audley could nod. But there was still one thing he wanted to know first. "How long have you been aware of . . . whatever it is you are about to tell me? Why have you sat on it all these years?"

"I haven't sat on it. I haven't even thought about it . . . 'all these years', as you say." Richardson's lips curled, "But you've just reminded me of it, that's all, David."

It had to be Lukianov. No matter that Prusakov had been the brains, or that he and Kulik between them had fixed their computers and set the whole plot in motion in the first place so recently. Because this was fifteen years ago, what Richardson was remembering. And fifteen years ago they would have been back-room beginners somewhere in the bowels of their respective KGB and GRU headquarters. Whereas a much-younger General Lukianov would have been in the field, at the sharp end.

"You've remembered Lukianov?"

"No. Or maybe." Richardson shrugged the name off disappointingly. "I don't know. I don't really know what's happening now, do I? To me, anyway."

"So what do you know, then?"

Richardson stared at him for a moment again. "You got quite a lot of it right. I was in trouble, when I got your message. I'd . . . had a long run. And I should have quit long ago, I suppose. But there it is — I didn't . . . It gets to be a habit, you know."

Making money? Taking risks? Having two separate lives, very different from each other? But that didn't matter right now. "The Mafia was after you."

"And the *Guardia di Finanze* . . . I was about to take a trip, anyway . . . when these people turned up, asking for me. Not the *Guardia* — and not the Mafia either, my people thought. Only, when they didn't find me they left a message, with something they knew I couldn't resist in it. But then . . . fortunately — very fortunately — I got *your* message." The stare became bleak. "And I don't believe in coincidences, David. Not when they involve you."

"So what did you do?"

"I thought I'd put matters to the test. I have a good friend on Capri, with a house just near the Villa Jovis. So I invited you both up there, to see how coincidental you were."

God Almighty! "I see. And we weren't." Audley cut his losses. "What was this thing you couldn't resist, Peter?"

176

"Does it matter? I decided you were my best bet. So I'm here — and you're here. And we've made a deal. Isn't that enough?"

"No." He could never rest easy with that Borgia smile at his back. "It's personal. It doesn't concern you. And you wouldn't understand, anyway. You of all people."

Given time he might be able to extrapolate from that insulting clue to the truth. But with Buster out there wolfing his dinner, time was what he didn't have. "There's no such thing as 'personal' — you should know that from the old days. 'Personal' is what causes avoidable accidents —"

"Accidents?" Richardson cut him off, but then stopped. And there was something about his mid-winter expression which warned Audley not to push into the man's silence, but to let it work itself out.

"I had an accident once." Richardson was as unmoving as a statue, and as cold. "Remember?"

"Yes. But, it was after . . ." Suddenly, it was like being on a high place, from which he could see everything but had been looking in the wrong direction ". . . it was after you left us."

"I was in a hospital bed, chatting up the nurses, when I got the telegram telling me my mother was dead." The statue swallowed, but still didn't come to life. "I discharged myself." Another swallow, almost painful. "She took an overdose. By accident, they pretended. They were . . . very understanding, you might say. Did you know that?"

Audley waited until the ensuing silence forced him to answer. "Not at the time, no." But he could see that wasn't enough. "Not in that detail, I mean."

"Yes. Of course." Something flickered in Richardson's eyes. "I had left you by then, of course. So it was only personal."

Audley realized why he, of all people, was not expected to understand any of this painful litany. Richardson had adored his legendary Principessa-mother, who had returned to her sunny *palazzo* after her husband's death — that was common knowledge. Whereas he himself had no memory of his mother, only of a succession of his father's colourful woman-friends. And, presumably, that bit of personal information had reached Peter Richardson somehow, never to be forgotten, like every other unconsidered trifle.

But the hell with that! "Peter ——"

"They calculated it exactly right, the Russians did: nobody was going to ask any questions, after that — not even me. Least of all me, the way things were. You've got to admire them for that." Richardson nodded at last, almost as though he was relieved. "But, anyway, the message was . . . that if I really wanted to know how my mother died, they were ready to meet me." Once he started to nod he couldn't stop. "And then up you popped, David. Only then I didn't need to know *how*. What I was interested in was *who* . . . and *why*. Which of course, is what you want. So you can have what I know for free." Now he actually almost smiled. "It's only a spade, David. Just a spade."

The almost-smile had also been almost-Borgia. "A . . . spade?"

"That's right." The almost-smile was there again. "I have the spade. You have the grave-diggers. Between us we should be able to manage a grave or two to my satisfaction, I reckon. Eh?"

PART THREE

No Trouble

I

IT WASN'T QUITE true that Paul Mitchell had eyes only for Peter Richardson when they met at last: he had one eye for Richardson but the other for his Porsche. And, having more-or-less satisfied himself about the near side, he walked slightly sideways with a curious crab-like bias, so that he could also take in the back as well, to make sure that it — *Que culo d'angelo!* — was also undamaged.

"Huh!" And even now Mitchell wasn't altogether happy: he wanted to take in the other side and the front as well. "Well, you've led us a pretty dance, David! To this god-forsaken place!" But then he remembered his duty and his manners. "Major Richardson, I presume?"

"Mr Mitchell?" Richardson was superficially much more relaxed. And, even though Mitchell wasn't even a name to him, his unfailing memory of what Audley had said the night before pinpointed the identification beyond doubt. "It is a pleasant car to drive. But you should try a Ferrari. Or a Lamborghini, Mr Mitchell."

"Oh yes?" Mitchell had decided to dislike Richardson on first sight even more than *in absentia*. "It's 'Dr Mitchell' actually, since we're into meaningless titles, Major."

"Oh yes?" The wet wind ruffled Richardson's hair as he looked away, pretending to study the glorious wreck of Tintern Abbey across the road. "Not a Doctor of Divinity, evidently." He nodded towards the ruins. "Only god-forsaken in god-forsaking times, perhaps?" But then he couldn't resist looking directly at Mary Franklin beyond Mitchell's shoulder.

"Franklin, Major Richardson." Mary Franklin wasn't impressed either. But she let Richardson take her hand nevertheless.

"Miss Franklin." Richardson shook her hand like an Englishman,

181

and then noted the absence of rings on its fingers, like an Italian. "You are another of my successors in Research and Development, I take it?"

"No, Major Richardson." She studied the man coolly. "But don't let it worry you."

"I am not worried, Miss Franklin. I have nothing to be worried about — at least, not in England." He glanced at the abbey ruins again. "Or, is this Wales — on this side of the river?"

"Except illegal entry."

"Travelling on a false passport." Mitchell supplemented the charge.

"You might find that hard to prove, Mr Mitchell — Dr Mitchell . . . Miss Franklin." Richardson studied them in turn. "But does it matter, now that I'm on your team again? And by . . . invitation, shall we call it?" He settled on Mitchell. "It was you that David here phoned last night, wasn't it, Dr Mitchell? To give you your orders? Oughtn't you to be reporting to him now — rather than wasting time with me?"

Mitchell breathed in deeply. But then controlled himself. "David ——"

The rasp in Mitchell's voice had sounded too much like steel leaving its scabbard. "All right, Paul." But Audley knew he had to make allowances for what must have been a long night. "Major Richardson will be with us, for the time being."

"He still needs me, is what Dr Audley means." Richardson had evidently recognized the sound too, but was making no such allowance. "So you must make the best of it . . . for the time being. After that . . . we'll see, eh?"

"Yes." Mary Franklin took centre-stage diplomatically before Mitchell could accept that challenge. "But, in that case, Major, why are we meeting here, and not in London? Is this 'the best of it'?"

"Good question, Miss Franklin. The best — and perhaps the worst." The wind ruffled Richardson's hair again. "This is fine country — the borders, the Welsh marches. *My* country, it used to be, I thought . . . I used to come this way, up from the south, where

my regiment was stationed after I left Sir Frederick Clinton's service
— your service, Miss Franklin? No?" He shook his head. "Never
mind! I used to come this way to visit friends at Pen-y-ffin up the
road, en route to Hereford, when I was cultivating old SAS friends
there, to get a transfer to them —" he cocked his head at her this
time "— SAS headquarters being at Hereford, you know? And all
this being one of their stamping grounds, where the English and the
Welsh used to raid each other in the olden times —

> *The mountain sheep are sweeter,*
> *But the valley sheep are fatter;*
> *We therefore deemed it meeter*
> *To carry off the latter.*

Do you know the poem, Miss Franklin? It gets very bloodthirsty
after that. Did you bring General Lukianov's picture with you, like
Dr Audley asked?"

"Yes." But she didn't move. "What's he got to do with it?"

"This could be his country too. But I won't know for sure until I
see his picture." Richardson put out his hand. "Please —?"

She took a stiffened envelope from her shoulder-bag. "This is a
recent photograph, Major."

"Of course." The wind fluttered the photograph as he slid it out.
"I'll make the same allowances as I do for myself, when I look in the
mirror."

They all waited.

"Handsome fellow." Richardson smoothed the print, holding it
with both hands against its envelope. "Typical *Spetsnaz*."

"Yes?" Mary Franklin exchanged a glance with Mitchell.

"Yes. Anglo-Saxon type . . . or, presumably, Scandinavian or
Germanic, from the north-west. Could be one of ours, from much
the same stock, way back . . . the same way as I can pass for a
foreigner, coming home." He held Lukianov at arm's length.
"Yes . . . a much-favoured type for missions in the west, eh David?"
He offered the picture to Audley. "You've seen this?"

"Do you remember him, Major?" Mary intercepted the picture.

"No. But, then, I didn't expect to." Richardson let go of it. "It doesn't change anything."

Mitchell sniffed. "I didn't know you were a *Spetsnaz* expert."

"No?" Richardson enjoyed Mitchell's not-knowing. "Not in my file, eh?"

"Not in your file, no." But Mitchell had recovered his poise. "Are you?"

"Not really. But I did do a bit of private study on them while I still had clearance — in the Barnet House records, as well as our own — like David's profile of General Kharchenko, from the late sixties . . ." Richardson smiled suddenly. "It was when I started to plan for my SAS-transfer later on, *Spetsnaz* and the SAS being mirror-image organizations, in some respects —" The smile became lop-sided "— except they are about a hundred-times bigger . . . But Kharchenko was a great SAS-admirer — ask David." Then the smile vanished again. "I just thought if I had a bit of inside-knowledge about them — *Spetsnaz* . . . it might have increased my suitability, that's all Dr Mitchell. Because I was a bit long-in-the-tooth for a transfer, maybe. But I didn't much fancy regimental duty — Salisbury Plain, Ireland, Germany . . . Salisbury Plain, Germany, Ireland. My time with Research and Development had spoilt my taste for playing that sort of soldier, what was left of it originally. Okay?" He took in Mitchell and Mary Franklin together again. "Does that answer your question?" Then he nodded at Mary Franklin's handbag. "Typical *Spetsnaz*, as I said. Turn his clock back fifteen years and you've got another of those clean-cut Russian boys in Afghanistan I've been seeing on Italian newsreels, is what I mean. Only he would have worn his hair longer. And no one from here to Hereford would have given him a second glance . . . except maybe the girls."

Neither Mitchell nor Mary Franklin looked at each other this time.

"Okay." Richardson accepted their silence. "So I've come clean on *Spetsnaz*. And I heard David on the 'phone to you last night, Dr Mitchell. So what have you got for me, then?"

184

Mitchell didn't fancy that final arrogant 'me' any more than he fancied the man himself. And it was more than a simple chalk-and-cheese, like-but-unlike, post-Capri reaction, Audley realized. More simply still, because of his own past and background Mitchell disliked the sum of Peter Richardson, everything he stood for and everything about him, from his distinguished good-looks to the way in which he'd twice abandoned his military career (never mind an equally promising one in intelligence) when it didn't please him sufficiently: that last, for Paul Mitchell, would be a betrayal beside which the man's retirement activities were a mere aberration.

"For you?" Mitchell's lip twisted with distaste.

"For me." Audley pushed the words between them before Mitchell's irritation got the better of him. "Have you traced the policeman?"

"Yes."

"Yes." Richardson wasn't interested in Mitchell's likes and dislikes. "Well, seeing as I supplied his name that can't have taxed you much." He lifted his head slightly. "He'd be retired by now, of course — eh?"

Mitchell ignored him. "Yes. We've traced the policeman, David."

"He wouldn't be dead, by any chance?" Richardson refused to be ignored.

"He lives with his widowed sister in a village near Hereford, David," said Mitchell pointedly. "We have arranged for you to talk to him this morning."

Richardson leaned forward. "Did you talk to him, Dr Mitchell — last night?"

"Yes, Major." Mitchell bowed to the urgency in Richardson's voice. "We got him out of his bed at midnight. And we talked to him."

"Did you ask him about the spade?"

Mitchell looked at his watch. "We've got a good half-an-hour's drive, David. Shall we go?"

"Did you ask him about the spade?" Richardson refused to be gainsaid.

185

Audley nodded to Mitchell.

Mitchell stared at him for a moment, then turned to Richardson again. "Yes, Major Richardson — we asked him about the spade."

"And — ?"

A stronger gust of wind swirled over and around them, carrying the word away up the valley.

"We also checked up on your own little accident, in London. And that was a lot easier. We only had to wake up a succession of irritable civil servants, as well as policemen, and pull rank on them. Plus the Defence of the Realm and the anti-terrorist regulations, and the Third World War." Mitchell took his revenge steadily. "And we established that you'd had an accident which wasn't your fault. As a result of which an Irishman named Murphy was fined £15, with £25 costs, after pleading guilty to careless driving. Although his present whereabouts — and the whereabouts of a million other Murphies —"

"The devil with my accident, Mitchell!" At the third try, Richardson got his word in edgeways. "What about the spade?"

"The spade?" Mitchell decided not to settle for one small victory, even for the time being. "That was PC Jenkins, retired. And you know how many Jenkinses there are in Wales — retired and unretired? Even Policemen Jenkinses? 'Daft', they thought I was, at first. And then 'bloody daft' when I told them you'd lost a spade fifteen years ago, maybe. But now you wanted it back, and —"

"Paul —" Audley cut him off sharply "— that's enough. Just tell us about the spade."

Mitchell looked at him, not so much twitchingly now as tired. And angry with it. "Right, David. So . . . I won't tell you the rest of it, then — not even when I had to get Henry Jaggard to phone up the Chief Constable? After the Duty Sergeant told me to piss off —?"

Just for a spade! thought Audley. *With no poor crooked scythe to go with it — never mind any hammer-and-sickle. But . . . six men, in two countries, had died because of that spade, maybe. And, but for Jack Butler's 'error of judgement', and then Colonel Zimin's possible error, he himself might have been one of them, by God!*

"No." There might come a time to make a joke of this, if they outlived this day, and came safe home: Normandy had been like that. But this was neither the time nor the day. "Just tell us about the spade."

"Okay." Mitchell shrugged at him, and then at Richardson. "He didn't remember the bloody spade — not at first . . . He didn't even remember *you*, Major — not at first, when we gave him *your* name, no matter that you remembered *his*: he thought we were 'daft', too." Against all the odds, Mitchell brightened slightly. "But then, in the end, he did remember. Only not because of you, Major. It was the owners of the spade he remembered. Because they were unfinished business — that's what he called them: 'unfinished business' —"

"What owners?" Richardson was calm now, almost ingratiatingly so.

"The owners." Just as suddenly, Mitchell forgot to be angry. "The owners of the crashed van you reported —? It was their van . . . and they'd reclaimed it. And then they came back for their spade —" Now he was calm too. "Yes —?"

"Were they the drivers?" Richardson shook his head. "When I came on that van, it was on its side, in the road, with no one in it. And the windscreen was broken — it had hit the bank, and turned over . . . And there was blood all over the front seats. And . . . there was the spade there — on the floor —?"

"So you called the police, like a good citizen." Mitchell nodded. "But the owners said it was stolen. And the police never found the drivers. But that was what PC Jenkins remembered, eventually: he thought they'd be in the local hospital, cut-and-bruised . . . or, preferably, worse. Like, detained for observation, with suspected fractures, to make it easy for him. But they weren't . . . which he thought was odd. But . . . the spade wasn't odd, Major."

Richardson frowned at him. "But I told him to show it to his boss — to find out who it belonged to. I told him what he ought to do, in fact, damn it!"

"Well, he did find out that." Mitchell stared back at him defiantly. "The owners came in to collect it. And he only remembered that because he already knew them: they were a couple of 'general dealers'

from Abergavenny. Two right old lags he'd known for years . . .
receiving stolen property, plus a bit of sheep-stealing, and all that.
And he'd reckoned at first, once he'd traced the ownership of the
van, that they'd be the ones who'd turn up black-and-blue — that
they'd both been pissed when they crashed the van, and had run off
so that they could sober up and establish an alibi . . . Which they
had, of course — had an alibi: they said the van had been nicked from
their yard, and they didn't even know it was gone until the police
phoned them up." He shrugged again. "So there wasn't anything he
could do then. Because they clearly hadn't been bashed-up in any
accident — not on that occasion, anyway."

"Not on . . . that occasion?"

"Uh-huh." Mitchell grinned. "The real reason why he remembers
the pair of them was that he *did* get 'em in the end — for drunk-
driving, that is." He nodded. "It was about eighteen months
afterwards. Only this time they ran out of road in a more public
place, not on a little back-road. And this time it wasn't a van they
were in — it was a damn great three-year-old Jaguar. Which turned
out to be theirs. And that also surprised him, because they had been
near-bankrupt for years. But he reckoned they must have pulled off a
big burglary somewhere off his patch, probably over in England, and
got clean away with it. Which was another reason why he started to
remember everything. Because it narked him that they were able to
pay the drunk-driving fine so easily, after the magistrates threw the
book at them. And not even the five-year driving disqualification
hurt them, either. Because they then de-camped off to Spain after
that, to the 'Costa del Crime' where all the rich villains go. While the
poor old honest PC Jenkins himself retired on his police pension to
keep house with his sister —" Mitchell broke off as he realized that
Richardson was no longer listening to him, but was nodding to
Audley.

"That just about wraps it up — eh, David?"

"The spade ——" began Mitchell sharply. But then he broke off
again as he began to interpret his own story.

"They were sent to collect it." Richardson stared through Audley.

"They must have spotted me — *someone* must have spotted me . . . After all, I was hanging round for about an hour or more, that afternoon . . . late afternoon, early evening — I was late for dinner with . . . my friends at Pen-y-ffin." He focused on Audley again. "Being a good citizen! This is what I get for being a good citizen, David!" But there was no amusement in the reflection, only bitterness. And then the glazed stare returned. "The Russians couldn't have known for sure that I'd spotted it. So they had nothing to lose, and maybe everything to gain, by sending their two locals to pick it up . . . But they couldn't be sure —" He stopped as abruptly as Mitchell had done. And then his face became stone as his teeth clamped together. "So that wraps it up."

It did just about wrap it up, thought Audley — and not 'just about', either: the two venal 'locals' (*always go for professional petty criminals, that was what the book laid down: they were more easily scared into absolute obedience if you chose them carefully, balancing their relative lack of intelligence against their cost-effective greed and more limited ambition — and, most of all, the limits of their curiosity!*); and, indeed, the proof-of-that-pudding was there in this whole sequence of dusty events from long ago, from a minor accident on the Welsh border, via another one in a London street, to the presumed suicide of an elderly and impoverished Italian lady in her heavily-mortgaged *palazzo* on the Amalfi coast. Only, until now, it had been an unconnected sequence. And now that it was connected it looked quite different. "Yes, I suppose it does, Peter. So far, anyway."

"Wraps up what?" Mary Franklin looked from Richardson to Audley, understandably irritated by them both.

"I don't really need to see PC Plod — Constable Jenkins." Richardson ignored her. "Like I said last night, David . . . our best bet is the SAS at Hereford. All this territory is theirs, pretty much — it used to be, anyway. From the Forest of Dean and the Black Mountains, northwards . . . And they'll have contingency plans, you can bet — for the IRA, if not the Russians. And ——"

"*Dr Audley!*" Mary Franklin had graduated from annoyance to anger. "What is all this about?"

"The spade, Mary." It was Mitchell who spoke, nodding to her as he did so. "Major Richardson's little all-purpose spade. That's what it's all about — eh, David?"

Little spade — Mitchell had got there, then!

Little *all-purpose* spade, from long ago, carelessly lost — criminal carelessness, that would have been. But quickly recovered, nevertheless. And, meanwhile, that original mixture of bad-luck-accident and criminal carelessness had been attended to with the appropriate antidote of well-calculated ruthlessness —

"Every Russian soldier has a spade." Mitchell nodded to her again, almost dreamily. "Eh, David?"

It wasn't really surprising that Mitchell had got there on his own, any more than Mary Franklin's present incredulity was unsurprising. Getting there was what they were both paid to do, but Mitchell's private obsession with all things military had given him the edge this time. Indeed, if he hadn't been so stretched by other events, and so plain dog-tired, he might have got there last night, when the little all-purpose spade had surfaced again, at last.

"It was a *Russian* spade?" Spades, evidently, were tools in garden-sheds to Mary Franklin, with which gardeners dug gardens. "How do you know — ?" She spread the question among them. Only now she was less angry and surprised than frankly curious, to her credit.

"A *Spetsnaz* spade?" This time, at last, Mitchell addressed Richardson. But it wasn't really a question: Mitchell was moving on already, to unwrap what had been wrapped up, with all the excitement of understanding animating him, after all his recent humiliations, through not-knowing what was happening down to having to ask for help from Henry Jaggard last night, when all else had failed.

"What's a *Spetsnaz* spade?" Mary Franklin was on the same road now, but still at its beginning.

"Same as a Russian army spade, Mary." Mitchell still concentrated on Richardson. "Every Russian soldier's most important possession, after his Kalashnikov: the moment he stops shooting, he starts digging. Or paddling. Or cutting up his bread. Or . . . he sharpens it up, just in case?" Now it was Richardson who got the nod. "This one would have been *Spetsnaz*-sharp — right?" Then Mary Franklin got her nod again, at last. "That's for *throwing*, Mary. Because it's so well balanced that it's also one hell-of-a-weapon, in its own right —" Then Audley himself got the rest of the nod "— the best entrenching tool since the Romans, David? Isn't there some ancient text about a Legion driving off the barbarians with their spades, when they were attacked while building one of their forts, eh? You're our resident Roman expert —?"

"And you are our resident *Spetsnaz* expert, Dr Mitchell?" Richardson's voice had lost all of its animosity. "As my successor?" But then he smiled his old easy smile at Mary Franklin. "Dr Mitchell is absolutely right, Miss Franklin: it was a razor-sharp little spade I found. And it was . . . really, quite distinctive. Because it's a ruler, to measure . . . whatever needs to be measured — the length of the handle, and the length and breadth of the blade: 32 plus 18 equals 50, by 18 . . . centimetres of course. And matt green, overall." The smile faded slowly. "They've got one at Hereford, in their collection —" He looked around suddenly, first at the ruins, and then at the wooded hillsides above them "— I'd be delighted to show the Hereford one to you, if you still doubt me — and Dr Mitchell, Miss Franklin —?" Having made his point, he came back to Audley at last. "So, now that I really am one of your team, Dr Audley . . . shall we go, then?"

Audley felt the first spots of rain in the wind spatter his face, out of the darker clouds which had been drifting like smoke among the topmost trees of the ridges.

"Ah — David . . . Dr Audley —" Mary Franklin had assimilated everything she hadn't known before, both about Russian military entrenching-tools and about Major Peter Richardson. So now she was as sharp as a *Spetsnaz* spade turning over in the air before it struck "— I must report in, to say where we're going."

And she must do bloody-well more than that, now they had wrapped up fifteen-years-ago, to give Henry Jaggard all he needed for his horse-trading. "Yes, Miss Franklin." Apart from which, he badly needed to know what Henry Jaggard himself was doing, after his own advice from last evening, which not even Jaggard could safely have ignored; but which, equally, he couldn't ask for now, in front of Richardson, who wanted blood, not *glasnost!* "And perhaps you can also ask Henry to alert Hereford — the SAS — to expect us, while you're about it."

"And to get them off their arses, too." Outwardly, Richardson nodded, prudent, one-of-the-team-again commonsense, in agreement. But Audley caught more than that in his enthusiasm. "We need to seal off this whole area, if Lukianov is back in it. But not crudely, Miss Franklin: we've got to make sure he gets *in* first. Otherwise he'll back off — do you see?"

"Yes." For the first time Major Richardson got a Mary Franklin smile. "I do take your point, believe me." Then Audley received a Mary Franklin frown, which froze him with his mouth slightly open. "We have a phone cleared here, Dr Audley. So . . . if you would stay here — or, maybe get into my car, perhaps?" Mitchell received the rest of the frown. "And, if you care to go with the Major, Dr Mitchell — to Hereford? After I have reported in —?" The frown reversed itself, quite dazzlingly, as the original smile hit Richardson between the eyes again. "I'm sure Dr Mitchell knows the way, Major. And I will follow you, with Dr Audley."

She might not know about spades. But she knew what she wanted — and how to get it exactly, with that movement order, which split them neatly, beyond argument.

No trouble, Charlie had said.

But . . . *what a waste — that loyalty to Henry Jaggard!* Audley thought. "Very well, Miss Franklin. Right, Peter —?"

II

"Damn this weather." Mary Franklin squinted through the rain-blurred windscreen at the rear lights of the Porsche. "And we shouldn't be doing this, anyway. It isn't necessary."

"No." Audley settled back comfortably for the first time in days. And she smelt good, too. "Is that what Henry Jaggard said?" He could imagine what Henry Jaggard had said: *Don't let the bastards out of your sight, Miss Franklin.* "Don't worry, Paul will look after the Major. And I know the way, if we lose them. I know all this country quite well, as it happens. From my old days."

"Yes?" In spite of what he'd said (but because of what the egregious Jaggard had said?), she was determined not to lose the Porsche. But she gave him a quick glance, nevertheless. "How was that? You've never had anything much to do with the SAS, have you?"

It was hardly a question; she had his long professional *curriculum vitae* at her fingertips for sure, Jaggard would have seen to that too. "No, not much — hardly anything, really. But I meant the *old* old days, Miss Franklin . . . may I call you 'Mary', Miss Franklin?"

"Of course, Dr Audley." She had the measure of the Porsche now: she was a good driver, predictably. And the Porsche was also slowing down somewhat — also predictably, as its occupants began to talk to each other, each having no doubt decided that there was more to be gained from the other by a temporary alliance than by chalk-and-cheese antagonism. "What 'old' old days?"

"When I was a student. And after." The past pointed conveniently to the present. "The Middle Ages was my special period. And the Welsh Marches are very . . . medieval, Mary. Lots of big castles . . . Chepstow, Raglan up ahead . . . Pembroke, to the west."

"Yes?" She nodded politely into the murk. "You wrote a book about the Earl of Pembroke, didn't you?"

"William Marshall — yes." That would have been in the CV. "And lots of smaller castles. And middling ones, like the 'quadrilateral' — Skenfrith, Grosmont, White and Maerdy, from Marshall's time. Although Hubert de Burgh held them then, of course." He threw the names in deliberately. "They control the Monow valley, which is the way into Wales from Hereford. And out of it, into England — Hereford–Worcester, Hereford–Gloucester . . . and Cheltenham."

"Cheltenham?" Her interest stirred, as he intended it should.

"Indeed. And do you enjoy working for Henry Jaggard, Mary?"

The rain slashed down more heavily. "I thought we were talking about medieval castles, Dr Audley?"

"You ought to work for Research and Development. You'd have much more fun . ¿ . Did you do what I asked, last evening? Has Henry made contact with the Russians?"

She reached forward to increase the speed of the windscreen-wipers. "A meeting has been arranged for this afternoon. At 4pm —"

Audley frowned. "As late as that?"

"Is that late?" She peered at a signpost. "'St Briavels Castle' . . . Is that one of your 'middling' castles, Dr Audley?"

The Russians were in no hurry to talk. "They're still looking for Lukianov, I take it?"

"Yes." She shrugged. "It seems so. But Mr Aston and Mr Renshaw are both insistent that we don't do anything without consulting them." She glanced at him meaningfully. "Nothing must be done to disturb Gorbachev's visit to London after he's spoken to the UN in New York."

Bloody politicians. And also, perhaps, *bloody Henry Jaggard*, too. "Did Mr Jaggard let slip that I was close to finding Major Richardson, as I suggested?" He could see the river through the bushes, close to the road. But it was muddy and fast-flowing after the night's rain, not at all the sylvan Wye of his memory and the poet's imagination. "Did he?"

"I don't know, Dr Audley." Her lips tightened.

It wasn't like working for Jack Butler. Although even Jack might have had scruples about rocking the boat, the way things were. And that left only Jake Shapiro. But it wasn't going to be so easy to get through to Jake with Mary Franklin on his own back again.

"So what do you know?" He heard the snap in his voice. "Is there nothing new on Lukianov? Or the others — what they were up to, between them?"

She relaxed slightly. "We've heard from Washington . . . they believe Prusakov and Kulik sabotaged their respective computers, to remove information from them. And either they, or maybe General Lukianov shredded certain files in their Central Records. But that's all — except there's been a joint KGB/GRU committee set up, to try and reconstruct what's missing. And that's been working round the clock —" She frowned at him suddenly "— but you said —?"

That about wraps it up? Or does it? *Damn Henry Jaggard!*

The brake-lights of the Porsche glowed ahead, almost as though its driver had heard his uneasy thoughts. But other brake-lights were also winking on and off: they were approaching the junction of the Monmouth–Gloucester (and Cheltenham!) road, with the old bridge and the fast road to Hereford just ahead. And this early, in this weather, both the junction and the old bridge would be jammed with traffic.

"You said — " The movement of the Porsche once more cut her off. Keeping up with Major Richardson was still part of her priorities, until she'd got him safe under SAS lock-and-key. Or, him and that other bastard, Audley, for an informed guess.

"Yes." There was a jam of vehicles ahead of them. And one element of it, on the main road which they were trying to join, was a tail-back of military vehicles which was not giving way, complete with a goggled motor-cyclist who was holding back the traffic on the side road in his unit's favour. "Castles, I was saying: how the 'quadrilateral' group controls the road into England, to Hereford and Cheltenham — yes? Very interesting, they are, too. Skenfrith and Grosmont are in the middle of villages. But White and Maerdy are in the middle of nowhere, pretty much. Particularly Maerdy, up beyond Monmouth a few miles."

"Dr Audley —" Mary Franklin's fingers drummed on the steering-wheel impatiently "— you said —"

"To Hereford and Cheltenham, Miss Franklin — Mary. A few days' march, in the old days. But only half-an-hour's drive to Hereford now. And little more than an hour to GCHQ Cheltenham, using the motorways. Right?"

"What?" The last of the military convoy was passing. And maybe . . . it was at least just possible that he had done Henry Jaggard an injustice, at that. Or even that Henry Jaggard knew more than he'd let on, and was actually hedging his bets —?

"What are you saying, Dr Audley?" She was torn down the middle by his sudden shift from ancient to disturbingly modern, and the crawl of the Porsche ahead.

He smiled at her. "Up ahead, north beyond Monmouth, on the Maerdy road, Mary — that's where Major Richardson chanced upon that crashed van, with the *Spetsnaz* spade in it. So it was somewhere up there where they must have planted one of their arms dumps, back in the early 1970s, it looks like."

The Porsche was moving and they were moving with it, as though at the end of an invisible tow-rope.

"The old days, Miss Franklin." He spoke into her ear. She had a beautiful little shell-like ear, which didn't need an earring. "You won't remember them. And they probably wouldn't have been your concern, anyway. Just as they weren't mine . . . or Peter Richardson's as it happens. But everyone knew the theory of it, of course — it was a theoretical near-certainty that they had to be establishing such dumps, little by little."

They were on the bridge now, although still moving only yard-by-yard with the town beyond shrouded in rain-mist. So this would have been dangerous weather in the very old days, when the war-beacons, burning in the Black Mountains ahead to warn that the Welsh raiders were coming, would have been blotted out.

"Those were the Brezhnev days, Miss Franklin — post-Vietnam,

196

early Brezhnev . . . the deep Cold War days." *The days of Audley*, he thought: *the years of endurance!* Not like now — eh, Audley? "The targets were obvious. Like, the early warning stations. And the communications centres. And, of course, SAS headquarters and GCHQ Cheltenham — those were both prime targets, inevitably, for *Spetsnaz* assault groups. But their problem wasn't getting the men in, ahead of D-Day: there are a thousand ways of getting in good-looking fellows like General Lukianov — or Captain Lukianov, he would have been then . . . Lorry-drivers, tourists, mock-Irishmen to Milford Haven and Holyhead and Liverpool . . . sailors with a bit of shore-leave, with friendly passports." He paused. "The problem was their weapons and equipment — machine-guns and mortars, rocket-launchers and the rest. And plenty of Semtex, naturally."

The traffic had clogged up completely, so that she was able to face him again at last.

"A complete do-it-yourself arsenal, Miss Franklin. All neatly packed and ready to use — worth a fortune to any terrorist group." He could see from her lack of colour that every word had entered that pretty ear. "Arabs — why the PFLP, or Abu Nidal, you're going to ask? Or maybe it would suit the Arabs to make a deal with the IRA, on the side. Or they've got an export-cover of some sort — who knows? And they want to queer Yasser Arafat's pitch, if he gets too close to making a deal with Israel."

She drew a breath. "How do you know this?"

"I don't know it — any of it. But Lukianov was *Spetsnaz*. And no *Spetsnaz* arms dumps have ever been found. Only a couple of communications outfits, in North Wales and Yorkshire. And then only by pure accident." He shook his head. "I'm simply trying to string all that together, with what we've got, to make some sort of sense of it —" He frowned ahead. "What the hell's happening here, in the meantime — ?"

"I think the traffic-lights have broken down." She shook her head helplessly at him. "But . . . the spade, David — ?"

"Ah! That was the start of it, yes." He could see Mitchell nodding at Richardson through the rear-window of the Porsche. "What I think is, one of Lukianov's pals — or his men, rather — ran out of road one day, purely by accident. Because some of those little back-roads are tricky, believe me . . . But he'd maybe been making a delivery. And he was hurt, but he didn't want to hang around." He turned back to her. "He shouldn't have had his spade with him, that's for sure. But he did have it. And he was sufficiently knocked-about to forget it. And then he remembered too late. Because the police were there. And Peter Richardson."

The car jerked forward this time, reminding Audley of Mitchell at Naples. But then it stopped again. "Wasn't that a remarkable coincidence, Dr Audley?"

"If you like to call it that." She had been taught to mistrust coincidences. "I'd prefer to call it carelessness, plus accident, plus bad luck. Richardson was visiting one of his girlfriends, at Pen-y-ffin, just up the valley, on the way back from one of his trips to Hereford. Coincidence or not, that's what happened." But that, of course, had been the whole point: they *had* been taught the same thing — the Russians too. "When they sent someone back, the police were there. And so was Richardson. And once they'd picked up his name — or maybe even someone identified him, for all I know . . . Because they'd sure as hell be on the look-out for anyone who wasn't local, sniffing around the Maerdy area: you can be damn sure of *that*, anyway . . . But, when they picked up his name *or* his face they'd have checked up, one way or another . . . then they'd ask exactly the same questions, Miss Franklin: 'who's this Major Richardson?'. And then they'd start to wonder about coincidences, too. Just like you."

They were up to the far side of the bridge at last, and the cause of the confusion was instantly apparent.

"How's that for coincidence?" He craned his neck to emphasize what she could hardly miss. The traffic-lights had failed, and there were two angry drivers blaming each other for their recent collision, while a rain-soaked policeman attempted to sort out the doubled traffic jam. "You were right about the lights. So what does that make this? It looks more like carelessness, plus bad luck and accident to me."

"Yes . . ." But for a moment she was more concerned to remain behind the Porsche ". . . maybe."

"No 'maybe' about it after that. They'd have had Peter Richardson on file. And me with him — because, we were at the sharp end in Italy the year before, Mary. And they certainly knew all about me. So when Lukianov decided to use his special knowledge, we were part of all the information which had to be erased from the record, just in case. Along with everything else from this other little episode."

"Erased —?" Mitchell was accelerating. But there looked like another related traffic jam ahead. "But . . . if they thought Richardson was on to them —" She slammed her brakes on, slithering to within an inch of Mitchell's pride-and-joy "— sorry! But . . . his accident, what about that?" She shook her head at him. "Why didn't they kill him?"

"Maybe they bodged it. Or 'Murphy' did . . . Or maybe they were smart."

"Smart?"

"They weren't sure about him. He'd resigned from R and D . . . And they'd got their little spade back. And killing him wouldn't have seemed so 'accidental', they might have reckoned — not if he *was* still working for us . . . It all depends how much they'd got in their dump, too: if they'd only just started they might have been able to re-locate. And then all they really needed was a little time — just to slow him up, and take his mind off his work." He nodded, as much to himself as to her. "Because that's what they damn-well did, anyway: they took his mind off everything, Mary, is the way it looks." The second traffic jam was moving again. "The proof of the pudding is always in the eating, don't you think?"

"Until now." She put her foot down. "But I still don't see why Lukianov was so worried about you and Richardson — after he'd removed you from the record."

"Yes. But now we're talking about Lukianov. And the other two . . . And that's quite different." They were almost free now, on the approach to a big new roundabout. "I don't know . . . It's possible that Lukianov wanted to get rid of his partners, as well as

Peter and me. And that would have been a neat way of doing it. Or he may have been afraid that there was still someone alive who could fill in enough of the blanks in the record to point the Russians back to the Richardson episode, if not to the location of his arms dump. In which case they might even try to make a deal of some sort with us — the sort of deal *I've* suggested to Henry Jaggard." He shook his head sadly. "Isn't that par for the course now?"

"What d'you mean?"

"What do I mean?" What he really meant was the old *Audley* days were very different from the new *Renshaw-Jaggard-Gorbachev* ones. But he could never explain that. "I suppose . . . they don't want trouble here, any more than we do. So . . . I was rather hoping they might just come clean and apologize. And then pool resources, for the good of *glasnost* and *perestroika*." He studied her beautiful pink ear again. "They must have some sort of idea what Lukianov is up to by now. And . . . Henry Jaggard would love that sort of deal — wouldn't he?"

But she wasn't listening to him: she was swinging the wheel furiously —

"What the hell —?" The car swerved violently, and the driver behind hooted at them.

"What —?" He had been momentarily distracted by the extension of his own innermost thought, which had filled him with sudden bitterness: *that these were the days of Henry Jaggard most of all, and that the days of Audley, when everything had been so black and white, were passing — if not already past?* "What?"

"He's not going to Hereford — Mitchell." She hung on to the Porsche's tail grimly. "He's going back into the town."

Audley looked around. They had been on a new dual-carriageway before the roundabout, neither of which had been there in the old days, any more than this maelstrom of modern traffic.

"No. It's all right, Mary." Memory came to his aid. "That must be the new route to Hereford. He's just taking the old one."

His own reassuring words relaxed her. But they turned him inwards on himself again, with their unintentional double-meaning.

200

The old roads he had travelled, in the days of Audley — of Audley and Sir Frederick Clinton — had been tortuous, and very dangerous sometimes too, at their black spots. But at least they had been mostly clear and well-signposted, and he had always known where he was going. Whereas on Henry Jaggard's congested multi-lane political motorways —

"No he's not," snapped Mary sharply.

No, he wasn't! They had twisted and turned. And now they were undeniably on a side-road . . . *going where —?*

Then he saw the little river beside him, and the question was instantly answered. And another one, as yet unasked, with it!

"This is the beginning of the Monow valley, Mary. We cross the river over a little bridge just ahead, to the left." Such a little river, to have so many castles: that was what he remembered. "Skenfrith and Grosmont are up ahead, then. With Maerdy and White to the west." And no prizes for guessing which, now. "But Maerdy's the nearest. And that's where they're going — Richardson's going to show Paul where he found the spade."

Mary slapped the driving-wheel angrily. "That's ridiculous!" She reached forward to flash the car-lights just as the Porsche disappeared round a corner ahead. "Damn them!"

"Yes." She wanted Richardson safely-confined. She wanted them all safely-confined.

"I said we'd be at Hereford by ten." This time she caught the Porsche. But Mitchell too turned his blind eye to the angry flash in his mirror, just as Audley had expected him to do. "Damn! How far is this village — Maerdy?"

"Not very far . . . at this speed." With Richardson beside him, Mitchell was demonstrating his car's performance, it looked like. "It's not a village. It's just a ruined castle, Mary. With . . . I think there's a farm nearby, if I remember correctly . . . All private, not National Trust. Or it was —" How many years ago? God! Too many! "— or it was when I was last there, anyway." He could almost sympathize with her, But he had to remember also that she was Henry Jaggard's woman, not his. "We shouldn't be too late. Because it's only a few miles on to the Abergavenny–Hereford main road, near Ewyas Harold. And that's an interesting place, too: a pre-Conquest castle site, Mary. Before 1066 and All That. Very rare indeed. In fact —"

"Spare me the castles, Dr Audley."

"Very well." He had never subscribed to the theory that angry women became more beautiful until now. But he saw also that she was not just angry. "What I should have said is . . . from Ewyas Harold to Hereford can't be more than ten or twelve miles, Miss Franklin. It's just . . . some people measure distance from one public house to the next. But my knowledge of the Welsh borders happens to be historical. So I measure from castle to castle, I'm afraid —"

"You should be afraid of more than that, Dr Audley —" She was too busy matching Mitchell's fierce decelerations and accelerations to look at him, but her voice was as tightly-controlled as her driving "— you should be afraid because we don't know where General Lukianov is right now — *damn them!*"

"Lukianov?" As Audley peered ahead the brake-lights of the Porsche glared at him suddenly, and he caught a glimpse of the vehicle beyond which had forced Mitchell to slow down. "Yes . . . well I don't think you should worry too much there. Not any more."

"Why not?" They were suddenly on all of two hundred yards of straight road, down into a dip and then uphill towards a crest. So she could actually frown at him.

He mustn't smile. "Because he's finally caught up with that military convoy we tangled with near Monmouth." He pointed ahead. "See that truck just disappearing over the top — and the motor-cyclist? He overtook us a few miles back."

"Yes —" She had switched back quickly to the road ahead "but — ?"

"Nobody's going to try anything with the British Army leading the way — Lukianov or any of his clients. General Lukianov will be lying very low right now if he's anywhere on this road. Having the army ahead is providential, don't you think?" He paused deliberately. "Or maybe it isn't."

The army disappeared over the brow of the hill as he spoke, its place being taken an instant later by the Porsche. "What d'you mean?"

"I mean —" he hated the next bit "— maybe your Mr Jaggard hasn't been so slow off the mark after all. If he had any sort of informal contact with their new man in the embassy, and they have any sort of idea what Lukianov *might* be up to . . . They might have suggested that a military presence in this general area would be prudent, even if they don't know the exact map reference. Just vehicles and men swanning around would be enough . . . Not that it matters, either way — whether it's just our good luck or Henry being smart. It amounts to the same thing, because Lukianov won't know which. But he'll have to assume the worst — at least for the time being."

They breasted the hilltop in turn, and for a moment the countryside was spread out below them: a rich landscape fading into the rain-mist, as deceptively peaceful now as it would have seemed in those other treacherous times when the quadrilateral castles had been garrisoned to protect it from the Welsh — when Moscow had been no more than a muddy provincial town and the Middle East 'the Holy Land' of exotic crusading legend.

Then the rearmost of the army vehicles disappeared from sight among the trees and hedgerows, and the countryside closed in again on them as they descended on to the valley floor.

"Anyway, as long as we're behind them —" An idea struck him, out of nowhere, as he broke the silence to reassure her, cutting him short.

The idea blossomed, as he tested it —

(They were slowing down now, because Mitchell had been again forced to slow down himself, at the tail-end of the convoy, which had itself telescoped into what must have been its original compactness before the traffic jams around Monmouth had opened it out. And, sooner or later on this twisty road, long before they reached the main road near Ewyas Harold, it would surely have to stop altogether. *And that would be the moment —*)

"Mary . . . whatever they're doing here — the military . . ." He completed the test as he spoke: whether he was right or wrong — or half-right, half-wrong, or whatever . . . and even if these really *were* the last days of Audley, if he was wrong, it didn't matter. Just as it didn't matter whether this military presence was due to Henry Jaggard or pure fluke. "Most likely, if Jaggard hasn't had them ordered in, then they'll be on their way to an exercise in the Black Mountains." He stared at her. "So . . . why don't we pull rank and cancel their exercise?"

"*What —?*"

"Cancel their exercise. Put 'em into Maerdy Castle, as their headquarters. Patrols out — ten-mile radius." He nodded enthusiastically. "If Lukianov is still loose, there has to be some sort of emergency still in force. And if I'm right about Richardson and his spade, and a *Spetsnaz* arms dump . . . Charlie Renshaw said we weren't to cause any trouble. So this way we'll be preventing trouble — Lukianov trouble *and* Russian trouble, Mary."

She thought for a moment. "*If* you are right . . . But, if you aren't?"

"Then I shall have egg on my face." It would be Henry Jaggard who would have to accept the egg officially, that was what she was thinking. And while that only made the idea more attractive to him it would hardly further her career. "You can blame me."

"I'm not thinking about blame."

He kicked himself. "No — of course. You're thinking about Lukianov — quite rightly." He nodded. "Just as I am thinking also of Berlin. And Capri, too." That was a better line. "And Peter Richardson, Miss Franklin."

She stared at the car in front, without answering.

They slowed down to a snail's-pace now, crawling past a derelict little cottage, boarded up and forlorn, but still with the last flowers of autumn colouring its overgrown garden.

"No." Mary Franklin came to a decision. "If the Russians aren't in any hurry . . . we can arrange matters better from Hereford, Dr Audley."

They stopped altogether.

Audley also came to a decision. "Well, on my head be it, then."

It was just like with Elizabeth: when you were out of a car you were free. But he had to move quickly once again, before the convoy started up again. Even as it was, he could only see the two rearmost trucks, stationary on the bend ahead of the Porsche.

Mitchell lowered his window. "What the hell are you doing, David?"

The bend was a stroke of luck: there was no way Mitchell could overtake the army here. "You stay put, Paul."

He could feel the rain on his face as he approached the caped and goggled motor-cyclist at the side of the truck. "Where's your officer?"

The motor-cyclist pointed at the truck.

Audley walked round the truck. If there was an officer in it, he wouldn't be driving. Along the road now he could see several more vehicles, including a Jeep-like one with his hood up against the rain. It seemed more likely that the officer would be there, but he decided to start with the motor-cyclist's silent directions.

He banged the rain-smeared window. "Open up!"

The window came down slowly, revealing a young fresh-faced soldier in a combat jacket and a beret with the Mercury-figure badge of the Royal Signals. "Yes, sir?"

No indication of rank. But the voice was educated. "Are you an officer?"

"No, sir. Corporal, sir." The good old army smells of oiled metal and wet clothes accompanied this information. "Can I help you?"

"What unit are you?"

"Royal Signals — TA." As though to support the corporal, a radio in the cabin began to crackle. "Can I help you, sir?"

Territorial Army — therefore *not* Henry Jaggard. But that accounted for both the educated voice and the politeness: the young man was probably a British Telecom engineer when he wasn't playing soldiers. And since privatization they had all become gratifyingly polite. "Yes, you can, corporal." He pointed to the radio equipment. "Can you call up your officer on that."

The young man nodded. "I can, sir. But what is the trouble?"

Audley could feel the rain running down his face. "Call him up. Tell him that there is an emergency." He felt trapped by this useless helpfulness as the corporal continued to look inquiringly at him.

Then he heard the sound of footsteps on the road. Another TA man was striding towards him purposefully, heedless of the succession of muddy puddles beside the overgrown road-verge. And although he appeared less than overjoyed at Audley's intrusion, his scowl bore the stamp of authority.

But then the scowl vanished. "Can I help you, sir?"

Lord, another telecom recruit — same words, same voice! "I hope you can. Are you in command here?"

The soldier shifted position slightly, peering past Audley, first at the Porsche and then at the plebeian Vauxhall behind it. "No, sir." He came back to Audley, frowning slightly. "We are moving, sir. You will not be delayed on the road. We are moving." He started to turn away.

"Wait!" Audley heard his own long-disused army snap-of-command voice crack. But before he could start to feel foolish at the sound of it (as he had so often done all those years ago, when he had also played soldiers' games, as a lamb in wolf's clothing) he saw with relief that it still worked: the TA man stopped in mid-turn, stiffening automatically with the Pavlovian response of the regular soldier rather than a part-time amateur.

"That's better." The old army habit of bloody-mindedness-in-uncertainty came back to him as the soldier faced him again, expressionless now — still more like a regular. But that, perhaps, was what he had once been. "Now — I demand to see your officer. At once, man."

The soldier's expression didn't change, but the one hand which was visible beside his combat jacket clenched into a fist. "That is not possible."

"No?" Audley was aware that he was wet, and getting wetter all the time. But he was also soaked in genuine bloody-mindedness now, as he reached inside his jacket for his identification warrant. "Well, you will damn-well make it possible." He thrust the card at the soldier's face. "Right."

The soldier blinked at the thing for a moment. Then his lips began to spell out its contents, with word-by-word slowness until the sound of a car-door opening made him look up, past Audley.

"David — " Mitchell came into view " — what the hell are you up to?"

"I am enlisting the Army." He decided to enlist the ancient jargon as well. "It's called 'Aid to the Civil Power', Dr Mitchell." The phrase curiously re-animated a memory from the most distant past, much more than half-a-lifetime away, of a boring lecture at OCTU on military law, in which the equally bored lecturer had merely repeated what Officer Cadet Audley had read in the relevant pamphlet; but which, he had to admit to himself, had mostly contemplated workers' unrest, and nothing like the presence of General Lukianov and his Arab (or IRA) associates in a very different age of the world.

"What for?" Mitchell wiped the rain from his face.

"To re-garrison Maerdy Castle and this area, pending an outbreak of *glasnost* and *perestroika*, Dr Mitchell — " As he spoke he threw the words at the British Telecom supervisor/ex-regular. And then, from the gratifying effect they had, decided to go further " — until the Russians help us in this matter . . . with Lukianov still at large, Dr Mitchell . . . we must help ourselves."

That stopped Mitchell in his tracks as effectively as it had done the TA man, who was still gaping at him in astonishment, with all the metal fillings in his teeth showing. And, in the poor devil's defence, the only truly memorable thing that the OCTU lecturer had said (off the record) was that whenever the Civil Power turned to the Army for help the best place to be was somewhere else, preferably as far away as possible, because the Army always got the blame for the disaster which inevitably followed, as night follows day.

But now he was Civil Power himself.

"Don't just stand there, man." He snapped the card away from in front of the unfortunate man's nose. "You've read the words: I am authorized to call for assistance from members of Her Majesty's Forces as well as the civil police. And that includes you. And that is what I am now doing. So . . . go and get your officer — *on the double!*"

The TA man had closed his mouth. But his jaw was set firm now and for a moment Audley was aware of a battle of wills being fought in silence. And he couldn't let that continue.

"Did you hear —"

"Yes." The man almost spat the word, without any polite 'sir' accompanying it this time. So, for a guess, that anonymous combat jacket concealed sergeant's stripes, if not actually the sacred insignia of the unit's squadron sergeant-major, who was unaccustomed to such bullying, either military or civilian — and least of all in front of one of his junior NCOs whose pale face was a picture of astonishment framed in the window of the truck beside them.

"David —" As the hypothetical sar'-major turned away, breaking into splashing double-time as ordered, Mitchell pulled him away towards the rear of the truck "— David, have you gone crazy?"

Had he gone crazy? "No. I'm simply obeying Charlie Renshaw's orders."

"What d'you mean?"

In the end, it was Jake Shapiro's advice he was taking, Audley realized. Henry Jaggard might be sitting on his hands, practising a wait-and-see policy; and even the Russians themselves, hampered presumably by a similar need to avoid embarrassing trouble in England, also appeared to be playing for time. But Jake had been scared, and it had been Jake's fear which had disturbed his own sleep last night on the ancient and uncomfortable camp-bed in Sophie's attic. And, apart from all of that — and even if Jake's fear proved to be unfounded — what he was doing would irritate Jaggard most satisfyingly.

"This is supposed to be a preventative operation." He turned on Mitchell haughtily. "'No trouble' is what everyone keeps telling me. But we've already lost three days saying 'No trouble' to each other, it seems to me — three days since Berlin, and thirty-six hours or more since Capri, and we're still saying 'No trouble', as though nothing happened there. And Lukianov's still free as air." He observed a little red umbrella blossom beside the Vauxhall. "So, okay then! 'No trouble', is what I'm trying to ensure, by spreading these poor devils all around here as obviously as possible right now, in the rain, to slow Lukianov up if he's here —" And now Richardson himself was coming to join them: and 'No trouble' probably wouldn't suit him at all. But the hell with Peter Richardson! "— or, if he isn't —"

"If he isn't, there'll be hell to pay, David. Taking over the British Army, as though you're God Almighty —" Mitchell shook his head helplessly "— that is, if they're fools enough to be —" he stopped suddenly "— Christ!"

"To be taken over?" Audley swung towards another new sound, even though he recognized it instantly from his long-dead youth: the trucks were disgorging their unhappy occupants in the rain. He turned back to Mitchell and the others, who were staring wide-eyed past him at the explosion of military activity he had caused. "Well, it would seem that 'Aid to the Civil Power' still works, anyway. Even if it is only the Territorial Army. But that'll do for a start."

"The Territorial Army — ?" Words failed Mitchell.

"What's going on?" Richardson looked from side to side as two pairs of stony-faced Territorials doubled past them down the road, old-fashioned FN rifles at the high port, equipment squeaking and clanking unmusically.

"You may well ask, Peter." Mitchell paused as one of the soldiers stopped beside his car. "It would appear that we're being protected from General Lukianov and his Ay-rab legions — presumably with empty rifles . . . Is that what they are supposed to be doing, Dr Audley?"

That was actually somewhat embarrassing now, Audley decided as he watched the two men who weren't guarding their cars disappear into the hedgerows on each side of the road. But it looked very much as though the sergeant-major had assumed that his order had involved an instant emergency, however incomprehensible, while they must still be a mile or two from the Maerdy Castle turning. "How near are we to where you found the crashed van — and the spade, Peter?"

Richardson shrugged. "It's just up the road from here, I think."

"You think?"

"Yeah. I think." Richardson gave him a disinheriting look. "I don't expect they've erected a monument there, but I reckon I'll know the place. It was on a blind corner near a farm track, where the road dips down. A damn dangerous place if you're not careful. That was why I stopped originally, and hung on there. It was . . . this was my old shortcut from Hereford via Pen-y-ffin, to Monmouth and the Forest of Dean. I always liked to drive through the forest, to Gloucester, off the main road . . . if I'd had a few drinks with — with the person I used to visit." He looked around morosely, with the rain already plastering down his frosted black hair. "I used to admire the scenery. God only knows why!"

The motor-cyclist's engine roared into life, re-directing Audley's attention up the road, towards the sergeant-major, who was returning with his officer at last.

He squared his shoulders and moved to meet them.

"What the hell!" exclaimed Mitchell loudly behind him. "Get away from my car, damn you — !"

Mitchell's explosive anger spun him round on his heel, so that he caught the whole sequence of movement together: the TA man opening the driver's door of the Porsche — *and, another soldier appearing round the back of the truck — the fresh faced corporal who had been so uselessly polite —*

Only now he wasn't being polite.

"Halt!" The corporal's sub-machine-gun, as well as the corporal himself, barred Mitchell's way. And there was something about both of them that backed the command brutally, turning the world upside down as it stopped Mitchell in his tracks.

"You will come now." The voice of the hypothetical sar'-major/ British Telecom supervisor was like that of the polite corporal who had stopped being afraid as well as polite — no longer polite.

Audley turned slowly towards the voice, trying to steady himself as he met disaster face-to-face as he wiped the rain from his face.

"Ah! Colonel Zimin." That steadying slowness helped him to discipline his own voice. "I was hoping that it would be you —" But, critically, he could still hear the slur of fear in his words. So he must do something about that instantly "— but . . . I was afraid for a moment that your men might be trigger-happy, so far from home. I'm glad to find them as well-disciplined as this." If he could have smiled then, he would have done. But his mouth was still under orders from his guts. "I must congratulate you on them. In other circumstances they might have fooled me, even."

Zimin shook his head. "Dr Audley . . ." But then he stopped.

Audley caught the faint echo of his own words in the silence between them.

So far from home!

"Yes, Colonel." This wasn't Capri. And, also, he wasn't alone this time: whatever Zimin might suspect, he couldn't be sure. Or, even if his suspicions were close to certainty, his guts ought to be twisting just as much, by God! "But, I don't think you've met my colleagues — or have you?" He turned to Mitchell and Mary Franklin. "Mary —?" He decided to omit Richardson from the introduction. "Paul —?" Now back to Zimin, who must be expecting a third name. "Miss Franklin is representing Mr Henry Jaggard, of course. And Dr Mitchell is Sir Jack Butler's representative, as you must be well aware." *Now for Peter Richardson!* "And Major Richardson is why we're here — eh?" He nodded everything after Capri into the balance finally. "The Major and I are old comrades, you understand?"

"Colonel Zimin." Mary Franklin held her umbrella with both hands.

"Yes." A bead of rain ran down Mitchell's cheek as he looked down his nose at the Russian. "I hope that man of yours who's playing with my car also knows how to drive it, Colonel. Does he?"

Richardson, who was to blame for everything, said nothing.

Zimin assimilated those three different contributions to his problems without acknowledging any of them. "If you and your colleagues will come with me, please — ?"

"With pleasure." Audley hastened to accept the invitation on everyone's behalf. With that morning rush-hour in Monmouth behind them they had still been lucky that there had been so little traffic on the side-road, to complicate this meeting further. But even with that motor-cyclist behind them (and maybe another one ahead of him, speaking just as good Queen's/British Telecom English politely, to delay any late travellers-to-work), it would be advisable to co-operate. "Shall we go, then — ?"

He moved to follow Zimin down the line of vehicles, conscious not so much of the others behind him as of the *ersatz* Royal Signals sar'-major in the rear, with the corporal appearing in each gap, until the Russian stopped beside a truck with its canvas hood open for them. Then he stood aside.

Zimin assisted Mary Franklin into the truck, but then also stood aside.

"*Spetsnaz*." Richardson scowled the statement at him.

Paul Mitchell, for his part, looked as though he was still thinking more about his Porsche than his skin. "'No trouble', David — ?"

The inside of the truck smelt like the British Army, as of old. Which was interesting, academically, because that was what it was supposed to be, although not what it was. And that was another plus for *Spetsnaz*, because all armies had their own distinctive smell: wasn't that what that old general from 1916 had once said to him?

But then, of course, the old general had never envisaged quite this sort of experience.

III

I⊤ wasn't Maerdy Castle, of course: it would never have been anywhere so romantically appropriate for an arms dump (albeit not for the conquest and subjugation of Wales this time, Audley thought grimly). Although private and protected by its relative inaccessibility, the castle would never have been safe enough from interested trespassers (of whom he himself had been one, so long ago — long even before the days of Lukianov and Peter Richardson). Nor, for that matter, would its overgrown ruins either have offered any secure and weather-proof cover for the dump's contents or the necessary accommodation for its guardians.

Only a farm (a private house would have been too small, if not too obvious) would have answered all those needs. And perhaps that had been the starting point in the Russians' desperate reconstruction of that one vital piece of information which the computer conspirators had erased from the records with all the rest, both essential and inessential: the co-ordinates of its map reference.

Only a farm! But that was easy to say now that he was actually looking at it. Given time, perhaps he would have got this far, eliminating one possibility after another to pinpoint this place after Richardson had narrowed the search area. And yet that itself was only an excuse, in dismal retrospect: there was never enough time, and in spite of Jake's warning he had squandered what he had had of it: he had allowed himself to be trapped by self-admiration of his wonderful memory, which had come up with so many answers but had foiled him in the end.

"Dr Audley — can you help me?"

"Help — ?" He realized that he had forgotten everything else, and everyone else with it, in his contemplation of the muddy farmyard

213

and his own foolishness after he had climbed out of the truck. But what had been easy for him in the damp wreck of his second-best suit was proving not so easy for Mary Franklin. "Yes — I'm sorry, Miss Franklin."

She was light as a feather, and soft with it. And she still smelt good.

"Thank you, Dr Audley." Liberated from the discomfort of the truck, she immediately put up her little red umbrella again, smoothed down her skirt, and then looked around as though she owned the place, ignoring only the *Spetsnaz* corporal who was covering them again with his automatic rifle. "Where are we?"

She didn't just *smell* good, she *was* good. Because, for all that she must be bloody scared and was standing in thick mud, she hadn't lost her cool: she appeared as self-possessed as she might have been on an unfortunately inclement day at Henley or Ascot. And that served to concentrate his mind properly, away from self-pity. "Russian headquarters in Wales, Miss Franklin." He pointed towards another truck, which had been outside a tumbledown barn. "But I rather think they're busy pulling out now."

"Yes." She watched two curiously-garbed *Spetsnaz* men place a small metal container in a larger one, which was then itself hydraulically lifted, to disappear into the truck. "I suppose we should be pleased."

"Pulling out." Richardson joined them. "Just like Afghanistan, eh?"

It seemed that Mary Franklin had set the tone. Or perhaps he himself had pointed the way towards it, with his desperate bluff on the roadside, when Zimin had appeared. And they had had time to draw their own conclusion from that in the truck, while silenced by the corporal's presence as much as the muzzle of his rifle. Or (but with these three it was perhaps unlikely) it might be that old resignation he remembered from the war, when that curious jokey lethargy had set in before they moved up to the start-line on what looked like the dawn of a bad day: *When rape is inevitable,* 'Daddy' Higgs had always said, *you just lie back and enjoy it, sir.*

214

"But where are all the rest of them?" Richardson looked round at the otherwise empty farmyard. "I don't doubt that the farmer and his wife are heading for foreign parts by now — like those bastards who hired out their van for me to find . . . yes?" He came back to Audley. "Or are they going to load up one-by-one, and take the stuff somewhere else — David?"

"*My God!*" exclaimed Paul Mitchell. "*God, David!*"

Mitchell had come out last. But then he had taken several steps beyond them, towards the second truck, before being confronted by their own truck's driver and shepherded back towards them. And now he was staring at Audley.

"*David* —" Mitchell rolled his eyes at the corporal, whose rifle was pointed directly at him. Then the sound of Zimin's command car, rather than the rifle, cut him off.

Audley watched as the vehicle slowed slightly to negotiate the farmyard gateway. Then, without warning, it accelerated past them, spraying mud in all directions before it skidded to a halt blocking their view of the loading.

"*David* —" Mitchell's face and clothing were mud-spotted "*— did you see —?*"

"See what?" He had been halfway to reminding himself simply that Mitchell was still twitchy, and never with better reason. But that wasn't it at all.

"*Not guns, David.*" Somewhere on the other side of the vehicle Zimin was shouting orders angrily. But meanwhile Mitchell was hissing at him like a ventriloquist without his dummy. "And not Semtex either — you don't have to handle Semtex like that . . . Those containers, David — *it looks like Sarin, for Christ's sake!*"

Zimin appeared between their truck and his own vehicle, his anger still contorting his features quite uncharacteristically. "Inside the house, Dr Audley — at once, if you please."

Sarin!

"Yes, Colonel." Even without the corporal's rifle, he wasn't going to argue with that anger, now that they had seen what they had seen. Because Zimin had every right to be angry: either that loading should

215

have been completed, or it ought not to have been started, that anger betrayed. So now, whatever deep trouble they'd been in before, they were in deeper.

The farmhouse was mean-looking: a low stone building with dirty windows and flaking paint. And when his eyes became accustomed to the gloom of the kitchen he saw that its interior matched its exterior: the sink was full of unwashed pots, and the remains of breakfast hadn't been cleared — tell-tale signs of a recent occupancy which, after fifteen years, had ended forever this morning.

Then the gloom returned as Zimin's figure filled the low doorway.

"Colonel —" With no defence, he had to attack first "— I will not bore you with official protests. So shall we take them as read?" He heard himself speak in the same slightly too-precise English of Zimin's own *Spetsnaz* men, who had undoubtedly been chosen and trained to speak the language in support of their unremarkably Anglo-Saxon features. "And, in return, you will dispense with empty threats, eh?"

"Empty threats, Dr Audley?" Zimin had recovered his poise.

It was that damned Sarin which was the problem, thought Audley. But, then, that Sarin had been the problem all along: the problem . . . and the high card in Lukianov's hand, which had enabled him to make his own terms with any of the world's terrorist groups. And, for a guess, it wouldn't have taken the Russians long to realize as much, even while it had taken them longer to reconstruct the past accurately enough to bring them here. Indeed, that fully accounted both for their almost heedless urgency thereafter and their final success: guns and explosives — all the paraphernalia *Spetsnaz* units needed for their work — that would have been bad enough. But *Sarin* — Sarin in any one of its specialized varieties and delivery-forms — would have been as unforgivable world-wide when publicly traced back to them as it would have been dreadful beyond imagination in terrorist hands.

"Yes." That was the trouble; it *had* been beyond his imagination, even though it shouldn't have been. But . . . maybe it hadn't been beyond Jake's? That, at least, would account for the Israelis' urgent desire to help. And perhaps that now would have given substance to his bluff. "If you are contemplating a tragic road accident for all four of us, I wouldn't advise it, Colonel. We've always suspected that your *Spetsnaz* caches might include chemical weaponry — even before the Israelis reminded us, just recently. Nerve gas is such an economical weapon, isn't it?" He cudgelled his memory for informed window-dressing to back up his words. But his knowledge was too minimal to risk. "What did you say it might be, Dr Mitchell?"

"Mmmm . . ." Mitchell pretended to consider the question again for a moment. And then shrugged. "Back in the early seventies . . . Sarin-D would have been the chemical — that's a quick-dispersing variety. And then the warheads out there —" He jerked his head towards the window "— they can be used with ordinary hand-held RPG recoilless launchers. Or adapted Sagger wire-guided missiles, maybe. They're both about the right vintage. And there are a lot of launchers on the market now. The Russians have been supplying 'em to all their Middle East clients for years. Long before my time."

"Yes." But Zimin knew all that, of course. So now was the moment to unmask Jake. "You know my old friend Colonel Shapiro, of Mossad, is back in London, Colonel? He's been very helpful to us. Because his country feels particularly vulnerable, if any of your property fell into the wrong hands . . . Just as, of course, mine also does. Since the IRA has such good links with certain Arab groups, eh?"

Zimin stared at him in silence for a long moment. "What are you proposing, Dr Audley?"

"Ah!" Audley clasped his hands behind his back so that the Russian could not observe them shaking. "Well . . . like you, Colonel — like your Government . . . *my* Government wants neither trouble, nor unfortunate . . . accidents. That is why I am here." He nodded towards Mary. "With Miss Franklin as Mr Jaggard's representative, you understand?"

Zimin nodded cautiously. "That is indeed why I am here too, Dr Audley."

So far, so good. "And General Lukianov's Arab clients? Where are they?" He tightened his voice deliberately. "I do not doubt for one moment that your *Spetsnaz* unit is well able to handle them. But, since this is not your country, that might cause problems, don't you think?"

Zimin relaxed fractionally. "That problem has been dealt with."

"Dealt with how?"

Zimin shook his head. "It need not concern you, Dr Audley." The merest ghost of a smile crossed his lips. "Our problem . . . is our property. And when we have removed that, there will be no problem at all."

They were back to square one. With all due preparations made, the removal of one small truckload of nerve gas projectiles wouldn't pose any great insuperable problems for the Russians now that they had pulled out all their stops, judging by the smoothness with which this *Spetsnaz* unit had been activated — even though evacuation might not have been included in its original contingency plans. But that still left all four of them out on a very dangerous limb, thanks to his criminal complacency —

"That's not quite good enough, Colonel."

"Madam —?" Zimin had been watching him, so that Mary Franklin's snap caught him unprepared, from the flank. "Not —?"

"Not good enough — no." She pursed her lips. "We require more than that."

"Madam?" Zimin relaxed slightly, and the ghost-smile returned. And then he shook his head. "You . . . *require* —?"

It didn't necessarily mean that he was a chauvinist-pig, thought Audley even as he clutched at her confidence so desperately that he nodded agreement to it: it might simply be that he was married only to his career, and didn't know any better — that he had never seen that expression on a wife's face. Or a daughter's, even —?

"Colonel Zimin . . . you don't seriously believe that Mr Jaggard would send me here, with Dr Audley, like this —" The edge-of-contempt was razor sharp. "And Dr Audley after his meeting with you on Capri, Colonel. And after Berlin, too?"

Zimin stopped relaxing: now he looked as though he was remembering his lessons about pretty faces, belatedly.

"Miss . . . Franklin?" The Colonel was a fast-rememberer. Or a fast learner, maybe?

"We took Major Richardson last night, Colonel." Only the very slightest emphasis conveyed her contempt for all military ranks. "So we have been monitoring this area ever since, as a precaution. And . . . notwithstanding what Dr Audley has just told you, we still weren't sure whether it was conventional arms or chemical weapons — also, in spite of what Colonel Shapiro warned us of, *Colonel* — yes?"

That final rank-emphasis was inspired, thought Audley admiringly: what a perfect little liar she was! And —

"But Mr Jaggard insisted that we must take the worst-case view, Colonel Zimin." She continued before Zimin could get the first word out of his opening mouth. "And that was after your commanding officer delayed his meeting with him, to this afternoon — do you understand?"

"Madam —" The last three words had been not so much razor-sharp as *laser*-sharp, almost standing Zimin to attention "— madam —?"

"Yes." Instinct prodded Audley into support. "Perhaps you recall the traffic-jam on the bridge at Monmouth, after the lights had been turned off? That was *our* delay, to get our units in place . . . after we'd spotted a unit which had no right to be on the road — out of where? The Forest of Dean —?" He looked to Mary Franklin for confirmation. Then he shrugged at Zimin. "I forgot to ask. Not that that's important . . . now that they're going back home — eh, Colonel?"

"Thank you, Dr Audley." In return for his support he received a withering glance. "Colonel . . . the fact of the matter is that you won't get five miles from here now —" Mary Franklin consulted a tiny watch on her wrist "— if I fail to report in . . . at a particular time, within a very few minutes from now . . . and with a very precise form of words. *Do you understand now . . . Colonel?*"

God! It was like 'True Grit'! thought Audley, beyond admiration: *she reminded him of himself, long ago — before he'd taken it for granted that he was better than everyone else!*

"M ——" Zimin caught himself talking down to her just in time. "Miss Franklin . . . what are you proposing? What . . . is 'not enough', please?"

She nodded gravely, not triumphantly. (And, humiliatingly, Jake was wrong: the old ones weren't the best ones, by God!) "The Arabs are not a problem you said?" She didn't even wait for the Russian to nod. "And Lukianov —?"

Zimin actually slumped slightly. "He is no problem either, Miss Franklin. But . . . what are you proposing —?" He touched his own wrist, where his own watch lay. And that, for a guess, was because whatever he might be thinking about all of this, what was certain beyond all of it was that he was in a far country now, and far from home.

"No problem?" Not an inch — not a metric centimetre, or even a millimetre: she merely massaged her wrist-watch on her even-tinier wrist. "Why not?"

"Because we have him." No 'Miss Franklin' this time — never mind 'Madam': she wasn't giving him time to dig himself in, with his own little all-purpose spade.

"Where?"

"Not here —"

"Where?" No time even to cut the first sod of the next fox-hole!

"In France, Miss Franklin."

France was always the clearing-house. Even 'Mr Dalingridge' had headed for France first: if you weren't a French problem, then you had twenty-four hours — or even thirty-six. But if you were . . . then you'd already run out of time!

"So we're safe, here?" Even beyond certainty she was inexorable. "Very well, Colonel Zimin —" Only the briefest nod, beyond certainty "— you must leave at once —" The nod included what was happening beyond the door and the dirty kitchen window "— How soon will you be away, with your . . . property?"

No trouble! thought Audley, with a mixture of relief and bitter-ness: *the days of Audley were gone.*

Zimin nodded: the days of Zimin were the days of Jaggard. "Before nightfall, Miss Franklin . . . If there are no obstacles to our passage —" But then a hint of remembered doubt intruded "— Dr Audley —?"

It was like the poet had foretold — *not with a bang, but a whimper!* Yet all this, after they had taken Lukianov, had only been because they had feared that 'the celebrated Dr Audley', once roused, might have nosed out their *Spetsnaz* dump.

"That's the way it is, Colonel." He tried to make it sound the way he would have once said it. But it still tasted like ashes. "For what it's worth . . . you have my word on it."

For a time, after Zimin had gone, no one said anything. Not even Peter Richardson, who was full of unsaid things.

Then, when the last sound outside had faded into the rain, Mitchell went to the window and peered out of it.

"Phew!" He looked at Audley. "Your word's good, is it?"

Audley could only look at Mary Franklin. Not-knowing was where he'd started, so not-knowing at the end turned full circle. "Well, Miss Franklin —?"

As though suddenly domesticated, she was exploring the filthy kitchen. She had found a packet of tea, and there was a half-full bottle of milk and a bowl of lumpy sugar already on the table. And now she'd discovered an old-fashioned electric kettle, with a frayed lead still connected to a switch in the wall, which was itself at the end of a crudely-stapled wire running out of the ceiling.

"What —?" She turned towards him as she filled the kettle at the sink.

"What happens now?" Mitchell let the curtain fall on the silence outside. "They have a clear run, do they?"

"Yes . . ." She scanned the kitchen. "What I want is a teapot. And some cups . . ." She wrinkled her nose at the mess in the sink ". . . can you see any, Dr Mitchell?"

"They have a clear run?" Richardson snarled the words at Audley. "Things have changed since I worked for Fred Clinton, by God!"

"So they have." Mitchell opened a cupboard door. Then closed it, and opened another one. "You're still alive, Major — Peter . . . Be thankful for that!" He reached into the cupboard. "It's David here who has to worry now: he has to live down enlisting *Spetsnaz* . . . 'in aid of the Civil Power' — eh, David?" He unhooked a succession of mugs from the cupboard. "Here you are, Miss Franklin — will these do?"

"Yes." Mary Franklin had found a teapot. "But nobody is going to have to live down anything, Dr Mitchell."

"No?" Mitchell handed her his fourth mug.

"No." She fixed him with the mug between them. "Not if you want to keep your job, Dr Mitchell —" She turned towards Richardson "— and not if you want to enjoy your ill-gotten gains, Major Richardson. Because we can always give you back to the Mafia, if you don't. So all this never happened. Right?"

No trouble was her bottom line, thought Audley — no matter what humiliation that entailed: no matter, for Richardson, that it left him and his mother both unavenged . . . or the Russians in the clear. Or, maybe, even Dr Audley himself as a survivor again — at least for the time-being, anyway.

But, then, that was what obeying orders was all about. And, in this case, that was also what survival was all about. And, whether you were young and beautiful, or old and stupid . . . survival was a virtue.